Mandy Magro lives in Cairns, Far North Queensland, with her daughter, Chloe Rose. With pristine aqua-blue coastline in one direction and sweeping rural landscapes in the other, she describes her home as heaven on earth. A passionate woman and a romantic at heart, she loves writing about soul-deep love, the Australian rural way of life and all the wonderful characters who live there.

www.facebook.com/mandymagroauthor

www.mandymagro.com

MANDY MAGRO

Rosalee Station

mira

This edition published by Mira 2018
First published by Penguin Group (Australia) 2011
ISBN 9781489251381

Published by
Mira
An imprint of Harlequin Enterprises (Australia) Pty Ltd.
Level 19, 201 Elizabeth St
SYDNEY NSW 2000
AUSTRALIA

A catalogue record for this book is available from the National Library
of Australia
www.librariesaustralia.nla.gov.au

Printed and bound in Australia by McPherson's Printing Group

For my darling Chloe Rose and my parents, Gaye and John, I love you all dearly. And in memory of my beautiful Nanna Edie, Grandad Victor, Uncle Jack and Leanne.

CHAPTER

1

It was only six a.m. and already the air was so thick you felt like you couldn't breathe. Sarah Clarke had been lying in bed for a good ten minutes, staring at the fan above her spinning madly out of control. It was squeaking and waving about like it was a missing person trying to attract attention from rescuers. She sometimes had visions of it spinning straight off its bearings and landing smack down on top of her in the middle of the night. Scary thought. The thick, humid air it was blowing down was not really doing much good, but it was better than nothing. As soon as the air was still it was like standing in front of a hot oven with the door open, but after years of living with the heat of the tropics you got used to it.

She kept asking her dad to get her air conditioner fixed but the electrician, a family friend, had still not turned up. Sarah could fix most things herself, but going anywhere near something that threw out 240 volts of electricity was just not going to happen. She would rather sweat it out.

Summer in Mareeba was close to unbearable at times. Some days the sun tipped the gauges at well over forty degrees. Today Sarah was already swatting at an endless stream of flies, annoyed that they were in her space so early in the day. It was a pretty good sign it was going to be stinking hot.

Oh well, Sarah thought, *I better get up and start the day's work down the packing shed.* She threw her tanned, slender legs over the edge of the bed and felt the cool timber floor creak underneath her feet as she stood up and stretched her arms. She let out a huge sigh. She was getting tired of the same work, day in, day out. She knew it was time to try something new.

As she walked to the window, Sarah's mind turned to Brad, her boyfriend, who was a chopper pilot. He worked a fair bit away mustering cattle out on stations in the chopper, and she missed him when he was gone. She knew from the stories he told her that the times out on the stations were tough, but she would give almost anything to give it a go. She'd always loved cattle and horses, and it would be amazing to experience mustering in the heart of the cattle country, amongst the dust and bellows of the cows, in the saddle of an Australian stock horse.

Sarah let out another drawn-out sigh, bringing her thoughts back to the reality of the day. *It's okay to dream, I s'pose,* she thought to herself as she flung open her heavy curtains, letting in the sunlight that had been playing peek-a-boo through the cracks. The sun thrust its rays into Sarah's room, hitting the crystal sun-catcher she had hanging off the curtain rod and bouncing a spectrum of colours across the walls and furniture of the room. Sarah admired the beauty of it for a split-second before her gaze turned back to the bay window, which had a perfect view of the fruit paddocks behind the house. Outside there were fruit trees as far as the eye could see, beneath netting that had been expensively erected a few years back to stop the birds and the bats eating the crops. Mother Nature was already hard at work as bees buzzed industriously around the fruit flowers, doing their job of helping the fruit set, while sunshine kissed the flowers, helping produce the future mango and lychee crops. She smiled as she watched a kangaroo go bounding through the back yard with its joey in tow, relieved to not see Duke, her beloved dog, chasing them for a bit of fun.

Sarah dragged her gaze away from the window and pulled on her regular work gear of jeans and a Bonds singlet before tipping her head upside down and ruffling her fingers quickly through her mane of platinum-blonde curls. People said they matched her personality: bouncy, free-spirited and full of life. Brushes were her worst nightmare – she just ended up looking like she had put her finger in an electrical socket. Maybe in the eighties it would have been a fashionable look, but not now.

Sarah had worked on the family fruit farm since she had left school. The Clarkes had 800 hectares and employed over eighty staff in the fruit-picking season. The family business pumped out over 3000 tonnes of mangoes, lychees and Chinese longans every year.

It was a good life all in all. Sarah worked really hard for six months during harvesting and then got to work at a nice pace the rest of the year when the main jobs were just pruning, slashing, watering and fertilising the crops. She loved the time she spent in her John Deere tractor. It was a cruisy job, sitting in an air-conditioned cab with country tunes blaring from the stereo as she drove up and down each drill feeding the crops to produce a massive harvest.

Her two older brothers Peter and Daniel worked on the farm alongside her dad, Jack. Sarah had always worked as hard as the men in the family but she constantly felt like she had to try harder than her brothers to get appreciation from her dad. She knew deep down that her father worshipped her like flowers worshipped sunlight but he had a tough exterior and didn't show his emotions too freely. Sarah blamed his time in prison for that. When Sarah was a baby, Jack had been caught growing marijuana. He'd been farming tobacco and had a bad crop for a few years running. With the naïve confidence of youth, he thought growing illegal drugs might get him through the hard times. He couldn't bear to lose the family farm that had been handed down through two generations. Jack had never even smoked pot but had used his skills as a farmer to grow a massive, thriving crop. But then he was caught red-handed, arrested and locked up in Townsville maximum security for five long years as an example to the community. Sarah knew it must have been a hard time for her mum, Maggie, especially with three young children, and Jack still lived with the guilt of not having been there for his family.

Sarah didn't have time for anybody stupid enough to touch drugs, especially marijuana – she knew how much it could hurt people's lives.

'Sarah!' Maggie yelled from the bottom of the stairs. 'Lily's on the phone for you, love.'

Sarah raced down the stairs, tripping over Harry, the family cat of nine years, on the way down. 'Do you always have to sleep right in the middle of the stairs, Harry?' Sarah asked him once she had found her footing after sliding down three steps. Harry looked up at her, yawned, and went back to sleep. The only thing that got him moving was the sound of his canned sardines being spooned into his dish.

Sarah grabbed the phone from her mum, kissing Maggie on the cheek. 'Morning, Mum.' She put the phone to her ear and scrunched her shoulder up to hold it there while she zipped up her jeans with her free hands. 'Hey, Lily. How are ya, mate?'

Lily's voice sang cheerfully into the receiver, 'Great, Sarah. Almost your birthday! Hey, I just wanted to know what time we're going to head down to the rodeo tomorrow?'

Sarah sat her bum down on the bottom step of the stairs. 'Daniel's gonna be out in the arena about five-ish so I'd like to be there to watch him give those bulls a good go. Let's just pray he doesn't draw Devil's Grin!'

'Exactly! That sounds like a good plan to me. I'm so looking forward to watching Daniel ride. And we'll have to party like there's no tomorrow – it's not every day you turn twenty-three. I'll be at your place about four, okay?' Lily said, bubbling with excitement.

'Great! I'll see you then. I gotta run, or I'll be late down the shed and Dad'll be in a right huff. He's a pain in the arse to work with when he's in a mood. Catch you tomorrow.'

'Have a good day, Sarah. Catch you, matey!' Lily said as she hung up.

Daniel rode bulls at the local rodeos, and Sarah always went and cheered him on, either in the crowd or at the back of the chutes. He was one of the top riders in the circuit, and had a few scars to show for it too. It was great timing he'd be riding on the day of Sarah's birthday.

Sarah's mate Greg supplied the bulls for most of the big rodeos and she liked to catch up with him for a drink and a laugh whenever he had a minute spare. He had let her name one of the bulls last year. She had been honoured, and proudly named the bull Devil's Grin. He'd turned out to be one of the most feared bulls on the rodeo scene: a big, burly brute that didn't like any bugger on his back. Not one cowboy had been able to ride him past four seconds. Once free of the chutes he went off like a cracker on Chinese New Year.

Sarah strolled into the kitchen to the warm and welcoming smell of her mum's cooking. Maggie was a brilliant cook. Her friends were always madly scribbling down recipes after enjoying one of her home-cooked meals. There was only one recipe she refused to give out: her very own famous lemon meringue pie. All the neighbourhood women requested it every time they were invited to a barbecue and there was always a friendly debate amongst the men over the last piece of pie.

'Hey, Mum,' Sarah said as she sat down on the kitchen bar stool.

'Good morning, Sarah. Sleep well, darling?'

'As well as I could in this heat.'

'Sorry, hon. I'll call the electrician again for you today. You think he'd make more of an effort. Your dad is too bloody soft on him. I'll put the wind up him about being slack when I talk to him.' Maggie pointed her finger into the air as if poking the electrician then and there.

'Thanks, Mum. I better run or Dad'll get his knickers in a right knot. You know how he gets.'

'I know, love, but he doesn't mean it. He just gets really stressed out in the season. You know he loves you to bits,' Maggie said, passing over some foil-wrapped parcels. 'Here's breakfast for you. Give these ones to Daniel and your dad, would you? I have to catch up with some of the housework and then I'll be down the shed to help out.'

'Righto, Mum. Thanks for the brekkie. You're the greatest! This is probably going to be the only thing I'll have time to eat today – there's so much fruit to pack.' Sarah took the parcels and stood up. 'The pickers have been working their nuts off to get the fruit off the trees before the rain sets in. We're gonna be as busy as blowflies at a barbie, us lot!' She gave Maggie another kiss and headed towards the back door.

Sarah was proud of the way her mum and dad loved each other with an intensity that not many marriages had left after twenty-nine years. She hoped that one day she would have a marriage as loving as her parents. She cared deeply for Brad, but she hadn't really thought about the future. Or was it that she avoided thinking about it? Sarah had seen too many of her friends and neighbours go through divorce, and the pain it put the children through was heartbreaking to watch. Farming could be financially and emotionally challenging and it broke families into pieces when they weren't strong enough to cope. Despite the hard times, Maggie and Jack had survived, loving each other more and more with every hurdle they jumped together through life.

Duke, Sarah's dog, was at the back door waiting for her as he did every morning. She had saved him from the local RSPCA six years ago. He was a border collie cross kelpie, which naturally made him as mad as a cut snake but Sarah adored everything about him. She could not imagine her life without him. He was her best mate.

He was always as happy as a worm in a tin can on the way home from a fishing trip when he saw her, especially when he got the crusts off her breakfast sandwich like he knew he would – he did every morning. Sarah hated crusts. The old wives' tale didn't work for her – her hair was full of chaotic curls without the aid of one single crust.

Sarah crammed her weatherworn akubra on her head and pulled on her tattered R.M. Williams boots before heading off in the direction of the shed, Duke blissfully trotting beside her. She said hello to Cookie the kookaburra in passing. He was perched on the timber fence around the house, feasting on a bowl of mince that Maggie must have put out earlier this morning. Cookie had been visiting Sarah and the family for five years now so he was like a family pet. She sniffed the morning air as she walked; the faintly sweet smell of mango flowers floated up her nostrils, making her smile. A congregation of rosellas was perched happily on the branches of the star fruit tree, gorging themselves, their chirping filling the morning with beautiful song. A flock of galahs flew overhead, their loud conversation capturing Sarah's attention. She looked up to the azure-blue skies, squinting from the harsh rays of the sun, and watched them fly out of sight. Sarah's boots crunched on grass underfoot, which was aglow with early morning dew, the sunlight making it glimmer like webs made of diamonds. Maggie used to tell Sarah that the dew was angels dancing in the sunlight. Maggie had made the world such a magically enchanting place when Sarah was growing up.

Despite the beauty of the morning, it was already hot, and Sarah breathed a sigh of relief as she stepped into the shade of the vast packing shed. There was farm machinery everywhere, parked haphazardly around mountains of packing boxes and pallets of fertilisers and chemicals.

Sarah caught a glimpse of Johnny Marsh, the paddock manager, approaching in the old farm ute that was already stacked high with fruit ready to be packed. She gave him a quick wave. Johnny beamed out the ute's window as he skidded to a halt beside her. Sarah watched as the crates of fruit wobbled dangerously about but surprisingly they all stayed put.

'Mornin', Sarah. How's it goin', mate?' Johnny asked, a smouldering cigarette hanging from his lips as he slid himself across the vinyl seat, dodging cans and old chip packets, before escaping out of the passenger's side door.

'I'm great, Johnny. Doors still jammed, then, I see!'

Johnny rolled his eyes for effect. 'Yeah, the darn thing. I haven't had time to fix it yet so the only way in or out is through the bloody window or the passenger door, and I ain't even gonna try the window. Knowing my bloody luck, I'll get stuck!' Johnny laughed, pointing to his large rotund belly.

'I dunno, Johnny. Maybe if you just sucked it in you could get through.' Sarah patted Johnny on the belly. 'Anyway I better get in there and get my hands dirty, mate. Catch you later, hey?'

The first person Sarah saw as she opened the massive doors was Daniel on the forklift. She smiled and gave him a friendly wave.

Sarah's eldest brother, Peter, lived in his own place on the farm with his family, but Daniel still lived with Sarah in their parents' home. Sarah called Dan the piggy in the middle – not only was he the middle child, but he had an unbelievable appetite. You would never pick it, though, as he had a body that girls drooled over and they swarmed to him like ants to sugar. He was what most would call tall, dark and handsome, with mesmerising green eyes. Yes, Daniel Clarke had appeal – maybe too much for his own good. He worked hard and played even harder. But he had always been very protective of Sarah. No guys had dared go near her while she was growing up. They were all too afraid of what Daniel might do to them if they were to break her heart. Sarah secretly liked it – she was a bit of a tomboy and liked to be mates with the boys, so Daniel's protectiveness worked in her favour. None of them ever tried anything on with her. That was until Brad came along.

Daniel was loading yesterday's pallets of fruit onto the waiting truck parked up in the loading bay. The fruit would be transported to the markets down south and most of the time, stupidly enough, would then be transported all the way back up north again for sale. Sarah could never understand the concept. It was time-consuming and expensive, but that was the way the farmers had to do it because all the markets were down south.

'Morning, sis. I'm that hungry I could bite the balls off a low-flying pigeon! Got some food there for me?' Daniel said as he drove so close to her on the forklift he nearly ran over her toes.

'Nope, I ate it all,' Sarah said, rubbing her stomach teasingly.

Daniel looked like a kid who had lost his lollipop.

'Of course I do! Don't I always?' Sarah said, laughing as she passed him his bacon and egg sandwich. Daniel grinned widely as he unwrapped the foil in seconds, practically inhaling the contents.

Sarah headed over to her dad, who was sitting at his desk doing the daily paperwork.

'Morning, Dad. Here's your breakfast.'

'Thanks, love. We've got a big day ahead. Have to get all the work done so we can have the weekend off for your birthday and the rodeo.'

'No rest for the wicked, as they say,' Sarah said as she headed for the checking and stacking station in the middle of the massive shed floor. Her job was to make sure all the boxes of fruit were packed to the highest of standards so they got the best price at the Brisbane, Sydney and Melbourne markets. Once she was happy the boxes were perfectly packed, they were stacked onto pallets, then wrapped and stamped ready for their long journey south.

Sarah loved the buzz in the shed of a morning. All the packers were fresh and geared up for a full day's packing, and the forklift and trolley jack were moving things this way and that. By the afternoons it was a different story. Everybody was tired and aching from all the lifting and packing and all everyone wanted to do was get the heck out of the shed and into the last few rays of sunlight. They had a saying around the Tablelands to describe what happened during the harvest – mango madness. It hit them all at some stage. By the end of the season Sarah would be dreaming about fruit. Thank God the picking season only lasted for six months. They'd all be a bit batty otherwise.

'Hey, love. Brad's on the phone for you!' Jack bellowed over the noise of the shed.

Sarah tried not to run to the phone. Daniel would really give her jip then. But she hadn't seen Brad in three whole weeks. He was out on Rosalee Station, just near the Northern Territory border, preparing for the mustering season.

She grabbed the portable off the desk and walked outside. 'Hey, babe! I miss you. When are you home?' she asked affectionately.

'Hey to you, too, gorgeous. I'm flying home early tomorrow morning so I can be there for your birthday and the rodeo. I can't miss my lady's special day, now, can I?' Brad replied.

'Oh, Brad, that's wonderful! I can't wait! That has absolutely made my day,' Sarah said, smiling.

'I have some really exciting news for you, but I'll wait until I see you to tell you about it. You're gonna be over the moon. Also I have a surprise for your birthday. I hope you like it.'

'Tell me now, Brad, you devil. I *cannot* wait another day. You know what I'm like with secrets! I'll make it worth your while if you tell me now,' she said in her most seductive voice.

'You're not going to sweet-talk me into telling you now! I'll see you tomorrow morning, okay?' Brad answered, laughing.

'Okay. See you in the morning then. Have a safe flight back, honey.'

Sarah walked back into the shed in a daze – excited that Brad was going to be there with her for her birthday, but also burning with curiosity as to what he had to tell her. She knew it was going to play on her mind all day. The phone line had been bad, though – Brad's voice had sounded different, almost as though he'd had a few beers. Sarah shrugged it off – connections from the outback could be dodgy sometimes – and smiled to herself at the thought of seeing Brad again.

CHAPTER

2

Sarah woke to the reverberation of chopper blades slicing their way through the humid morning air. It was the best sound in the world to her – it meant Brad was here. He had his spot down in the spare paddock, where he parked the beast whenever he came to see her.

She quickly threw on her jeans and favourite old singlet and ran down the stairs, jumping over Harry on the way, and out the back door. Duke ran behind her barking, caught up in Sarah's exhilaration. He was an eager beaver whenever there was action and adventure to be shared.

Sarah raced to the four-wheeler motorbike and Duke jumped up on the seat behind her. She raced off down to the paddock, wiping the sleep out of her eyes on the way down. In her haste to get out the door she had forgotten to put a bra on, and bouncing along the dirt road with ample boobs was quite painful. She placed her hand over the top of them to curb their crazy romp beneath her thin singlet.

By the time she arrived, Brad had stepped down from the chopper, looking handsome as always. He was by no means tall, but his frame was well proportioned with muscles in all the right places from the physical work he did. From under the rim of his akubra, his blue eyes looked cheekily at Sarah. His Blue Dog jeans hugged snugly to his hips and his Wrangler shirt was missing the top two buttons, showing off his broad, tanned chest. He smiled as he walked slowly towards her. She ran up to him and wrapped her arms around his neck, kissing him smack on the lips. He melted into her, his muscular arms folding around her waist, and kissed her back.

When they finally pulled apart, Brad picked her up in a huge bear hug and spun her around. 'Gee, I've missed you, my sexy lady. Happy birthday.'

'Thanks, babe. I've missed you too. It means so much that you've come back for my birthday.' Sarah gazed into Brad's eyes before smiling mischievously. 'Now what was it you needed to tell me about? It is *killing* me not knowing!'

Brad winked at her. 'Sorry, babe, you'll just have to wonder a little bit longer. Otherwise it wouldn't be a surprise, would it?' He smiled enigmatically and gave Sarah another kiss.

*

Maggie was in the kitchen looking freshly showered by the time Sarah and Brad got back to the house. She had on a simple yellow sundress that matched her bright and friendly personality. Her short hair was still wet and combed back off her youthful face. She hummed away happily to the song on the radio as she cooked them all breakfast, her floral apron tied firmly around her childbearing hips.

Jack was sitting at the table reading the morning paper with a steaming cup of tea in his hand. His brows furrowed in concentration whilst he read about what was happening in the big, wide world. He was muttering to himself about how the government was all bullshit and that if he ran the country he would put farmers first.

Maggie immediately dropped what she was doing when she spotted her daughter, and ran over to Sarah to give her a birthday kiss.

'Happy birthday to you, my beautiful girl. We have your present down the shed for you, so when we finish breakfast we'll all go down there and you can unwrap it, okay?' Maggie beamed.

Jack stood up from the kitchen table. 'Yes, happy birthday, darling. You're another year older and wiser, hey?' He wrapped his daughter up in his strong arms, kissing her on the top of her head. He always gave brilliant hugs.

Jack turned to Brad and shook his hand a bit too determinedly, without releasing his grip as he spoke. 'G'day, Brad. Welcome back to the fun house. Hope you're up for a big night tonight – the girls have been planning like mad.'

'Lord help me,' Brad said, quickly pulling his hand away before Jack succeeded in squishing the life out of him.

Jack had known Brad for years, but they still weren't at ease with each other. Brad had been best mates with Sarah's brother Peter – right from the beginning in Grade One, when they were still sweet and innocent, through to Year Twelve, when they were a pair of absolute ratbags.

Brad had also done some work on the family farm in the school holidays, which was how Sarah had got to know him. Brad had been a good mate of hers for as long as she could remember; it was only a year ago that they'd hooked up. She was never too sure what brought them together – maybe it was because they knew each other so well and were comfortable in each other's company. Whatever the reason, she was happy with Brad, but didn't want to think too much about where their relationship might be going. Jack wasn't too pleased when she had announced that she and Brad were together. When she had reacted to his displeasure by reminding him that Peter had been friends with Brad for years, Jack had simply replied that *that* was different and he didn't want his daughter falling in love with a man he couldn't trust to take care of her. He said Brad couldn't even look after himself. It was true that Brad had had a few run-ins with the police, but it was only over minor things, like speeding and drinking in public. Sarah put Jack's reaction down to him being overprotective.

Daniel came into the kitchen and gave Maggie a huge bear hug. 'Hey, Mum. I thought I could smell your great cooking. What's on the menu this morning?'

'Chook bum nuts on toast!' Maggie teased.

Daniel licked his lips. 'Mmm, my favourite!'

'Food really is the way to your heart, isn't it, son?' Jack said, laughing.

'Happy birthday, sis. How old are you today – thirty?' Daniel asked cheekily.

Sarah tried to tackle him but he ducked and she landed flat on her arse. Everyone burst out laughing.

Over breakfast the family sat around the table sharing yarns about the week gone by, before deciding it was time to give Sarah her present.

'The present's from all of us combined this year,' Maggie said with a twinkle in her eye as they walked down to the shed. When they got there everybody but Sarah kept walking past.

'Hey – you guys, I thought my surprise was in here?' she called after them.

'Well, it's *near* the shed. Sorry, we should've told you that – but then you might have guessed what it was!' Daniel teased.

They all walked another ten metres to the stables and stopped. Sarah's heart skipped a beat. No, it couldn't be, she thought to herself. Only five months before Sarah had had to put down her horse of eleven years. He had cancer and was in too much pain. She'd cried for days and still got a lump in her throat when she thought of him. Ned had been not only her horse but her mate as well. She had got him for her twelfth birthday, and had basically grown up with him.

Jack put his arm around his daughter's shoulders and slowly opened the door to the stables. Sarah closed her eyes, holding her breath. She opened her eyes and gasped. There in front of her was the most beautiful chestnut Australian stock horse she had ever seen. He was about fifteen hands high, just the right height for Sarah's short but athletic frame.

Sarah burst into tears of joy. Maggie ran to her side and wrapped her arms around her while everybody sang 'Happy Birthday'.

Once the song was finished, Sarah kissed Jack on the cheek so many times he laughed and told her to stop before he started blushing.

'I'm happy he makes you happy, love. Go on. Go and make friends with him.' Jack gently pushed Sarah towards the horse.

She walked very slowly up to him. She didn't want to frighten him with any sudden movements. She wholeheartedly believed that horses were one of the most intelligent creatures on earth, and no matter what any bugger said, they never, ever forgot if somebody put the wind up them on their first encounter.

Sarah let the gelding smell her hand. He put his head down and sniffed her hair and then took a step towards her.

'I think he likes you, sis,' Daniel said. 'What are you gonna name him?'

Sarah thought about it for a few seconds and then it just came to her. 'I'm going to name him Victory, after our amazing granddad Victor. If he's looking down on us he'll be chuffed that I named a horse this fine in his memory.' Sarah and her granddad had been the best of mates and she missed him terribly.

Maggie clapped her hands in agreement. 'That's a wonderful idea, darling. I'm so glad you like him. It took months to find the right one. He's come from a station out west and has been used for mustering for the last two years. He's only four, but he's been trained by the best. Daniel saddled him up for you earlier this morning, so you can go for a ride now if you want.' Maggie took her daughter's face in her hands and looked her in the eyes. 'We're not trying to replace Ned – he was one in a million – but we all thought it was time for you to get a new horse to spend time with. I know how much you miss riding.'

Maggie turned to Brad. 'My horse is all saddled up for you and ready to go now if you both like. We've packed a nice lunch in the saddlebags so you can take your time.'

'Thanks, Maggie. We really appreciate it.' Brad smiled.

*

Sarah and Brad were soon in the saddle and ambling away from the farm.

'So Victory was the surprise, you bugger! You knew all along! I love him, Brad. I can just tell he's a ripsnorter of a horse.'

'He's only part of the surprise, Sarah. Come on, cowgirl! Get that sexy butt of yours moving and we'll head out to the back dam for a swim,' Brad said with raised eyebrows, insinuating that he wanted more than just a paddle.

Sarah smiled but inwardly rolled her eyes a little. Brad was always up for nooky but he never seemed capable of expressing his feelings for her on the deeper level that she craved. She kept hoping that he would show his love for her in other ways as their relationship progressed, but so far it hadn't happened.

They rode slowly for the first half hour so Sarah could get a feel for Victory. Once she was sure that he was listening to her commands, she smirked at Brad and then took off in a gallop. Brad gave his horse the go-ahead and off he went, hell for leather after Sarah.

They both reached the dam at the same time, sweaty and exhilarated, with their horses in desperate need of a drink.

'Hey, Sarah, how about you take care of the horses for a minute while I get us a spot set up under the wattle tree?' Brad said, pointing.

'Okay. See you over there in two shakes of a lamb's tail.'

Sarah admired Victory while he drank from the dam. He was a fine-looking gelding with a beautiful nature. She could tell from the way he responded to her that he was happy to have her in charge.

'We're gonna have some adventures, us two. I think Ned would've approved of you, mate,' she whispered to Victory as they walked back to the shade of the tree.

When Sarah got over to Brad he was lying on a picnic blanket, looking up at the fluffy white clouds that were scattered across the blue sky. There were ham and salad sandwiches on plastic plates, with bottles of beer to wash it all down. Brad patted next to him, gesturing for Sarah to lie down beside him. Once she was comfortable he took a deep breath and started talking.

'I have a proposition for you, gorgeous. The station owners where I'm mustering for this season have asked me if I know of anybody who wants the job of station cook out there. The contract is for about four months, with the option of staying on to do other work around the station in the off-season. I reckon you'd love the job, seeing you love cooking so much. I've told them that you may be interested, and they're holding the job for you. What do you think about that?'

Sarah sat bolt upright. 'Are you serious, Brad? I'd love to come out there with you! I'd get to live and work on a cattle station. Oh my God, I cannot believe how much better this day keeps getting. I just hope Mum and Dad won't be too annoyed at me up and leaving them in the busy part of the season.'

'Brilliant! I'll give the station owners a call when we get back to the house and let them know you want the job.' Brad leant up on his elbow to give Sarah a kiss.

She leant forward and her lips met his. It was slow and lingering, filling them both with desire, making them want more. Soon Sarah was unbuttoning Brad's shirt while he slipped his fingers under the waistband of her jeans, exploring further until she could resist no more. They tore at each other's clothes and enjoyed a quickie under the shade of the willow tree, falling asleep afterwards wrapped around each other.

Sarah was the first one to stir an hour later. 'Last one in is a loser!' she yelled, jumping up and running butt naked to the dam.

Brad woke suddenly to see her mop of blonde ringlets bouncing around her back as she ran. He jumped up and ran after her, naked as the day he was born. With a crash he hit the water and grabbed Sarah playfully. They splashed and giggled together, talking excitedly about the new adventure ahead of them. 'I cannot wait to tell Mum and Dad,' said Sarah, ducking away from Brad as he tried to splash her.

'Yeah, I hope your dad takes it well. He's a big bloke with a big bloody gun!' Brad joked.

'Yeah, you better treat me right out there on the station, or he might just have to use it on you!'

Brad made a face of mock terror and lunged at Sarah as she squealed and ducked away.

*

When Sarah and Brad got back to the house, Jack and Maggie were sitting on the back verandah enjoying the afternoon sun; glasses perched on their noses, they read their magazines.

Sarah was trying extremely hard to contain her excitement. She wanted to talk to her mum first before telling her dad – she was afraid he might react badly. Jack looked up from his magazine and offered them both a cuppa.

'That'd be great, thanks, Dad,' Sarah said, hearing her voice quiver slightly from the exhilaration she was bottling up. She felt like fireworks were going off in her belly and her head was spinning like a loose hubcap.

Once Jack had gone inside, Sarah filled Maggie in on the job out on the station. Maggie listened intently, waiting until Sarah had finished before telling her how happy she was for her.

Sarah smiled, relieved. 'I'm so excited, Mum, but I'm worried what Dad's gonna think if I take the job.'

'Your father will be happy for you, Sarah. He knows you're ready for a change. All he wants is to see you happy and I know he'll support you. Why don't you tell him when he comes back? I promise he'll be fine,' Maggie said as she wrapped her arm around Sarah's shoulders.

Brad sat down beside Sarah. She noticed he was a little nervous, realising he was probably a bit worried about telling Jack too. She grabbed his hand and gave it a squeeze.

Jack whistled cheerfully as he came back out to the verandah, carrying a tray of coffees and fresh Anzac biscuits that Maggie had baked that morning. He placed the tray down on the table and settled himself back down.

Sarah turned to face her dad. She looked down at her hands and fumbled with her bracelet. 'Dad, I've got something to tell you, and I'm gonna get straight to the point. Brad has offered me a job out on Rosalee Station as the cook. It's only for four months to start. I would really love to do it, but only with your blessing. I feel bad leaving the family farm, but you have Daniel and Peter here to help you. I'm sure you'll cope without me.'

Jack's face dropped for a few seconds, but he regained control quickly. 'Love, you take that job. We'll miss you around here but I know it'll make you happy finally getting to experience station life, and if you're happy then I'm happy. Just make sure you ring us whenever you can and let us know how you're doing. Are you going to take Victory with you?'

Sarah wrapped her arms around Jack, her excitement no longer contained. 'Thanks Dad! It means the world that you're happy for me. Of course I'm going to take Victory! He's gonna be my right-hand man out there – along with Duke, of course.'

'Hey! What about me?' Brad said with a smile, happy that Jack had taken the news so well.

'You're my left-hand man, then!' replied Sarah with a giggle. Jack turned to Brad, worry creasing his brows. 'You take care of my little girl out there, Brad.'

Brad shuffled his feet nervously, Jack's firm stare putting the wind up him. 'Of course I will, Mr Clarke. She'll be my number one priority.'

Jack nodded his head. 'Glad to hear that.'

Sarah smiled meekly at Brad when he looked in her direction. She couldn't say a word. Jack was just being a protective father.

Brad decided to go say hello to Sarah's brother, Peter, and Sarah sat with her mum and dad on the verandah a little while longer. The view of the farm from there was glorious. Sarah was going to miss her home, but her dream was within reach now and nothing was going to stop her from achieving it. She smiled to herself and felt like the luckiest woman in the world.

CHAPTER

3

The night was warm and a soft breeze blew through the open window of Sarah's bedroom, cooling her down a fraction. She sat down on the edge of her bed and pulled on her favourite leather boots. She'd bought them over in Nashville and kept them for special occasions; tonight was definitely one of them.

She gave herself the once over in the mirror and was content with what she saw. She'd even put on a bit of make-up. She was normally an *au naturel* girl but tonight she wanted to make a bit more of an effort. Her jeans hugged her lean curves and her red top showed a hint of cleavage. Her blonde hair was out in full force, with disorganised curls framing her face. Sarah never had to blow dry her hair – she just tipped her head upside down, threw in some mousse, scrunched, flicked her head back, and the curls fell about in wild abandonment.

Sarah thought back to last year when she and Lily flew over to Las Vegas for the massive Professional Bull Riders event at the Mandalay Bay Hotel. Sarah was so excited about going that she had barely slept a wink for the three nights before her flight. It was eye-popping to see the extremes the organisers went to, endeavouring to create the perfect scene inside the luxurious hotel. They moved in hundreds of tonnes of dirt to fill the auditorium and the show they put on was one Sarah and Lily would never forget. There was a big tribute to the late Chris LeDoux before the beginning of the first day of events, and Sarah had to wipe tears from her eyes as she watched. Chris LeDoux had been a champion bull rider himself and an awesome country music legend. Her LandCruiser bumper proudly wore a sticker she had bought from the PBR that read *Save a horse, ride a cowboy!* in honour of the fantastic song by Big & Rich.

Sarah heard a noise and turned to see Lily come running into her bedroom with her arms outstretched, ready for a hug. 'Happy birthday, lovely! I'm so excited about tonight. We're going to have a ball!'

Sarah stood on her toes to give Lily a welcoming hug and kiss. Lily was nearly six feet tall, with long dark hair, a body most women would kill for and a smile that made even the most confident of men stutter. She had petite features with caramel brown eyes, and she knew how to work them to get what she wanted. Lily's favourite line to over-eager men was, 'Good cowgirls keep their calves together.' He'd have to be one hell of a special guy to win Lily Wright's heart, that was for sure.

Earlier that afternoon Daniel had casually asked Sarah if Lily was coming along tonight. Sarah knew from the way he acted around Lily that he had liked her for years now but Lily had never really showed much of an interest in him in that way. She seemed to treat him more like a brother than a lover. Sarah thought it best to keep out of it, not wanting to ruin any friendships if things went pear shaped between Lily and Daniel. Very occasionally Sarah would notice a little glint in Lily's eyes when she was talking about Daniel but it always vanished just as fast as it had arrived so she never had the chance to judge whether it was maybe proof of some deeper feelings Lily had for him. Lily had never spoken to Sarah about Daniel in any other way other than as a mate but Sarah knew her best friend and she was sure Lily liked Daniel just as much as Daniel liked her. Sarah secretly hoped Daniel would get over his nerves and ask Lily out one of these days. She reckoned Lily would surprise herself by saying yes.

You had to hand it to her, though. Lily played hard to get and was no easy catch for any man, even if she was interested.

'So how are ya? What's happening? Where's Brad?' Lily asked. Sarah laughed. Lily was so keyed up about tonight she was beside herself.

'He's already headed over to the rodeo grounds with Peter and Daniel. He thought Danny boy might need some support out the back of the chutes. I think they all just wanted a bit of guy time to celebrate without us girls.'

'Fantastic! That means we can have some girl time! So, how's your day been, birthday girl?' Lily asked as she sat down on the end of Sarah's bed.

'I have so much to tell you!' Sarah shrieked, radiating happiness. 'I just don't know what to tell you first. It's been such an amazing day. The family and Brad all put in and bought me a horse for my birthday. He's a gorgeous gelding with such a nice nature. I took him for a ride today and he rode beautifully. I know we're gonna be the best of mates. I'll be taking him on my big adventure out to the station.' Sarah deliberately threw in the last sentence, not knowing how else to tell her best mate that she'd be leaving Mareeba in a week's time.

'Whoa. Wait a second. What station?' Confusion was written all over Lily's face.

Sarah looked down at the floor, not wanting to meet Lily's eyes. 'Brad's offered me a job out on Rosalee as station cook. I'd be crazy not to go. You know it's always been my dream – and now I have my chance. I'll miss you though, Lily,' Sarah said sadly, finally looking up at Lily.

'Wow. You *have* had an interesting day, my friend. Of course you should go to the station. I'm going to miss you, though. Heaps! You're my bestest buddy, Sarah! I'm gonna be lost here in Mareeba without you.'

'Nah, it's not like I'm moving to another country, and I'll only be gone for four months, I reckon. You won't even have time to miss me before I'm back, annoying the crap out of ya!' Sarah said, relieved Lily had taken it so well. 'Let's hit the road – I'm dying for a drink. We'll catch a lift with Mum and Dad so we can have a few and not worry about parking. I'm not going to leave my Cruiser at the rodeo after what happened last year. Cost me 500 bucks to fix the dint in the back after that moron reversed into it.'

Sarah loved her Toyota LandCruiser. It basically ran on the smell of an oily rag. She'd bought it for a steal off one of her granddad's mates down the local pub. She and her grandad had spent hours working on it, and even though that was six years ago now, Sarah couldn't begin to think of parting with it after all the blood, sweat and tears her grandad had put into it.

The girls headed down the stairs chattering breathlessly about the day's events, both giving Harry a quick scratch on the way down. He purred in delight. 'Wish I was a cat sometimes,' Lily said, laughing.

*

The rodeo grounds were jam-packed. To see so much life in such a quiet country town was brilliant. It gave Sarah a buzz just being there. Jack drove into the carpark and the girls giggled in the back seat as a man with the belly the size of a wine barrel directed them, with the seriousness of a doctor about to embark on a life-saving procedure, to the next parking space. He then shoved a mouthful of sausage roll in his mouth and smiled to Maggie and Jack in the front, his teeth showing bits of pastry as he casually tried to pull his jeans up at the same time.

'Gee whiz. He's a charmer!' Lily said, laughing. They all chuckled along with her.

Sarah and Lily were itching to get over to the back of the chutes. The area was always pumping with testosterone-fuelled men, bulls and dust, with the smell of horses, cattle and leather wafting in the air. Only hardcore men could handle bull riding and their sex appeal was undeniable. The back of the chutes was a country girl's fantasy made into reality.

Sarah loved watching bull riding, whether on the telly or live in the centre ring, where you could practically smell the anticipation of the crowd. She had seen her share of bad injuries over the years too, which the riders took in their stride, all of them knowing full well the dangers of bull riding.

'Thanks for the lift, Dad. We're going to grab some tucker before going over to see how the guys are doing, so I'll catch you and Mum a bit later,' Sarah said as she and Lily took off in the direction of the goings-on before Jack or Maggie had time to answer them. Even from the edges of the car park Sarah could hear the announcer's booming, elated voice, with a country twang, letting the spectators know what events were coming up. The girls stopped at the main entrance to check out the last of the Beaut Ute Muster. The judges were picking out the Best Feral Ute, and Sarah and Lily had to have a laugh at the owner's expense when they saw the state of the winning ute. It was a mass of dings and dents from past bush bashing, with a stub where the antennae used to be, stickers from every rodeo and B&S imaginable, a patchwork of panel colours from previous repairs, a bull bar that had seen better days and the remnants of mud from at least a decade of filth. The girls watched as the winner took his trophy before hurrying on to the chutes.

Sarah felt exhilarated as she and Lily wandered through the sideshow alley on the way to the chutes. Their conversation was drowned out by the screams of adrenaline junkies being thrown about in the air by the huge mechanical arms of the rides. Others were crashing about like loonies in the dodgem cars, with country music pumping out of speakers at ten thousand decibels. It always amazed Sarah how much people put their trust into the safety of the topsy-turvy rides. She honestly would rather get on the back of a bull.

Sarah felt her belly rumble and her mouth water as the smells of the rodeo food wafted in the air, teasing her tastebuds. There were stuffed potatoes, pizzas, massive ribs drenched in thick syrupy sauces, burgers, hot chips, fairy floss, dagwood dogs, waffles filled with fresh cream, pancakes draped in generous lashings of cream and strawberries, and even a stall advertising deep-fried cheesecake. Sarah loved cheesecake but she thought the deep-fried bit was going overboard. Only one way to find out, she told herself, making a mental note to get a piece later on.

'Hey, Sarah, I *have* to grab a dagwood dog on the way past. I can never come to a rodeo and not tuck into one. Do you want one, mate?' Lily asked.

'Yeah, count me in. Make sure you get heaps of dead horse on it for me.'

'That's the best way to eat them, hey, dripping in tomato sauce! I'll be back in two secs,' Lily said, dashing off.

Sarah stood off to the side to wait for Lily, watching the enormous crowds wandering about. The action in the centre ring caught her eye, and she walked over to see what was going on. The grandstands were packed to the brim with people young and old, their eyes glued to the action. The steer-wrestling was sending *oohs* and *ahhs* soaring from the spectator's lips. Sarah liked the name 'bulldogging' better than steer-wrestling; it had a rebellious ring to it, signifying the strength and guts it took to be part of the sport. As Sarah watched, a horse-mounted rider pursued a steer before diving from the horse and landing in the perfect position to wrestle the steer to the dusty ground by its horns. It was all over in less than ten seconds. The announcer's voice dominated the loudspeakers once again, advising of a quick dinner break as the water truck came out to hose the grounds down before the bull-riding competition. The people who were regulars at the rodeo took cover as the jets at the back of the truck showered them with water, a commonplace lark on the part of the driver. The poor buggers who were new to the Mareeba Rodeo got an uninvited light hose-down, creating echoing laughter in the stands.

'Sarah Clarke!' Sarah heard someone yell. She looked around and saw Johnny Marsh's big round face coming in her direction. He was swaying slightly – probably from the amount of alcohol he had already thrown back at the bar.

'Hey, Johnny. How are ya, mate?' Sarah asked, smiling at her fellow workmate, the paddock manager of the farm.

'I'm well on the way to being as crissed as a picket, but enjoying every second of the journey, my friend!' Johnny said with a slight slur, his face glowing a shade of red.

'There are still a lot of hours left to party tonight, and I wanna have a birthday drink with you later on so pace yourself, mate. Otherwise you might find yourself in the same predicament as last year – asleep near the campfire by eight o'clock with no eyebrows and bright red lipstick all over your face!' Sarah grinned as she remembered. She had nearly wet herself from laughing when Johnny had walked into the bar for breakfast the next morning, unaware of what a fright he looked. Thank God Johnny had a great sense of humour.

'Oh, don't remind me,' he smirked, stumbling slightly to the left, then to the right, trying his hardest to stand still in a poor attempt to act sober. Sarah giggled at his antics.

He tapped his head as he spoke again. 'But don't you worry your pretty little head 'bout me, mate. I'll be there with bells on later to have a drink and a boogie with you. The band is going to be awesome. Wish Dan luck for me, hey? I heard he's drawn Devil's Grin. I reckon he's gonna need all the luck he can get, riding that crazy-arsed beast.' Johnny chuckled as he wandered off towards the bar area, unaware of the effect his words were having on Sarah. 'I'll catch you later on, mate!' he called over his shoulder.

Sarah couldn't answer him. Daniel had more balls than a game of Keno when it came to riding bulls, but with Devil's Grin that didn't make a bit of difference.

Lily arrived with two dagwood dogs dripping in a sea of tomato sauce.

'Here, Sarah, grab yours, would ya? I told the lady we wanted heaps of sauce and she's deliberately put half a bloody bottle on, I reckon.' Lily was too busy cleaning the sauce off her hands and arms to notice the look of shock on Sarah's face.

'Shit, Lily,' Sarah said. 'Daniel's drawn Devil's Grin!'

*

'Don't stress, sis,' Daniel said, looking surprisingly calm. 'I'm gonna be the first one to show that bull who the bloody boss is. You wait and see. I reckon I'll give Devil's Grin a good run for his money.'

'That's the spirit, Dan!' Lily said as she slapped him on the back.

Before Sarah could put her two bob in she felt a tap on her shoulder and turned around to see her old mate Greg, his Johnny Cash smile on his face. He always reminded her of the Man in Black – same age, same looks. Sarah loved Johnny Cash. No, more than that – he was her country music god.

Greg put his arm around Sarah's shoulder.

'Blondie, how are ya, mate? Brad's told me that you're off to Rosalee to be the cook. Good on ya, girl! I know Matt, the owner's son out there – I buy stud bulls off him occasionally. They're a top family, and from what I've heard, great to work for. I might see ya out there at some point.'

'Good to see ya, Greg. It's been a while, hey!' Sarah said, giving him a huge smile. 'Yeah, I can't wait to get out there. I'll woo them all with my fine country cooking. It'll be great to get my butt in the saddle too and learn the ropes of mustering.'

'You watch those boys out there, Sarah. They don't see fine young women like you in their parts very much. Brad'll have a bloody fight on his hands if he's not careful.' Greg had always been extra protective of Sarah, and she took it as a wonderful compliment that her mate cared about her so much.

'Don't worry, mate. I can look out for myself. I'm going next week, so that leaves me seven days, give or take, to get everything wound up here,' said Sarah. 'I got a beautiful chestnut stock horse for my birthday today, and I reckon I'll take him too. He used to muster so he'll be right at home on the station.'

'Oh shit, I nearly forgot it was your birthday – blame the old age! Happy birthday, sweetheart. We'll have to have a drink later.' Greg gave Sarah a kiss on the cheek then turned to open a gate, wiping his dusty hands on his threadbare jeans. 'Glad to hear you're happy with the new horse after losing Ned. He would've been a hard one to replace. You know me though; I'm more a cattle man myself. I reckon you never really know what a horse is thinking. At least with a bull you know what's on his mind: getting your sorry arse if he's in a bad mood and you're in his way!'

Greg started to push a few of the bulls along in the yards. One of the bulls thought twice about moving, but as soon as he saw Greg stomping towards him he changed his mind. Greg's bulls had a respect for him that not many people could earn. It was a testament to how well he treated his animals. All the people who rallied against bull riding probably didn't have a clue about how the animals were treated. If it wasn't for men like Greg, most of the bulls used for rodeos would have their lives cut short at the meatworks.

Sarah laughed. 'You bloody galah, Greg! I'll hold you to that drink. I might even be able to get you drunk enough to have a dance with me.'

'I'll embarrass you if I get out on the dance floor with you! I think I'm better off watching from the sidelines. Apparently I dance a bit like a drunken spider.'

'Oh, come on now, Greg. I don't believe that for a second. With a face like Johnny Cash, you gotta be able to dance.'

Greg smiled shyly, blushing at Sarah's comment. 'Yeah, well, we'll see. I gotta get going and get some work done here, or there'll be no bulls for the riders to put their arses on.'

'Rightio, Greg. Hey, before you run off, have you seen Brad about?'

'Yeah he'll be back in a minute or two. He just went to grab us all some grub. I haven't eaten a thing all day and I'm that hungry I could eat the — well, you know. I shouldn't speak badly in front of a lady.'

'I think I've heard it all before. You should know that by now, Greg. Can you let Brad know that Lily and I've gone to the grandstands to watch Daniel ride?'

'No worries, mate.' Greg's reply was almost swallowed up by a cloud of red dust as the bulls kicked up a storm.

Lily and Daniel were having a good old chinwag behind Sarah. Lily was leaning into Daniel's space to talk to him, and Sarah's gut instincts told her there must be some kind of spark there. She waited for them to stop chatting, trying to think of what to say to her brother ahead of his toughest ride yet.

'You give that bull all you've got tonight, Dan. I've got a good feeling about tonight and I just think you might ride him for the whole eight seconds,' she said, trying to sound confident.

'Thanks, Sarah. I'll see you out on the dirt in twenty minutes. After that we'll have a celebratory drink, I reckon.'

Lily suddenly leaned over and gave Daniel a quick peck on the cheek. Daniel blushed but quickly regained his composure. Sarah inwardly cheered at Lily's affectionate display. And without another word, Daniel was off towards his bag to finish getting ready, spurs chinking with each step, his chaps flapping around his legs as he walked. He blended in with all the other burred-up cowboys, dressed in their boots, cowboy hats and chaps, readying themselves for the rides of their lives. Cowboys were so close to the land, with most breeding cattle for a living and also riding the bulls for sport. It gave them a raw, untamed aura that a laptop and a suit just didn't give urban men.

Sarah and Lily made their way to the grandstand through the hordes of people. They exchanged an amused look as they saw the groups of dressed-up girls standing around the back of the chute area, trying to catch the attention of the riders. They were known as buckle bunnies for the simple reason that they chased bull riders, who of course competed for trophy buckles. Sarah wondered how many of them would get lucky tonight.

*

The speakers boomed to life as the MC introduced the first rider and the name of the bull he was riding. Sarah felt her belly fill with butterflies.

Daniel's mate Jimmy Turner had drawn the bull the Wizard of Oz. Jimmy was a chopper pilot like Brad, and mustered away on the stations in central Australia. Every second he had off from work he spent riding bulls. He lived for the sport and spoke about it constantly. Nobody had the heart to tell him how bad he was at it.

The door of the chute flew open and out came Jimmy, hanging on with every bit of strength he had. A Garth

Brooks song blared over the speakers, adding to the intensity of the scene. Jimmy looked like a rag doll thrown in mid-air as the bull bucked him off in three seconds flat. The rodeo clowns came running to divert the bull's attention while Jimmy got up off the dirt and made a quick exit, launching himself straight over the fence, his hat landing on the dirt beneath him. Seconds later the bull slammed into the fence, snorting and kicking.

'He just made it over by the breadth of a bee's dick,' Lily yelled over the cheering crowd.

The next rider drew the Joker and rode him for the full eight seconds. He made it look easy, bowing to the crowd after landing on his feet.

And then it was Daniel's turn. Sarah felt the gentle butterflies in her stomach become a frenzied flutter fest. Lily whooped with delight when Daniel's name was announced and she grabbed Sarah's hand. Sarah squeezed it so hard that Lily let out a little squeal of pain.

Daniel was sitting high up on the bull's back behind the gate of the chute. It was taking a bit longer than normal as Devil's Grin snorted and kicked, letting the men know he wasn't happy being confined to such a small area. Sarah saw Daniel nod his head to the men. Then it all happened in slow motion. The gate opened and Devil's Grin came out hard and fast, bucking so high there were times when all his hoofs were off the ground. Daniel and the bull looked like crazy dancers, suspended in mid-air, performing in some elaborate Broadway show. But Daniel stayed on, swaying and moving with every buck Devil's Grin threw at him. His form was perfect. The seconds ticked past like they were hours and Sarah found herself standing up, screaming out encouragement. The horn blew, announcing that Daniel had made the eight seconds.

'Holy shit, Lily! He did it! Oh my God, he did it!' Sarah screamed, her voice drowned out by the cheering crowd, her eyes glued on Daniel. 'Hang on, there's something wrong. Daniel's hand's stuck in the rope! He can't get his bloody hand out!'

Daniel was dragged along in the dirt beside the one-tonne bull while it bucked and kicked, trying to get at him. Sarah could see the panic on her brother's face. He was pulling and yanking, trying to get his hand free. The rodeo clowns worked to help him while also trying to distract the bull. Then, to her horror, Sarah watched her brother's body slip underneath the bull as his hand came free. Devil's Grin bucked and stomped on top of Daniel before the clowns lured the bull away. A silence fell over the grandstand as Daniel's body lay deathly still.

'He's not moving, Lily. This can't be happening. Daniel!' Sarah could feel tears pouring down her face.

The clowns continued to divert the bull's attention as the medics came running in with a stretcher. One knelt down in the dirt, feeling Daniel's neck for a pulse. Sarah held her breath until he nodded to his fellow medic, indicating he'd found one. Sarah crumpled into Lily's arms, her body shaking with relief.

'Come on, Sarah. I'll help you down the stairs and we'll go and see how Daniel is. Come on, mate, just hold on to my arm and I'll lead the way for us,' Lily said, wiping

Sarah's tears but unable to hide her own shaking voice and trembling hands.

*

Daniel tried to smile but the pain forced him to wince instead. 'Sorry you all had to witness that. I did it though. I bloody rode Devil's Grin for the whole eight seconds!' He tried to sit up.

'Stay put, Dan, until we make sure you're okay,' Jack said firmly, his face betraying his anxiety. He was standing beside Maggie, who was deathly pale and holding onto Sarah for dear life. Lily stood next to Sarah, along with Brad, who'd come running from behind the chutes as soon as the accident had happened.

Sarah and Lily had almost collapsed in relief when they found Daniel conscious, although in enormous pain, behind the chutes. It looked like he might have escaped with a few broken ribs and concussion, but he needed to go to hospital to make sure there was no internal bleeding.

Maggie finally let go of her grip on Sarah and sat down on the ground beside Daniel, touching his hand gently. 'Your dad and I are going to come to the hospital with you, okay?'

'Yeah, okay, Mum. But I don't want any of you clowns coming along,' Daniel said weakly to Sarah, Brad and Lily. 'I'll be back to have a drink for your birthday, sis. You can count on it.'

They watched as the paramedics slid Daniel into the back of the ambulance, shut the doors and drove away, staring at the flashing red lights until they were out of sight.

'I hope he's going to be okay, Brad,' Sarah said, wrapping her arms around her boyfriend's broad shoulders and burying her head into the curve of his neck. His scent was comforting, and she felt a safety in his arms that she desperately craved.

'He's one tough bloke, your brother. I'm positive he'll be fine and back to have a drink with us like he said,' Brad said, stroking Sarah's hair.

Jack took hold of Sarah's trembling hands. 'Love, you stay here and try to enjoy yourself – you have a lot to celebrate. Daniel's in good hands, and I'll call you as soon as we know any more. No use us all sitting around the hospital like a mob of stuffed chooks.'

'Please call me as soon as you hear anything,' Sarah pleaded.

'We will, sweetheart. I promise,' Maggie said reassuringly, as she and Jack headed off to the car.

CHAPTER

4

Lily hadn't spoken since the ambulance left.

'Are you okay, mate? You haven't said a word,' Sarah asked, concerned.

'Oh, yeah, I'm okay, Sarah, I think. It's just, I dunno … What happened to Daniel really scared me. I felt emotions flooding through me I didn't even know I had. It's like they've been hidden all this time and tonight they finally got the courage to surface. I mean, of course I've known Daniel most of my life. He's like a brother to me … but what I'm feeling isn't the way you feel about a brother.' Lily paused, looking extremely confused.

Brad gave a low whistle and raised his eyebrows as Sarah smiled and wrapped her arm around Lily's shoulders.

'You sound like you're not sure if that's a good thing, Lil – but trust me, it is. About bloody time! I thought I'd caught glimpses of something between you two here and there, but I didn't want to say anything.'

'Well, gee whiz, Sarah Clarke,' Lily replied, grinning shyly. 'How did you know before me?' Her eyes widened and she looked like she was in mild shock. 'But I'm not the one whose brother's in hospital. How are you doing?'

'I'm calming down slowly. I'll feel better when I've heard from Mum that he really is okay.'

They decided to distract themselves while they waited by watching more of the action from the grandstand. It was dark now, and floodlights illuminated the centre ring while a blanket of stars glittered in the black sky above them like jewels. The night carried with it a chill and people were wrapped in thick coats and blankets, akubras glued to their heads to keep them warm. The comedy clowns were halfway through their show, giving the three a much-needed laugh. Halfway through the next show, the state bull riding competition, Sarah's phone rang.

'Sarah, it's Mum. Daniel's going to be okay! He has a couple of fractured ribs and a sprained wrist. The doc says he's had an amazing escape and he just needs to rest up. The doc also told him to stay away from the bull riding for a while. As if that's going to happen!'

'Oh, Mum. I'm so happy to hear that. We've all been so worried,' Sarah replied as she gave the thumbs up to Lily and Brad.

'It's crazy, but he really wants to get back to you to celebrate. We'll drop him off on the way past but, Sarah, please make sure he behaves himself tonight. They've given him some strong painkillers so he shouldn't be drinking at all. Keep an eye on him, okay? And have a wonderful night. Love you, sweetheart.'

'Love you too, Mum. Bye,' Sarah said as she flipped her phone shut and shoved it firmly back into her jeans pocket. Lily was tapping her foot with anxious energy, waiting for the news. Brad listened intently as Sarah filled them in.

'Shit, he was lucky. I'm glad he doesn't need an operation. He'll be sore for a while, but at least it's nothing too serious,' Brad said.

'Thank God he had no internal bleeding. I'm looking forward to congratulating him on his ride when he gets back here,' Lily said, her voice flooding with relief.

'Poor Daniel. He's going to be sore for weeks. But I feel like I can relax a bit now and enjoy the night,' Sarah said.

They sat back to watch the last half of the state bull riding competition. In the end, Queensland won, and the three of them hooted and hollered along with extra energy, born of relief, when the Queensland cowboys came out to centre ring and threw their hats up in the air in triumph.

'Who's up for a bit of grub and a drink at the bar then?' Lily asked.

'A drink sounds good to me. I'm as thirsty as a drover's dog,' Brad answered.

'I could definitely go a burger and chips from the CWA stand. The ladies always make a ripper burger. I didn't think I'd be able to eat, but now I know Dan is going to be okay I'm suddenly starving.' Sarah rubbed her belly.

Lily and Sarah got a steak burger each and shared a cup of chips smothered in salt and vinegar. Brad picked at the chips and got a playful slap over the hand from Sarah. Afterwards, Sarah bought a piece of deep-fried baked

cheesecake for the three of them to share. They sat on a hay
bale near the bar, devouring the fat-laden dessert, licking
their lips in pleasure. It went down an absolute treat.

*

Later, in the bar, Sarah and Lily were dancing like loons and
didn't see Daniel arrive.

'Hey Sarah!' he yelled from the sideline of the bumping
and grinding mob.

'Daniel!' Sarah screamed with delight. She left Brad on
the dance floor with Lily and ran towards him but he put
his arms up to stop her crushing whatever intact ribs he
had left.

'Don't hug me too hard, sis. I'm damaged goods at the
moment. You gotta treat me with care, the doc says.'

'Oh, Daniel, I'm *sooo* proud of you. You were amazing
out there tonight! I'm so glad you're here. I love you!' Sarah
spluttered as she wiggled and bopped to the music.

'Somebody's had a few drinks, I think,' Daniel said,
laughing and wincing.

Lily had made her way over with Brad and was waiting
to get a word in.

Daniel looked at her and seemed momentarily lost for
words. 'Lily, how are ya, mate?' was all he could muster.

'Great, Dan. But how are *you*, more to the question?'
Lily flashed a seductive smile, the alcohol helping loosen
those inhibitions.

'I'm gonna survive. Just,' he replied, with a cheeky grin.

'What can I get you to drink? You deserve one, I think,'
Lily asked, yelling over the band that had just started.

'A can of unleaded beer will do just fine. I'm not going to be drinking you under the table tonight, Lily. The doc's told me not to drink at all.'

Brad had mumbled something about needing the loo, so Sarah jumped in. 'I'll get you one, Daniel. You and Lily wait here. Maybe you can hire her as your nurse for the evening.' Sarah gave a devilish wink.

Before anyone could argue over who was shouting the round Sarah was gone. She returned with four beers just in time to watch, wide-eyed, as Daniel put his hand on Lily's cheek and leant in to kiss her on the lips. The passion flew between them like a fireworks display. Sarah waited for them to pull apart and tapped Daniel on the shoulder. He came out of his trance-like state and turned to her, grinning from ear to ear.

Lily and Daniel stood there blushing, looking like a couple of rabbits in the headlights. They reminded Sarah of two primary school kids who'd just been busted snogging behind the tuckshop by the headmistress.

'Geez, what did I miss?' Sarah asked.

Daniel blushed, grinning wildly. 'I asked Lily to come to Cairns with me on a date and she accepted!'

'How could I say no to an injured man?' Lily said shyly.

'This is just great, you two. I'm so happy you finally got it together!' Sarah squealed.

Brad arrived back to hear the last part of the conversation. 'Did you guys get together? About time, I reckon!'

Caught up in the emotion of the moment, Sarah turned to Brad and gave him a passionate kiss. He returned it briefly before pulling away and avoiding eye contact. She was sure she could smell something strange on his breath. He was chewing on gum, though, so she couldn't really tell. Maybe she was just drunk and imagining things. Suddenly the band started playing 'Happy Birthday', and the crowd turned to Sarah. Delighted and embarrassed, Sarah cracked up laughing and then held her glass of Bundy and Coke up victoriously in the air, her curly blonde hair bouncing while she sang along.

Once the song had finished, Johnny Cash and June Carter's hit song 'We're Going to Jackson' pumped out of the speakers, and Lily squealed. 'Come on, Sarah! Your favourite song is on and we gotta dance!'

Just as they started dancing Sarah spotted Johnny Marsh coming for her. He was blotto – he'd evidently been drinking solidly since she had seen him earlier. She ducked the incoming bear hug, causing him to stumble and collect Brad on the way down. The guys rolled on the ground in stitches of laughter, beer and whisky all over them.

'You right there, Brad?' Sarah asked, as she gave him a hand up off the ground. She could barely speak she was laughing so much.

'Thanks,' Brad replied as he clutched his groin with one hand and grabbed Sarah's hand with the other. 'Johnny hit me fair in the jatz crackers!'

Johnny grinned sheepishly as he got up.

The four of them danced as Daniel watched, singing out tunes from Garth Brooks, Brad Paisley, Slim Dusty, the Sunny Cowgirls and Lee Kernaghan. Finally, the night was over, and as Sarah looked up into the velvety night sky at the millions of stars above and smiled to herself, it felt as though everything she had ever wanted and dreamt of was within her reach.

CHAPTER
5

The Clarke household was up an hour before its rooster, Frank, crowed his morning wake-up call. Sarah felt the pang of sorrow the minute she opened her eyes. Today she'd be leaving her family home. But this was mixed with anticipation about her new life on Rosalee Station. She lay in bed for a few minutes, enjoying the sounds of the house coming to life as her family pottered around downstairs, staring at her wonky ceiling fan as though hypnotised by it. She knew she'd miss her family. Having them there any minute of the day was something she'd taken totally for granted. She felt tears well up and run down her cheeks, letting them fall, wanting to express the heartache she was feeling in the privacy of her room. It was going to be so hard driving away, but also thrilling to be heading towards her new adventure.

Brad had left the morning after Sarah's birthday, and Sarah had spent the week running around like a headless chicken, getting ready to leave. The trip itself was taken care of – Lily and Daniel had offered to drive her out to the station. Sarah was so happy her brother and best mate would be joining her on her journey – it was going to be a slow one with Victory in the heavy horse float behind the Cruiser along never-ending, unsealed roads. Lily had managed to get a week's leave from her job at the local real estate agency, and she and Daniel were going to fly home from Mt Isa after spending a few days on the station to help Sarah settle in.

Sarah sniffed and wiped away her tears, deciding it was time to suck it up and get out of bed. As she packed the last of her clothes into her bag, Maggie walked into her room. Sarah swallowed the huge lump in her throat, noticing Maggie's eyes were red.

'I've packed some food for the three of you in the esky, love,' Maggie said as she helped Sarah zip up her bag. 'I don't want you getting stuck in the middle of Woop Woop without food. Who knows what your brother's capable of if he gets hungry enough!' Maggie's cheeriness sounded forced.

'Thanks, Mum. You always look after me. What am I gonna do without you?'

Maggie reached out to Sarah and they held each other close for a few moments, catching each other's tears on their shoulders. Eventually Sarah pulled away and smiled at Maggie, wiping away her tears on the sleeve of her shirt. 'That's enough from us two crybabies, Mum. I'm old enough to be out in the world now, and I promise I'll call you all the time. It's only four months.'

Maggie smiled admiringly at her daughter. 'You're right, darling. But I'll miss having a female in the house. You're leaving me here surrounded by the cave men! Now let's go downstairs and get you on your way.'

*

Sarah whistled out the driver's window and Duke jumped in the tray of the Cruiser. He licked the window of the truck to say his hellos to all inside before making himself comfortable on the rug Sarah had thrown there for him. Lily and Daniel were ready to go, sitting next to Sarah in the front.

Jack put his hand through the window and handed Sarah $300. 'Take this for the fuel, love. I want to help you, so no arguments, okay?' And with that he stiffly tucked his hand back into the pockets of his shorts. 'Have a safe trip and make sure you call us on the way when you're in phone service. Your mother will be worried sick until she knows you're there safely.' He leant in and kissed Sarah on the cheek.

Sarah could see the sadness in her dad's eyes. She knew she would not hear the words from him, but his face told the story. Sarah felt a tug on heartstrings but she knew her old man would not want a big tear fest.

'Thanks, Dad. I appreciate the money. You behave yourself while I'm away, and no wild parties, okay!' Sarah laughed, trying to keep the mood light.

She reversed down the drive and took one last look at the mango-wood sign hanging on the front gate. It read *Clarkes' Farm* in large tired-looking white letters. Sarah and her brothers had made it for their parents years ago as a Christmas gift. It was looking worn now, after all the years out in the harsh sun, but Jack had been so proud of it. He'd marched straight out the front, dressed only in his boxers, and hung it up for all to see.

Sarah took a long hard look at the house from the front, taking a photograph with her mind so she could engrave it into her memory. The double-storey Queenslander stared back at her as the sun rose idly behind it. The weatherboards were in need of a fresh lick of paint, but the place still held loads of charm. The big verandahs that snaked their way around the house were filled with flowering potted plants, thanks to Maggie's green thumb. The miniature windmill Lily had given the Clarkes a few years back sat in the middle of the big front garden, spinning lazily in the light early-morning breeze.

Sarah sniffed the air, wanting to get her last smell of the mango flowers before driving away, then threw the old girl into first and took off down the dusty dirt road, Lily and Daniel waving like schoolkids as Sarah honked the horn. Soon the only evidence of their passing was a huge trail of rolling dust.

*

'Would you like to pick a CD, guys?' Sarah asked.

Daniel passed her *Garth Brooks Ultimate Hits*. As she put it on, Sarah took a fleeting glance at the Mareeba rodeo grounds from the window. It was now a hushed, giant grassland with a big, empty arena, hibernating until the following year's rodeo. A few grey nomads had their vans parked haphazardly around, making the most of the camping grounds with hot showers and toilets.

Heads turned as the trio drove through Mareeba, singing at the top of their lungs, way out of tune. Duke lay in the back of the Cruiser with his paws over his head. Sarah smiled, in between belting out lyrics, as she drove down the main street of Mareeba. The footpaths were still fairly quiet and most of the shops weren't open, other than the servos, the bakeries and the two newsagencies, which drew a certain kind of morning crowd. The pub was closed, the guests in the rooms upstairs probably sleeping off hangovers.

In the blink of an eye, they were through Mareeba, heading towards Atherton, the greener side of the tablelands. Here the volcanic soil produced a red dust that stained everything in sight. The cows looked close to obese from the endless supply of lush green grass – the polar opposite of Mareeba. Sarah turned towards Inner Hot Springs, famous for its unique thermal mineral springs that were said to have healing qualities. She'd always meant to have a look at them on her way to Mt Garnet for the rodeo and now pulled in to have a quick look.

They piled out of the car to admire the steaming waters. Daniel stuck his toe in, quickly pulling back with a shocked look on his face.

'What mad bugger would wanna hop in there? It must be close to eighty degrees!'

The girls giggled as Daniel shook his head in disbelief. Sarah took a quick snap of Daniel and Lily arm in arm in front of the steaming springs before they jumped back into the Cruiser. Daniel unpacked some bacon sandwiches and they filled the gaping holes in their bellies as they took in the scenery, drinking cups of coffee from the thermos.

Not long after, they arrived at Mt Garnet, famous for its rich mining history and the annual rodeo. You could have sneezed and missed the place. Sarah instinctively wriggled in her seat as she read the road sign on the way out of the tiny town, informing her it was 430 kilometres to Hughenden. It was time for the long haul, where mobile phones didn't work, cattle were frequent obstacles on the road, there was no such thing as a traffic light or a roundabout and it was rare to see much traffic other than the odd road train. They drove through ironbark woodlands and swamps, where grey kangaroos drank thirstily, a beautiful sight in a vast land. Sarah watched as a pair of wedge-tail eagles circled above the car. They looked as though they were floating without an ounce of exertion in the infinite blue sky.

They had been driving for two hours when they pulled up for a much needed leg stretch and a sugar hit at the Oasis Roadhouse, famous for Queensland's smallest bar. Sarah whistled for Duke to jump down off the back and he ran straight for the first tree, relieving himself for close to a minute. Sarah, Daniel and Lily bought cold drinks and ice-creams, which melted as they ate them.

'Shit, it's hot, and it's only nine a.m!' Sarah declared while wiping the sweat from her forehead and managing to smear chocolate ice-cream across her face.

Lily giggled, talking with a mouthful of Golden Gaytime. 'Bloody oath it is. I reckon we'd die of heat exhaustion in a few hours out here without shade and water.'

Daniel shoved the last of his strawberry Drumstick in his mouth before wiping the leftovers on his jeans. 'I need to take a leak, ladies, so I'll meet you back at the Cruiser in a minute.'

'Rightio,' Sarah and Lily said in unison, yelling 'Ditto' at each other for doing so.

*

Lily and Daniel sat beside Sarah, singing along with the CD. They'd been inseparable since the rodeo. Lily had stayed with Daniel the whole week, only going home once to grab some clothes for work. Even in the few hours she was gone, Daniel rang her twice to tell her he missed her. Sarah had never seen Lily so happy with a bloke before, and Daniel was clearly head over heels. His ribs were still causing him grief, but the pain was lessening with each day.

Once they turned towards inland Queensland, they left the picturesque coastline of sapphire-blue oceans behind them and the landscape changed into a vision of weathered red dirt, with a glimmer every now and then of dams shining in the sunlight like jewels. Cattle stood in open fields, frantically swishing away the flies with their tails, trying to find shade under barren trees. Windmills spun slowly, attuned to the laidback attitude of the outback, each blade throwing off specks of sunlight. Houses were scattered along the way. Some were far in the distance, behind fields of horses and cattle, but others were right beside the highway. Their gardens were filled with bougainvilleas, native trees, shrubs and beautiful flowers. The land was so vast that

Sarah felt an amazing sense of freedom just watching the landscape pass her by. It was a feeling many city people never got to experience, and Sarah thanked her lucky stars that she was a country chick through and through. The bush was in her veins, in her very core, and she could never think of living anywhere else but on the land.

It was another long trek along an unsealed road where the three ate loads of lollies, sang country tunes at the tops of their lungs and peed on the side of the road under ironbark trees – there were no toilets out here. As they drove deeper into the heart of the country, they passed Porcupine Gorge, towering cliffs of coloured sandstone standing proudly above permanent waterholes with pockets of vine forests adorning the water's edges, a striking contrast with the plains that surrounded them. Lily squealed with excitement as an emu crossed the road in front of them at lightning speed. It was beginning to really feel like the outback.

They cheered loudly as they entered the town of Hughenden at midday, their bellies rumbling for some lunch. The locals, a whopping total of 1200, waved cheerfully at the newcomers driving through their town. Sarah found their warmth so reminiscent of every outback town she had been lucky enough to visit. She pulled into the local pub, making sure to park in the shade for Victory. He'd been a total breeze to travel with, seeming to enjoy his adventure on the road as much as Sarah was. She opened up the back of the float and led him out, giving him a scratch on the neck and telling him what a champ he had been. He whinnied back to her gently. Sarah looped his rope up to the side of the horse float and placed a fresh bucket of water near him that he could drink at his leisure.

Sarah sat with Duke in the beer garden while Daniel and Lily ordered fish and chips. The service was fast and they had their lunch within ten minutes.

'I'm so glad you guys came with me on this trip,' Sarah said, dunking a chip into the homemade tartar sauce. 'Otherwise I would have to talk to myself, and that could get quite boring!'

'You do that anyway, sis,' Daniel said.

Lily burst out laughing with a mouthful of Coke, spraying it out her nose. Sarah and Daniel joined in, and Sarah felt her heart swell with happiness. She was young, free and on holidays in the Australian outback.

It was Lily's turn to drive, and Sarah watched in amazement from the passenger's seat as the landscape transformed yet again, this time into flat, black soil plains with star burr and devil's needles scattered about, thriving in the dry and arid land. They all covered their noses to avoid the stench of a dead pig lying on the side of the road, probably killed by keen pig hunters who had dumped their catch.

'Oh, boy. Did you fart Daniel? That's enough to gag a maggot!' Sarah teased as she fruitlessly swiped the air. Daniel playfully reached across and slapped Sarah.

'Get real, sis, I don't smell that bad when I release a beast!'

The three stopped for a quick refuel in Richmond, keen to continue the trek through to Julia Creek, famous for its annual Dirt & Dust festival. It was 150 clicks away along bitumen road, which would make the trip more comfortable. The scenery didn't change much between Richmond and Julia Creek. The highlight of the stretch was taking photos of a gathering of over 200 galahs, who were squawking at ear-piercing levels while resting on a boundary fence near a shimmering dam.

They reached Julia Creek at four o'clock. The area was home to a rare and endangered marsupial, the Julia Creek dunnart, which not many ever saw because of its timid nature and nocturnal habits. Sarah's grandad swore he had seen one, but she never knew whether he was pulling her leg. Everywhere you looked there was evidence of the rich local cattle and wool industry. Sarah was especially impressed by the size and quality of the cattle saleyards – evidence the town was a vital link within the beef industry. The feel of the place took you right into the heart and soul of rural Australia with Queenslanders standing proudly amongst gardens filled with bottlebrush, banksia, flowering mallee daisies and weeping paperbark trees. Sarah was entranced by the stark beauty of the little town.

'Isn't it lovely here guys?'

Lily nodded her head as she gazed out the window. 'It's like a little oasis.'

'Yeah, it's great, girls, but I'm about to burst here. Do you reckon you could find a bloke a dunny?' Daniel squirmed in his seat.

'Geez, Daniel! You're worse than a sheila!' Lily teased.

Lily pulled up beside the public toilets and Daniel scrambled out of the Cruiser. The two girls followed, happy to stretch their legs after being on the road for so long.

Duke jumped down from the back and ran around like a madman, chasing the local wildlife to let loose some pent-up energy. Meanwhile Sarah made a quick call to her parents from the phone booth beside the toilets. They didn't talk long as she didn't have a lot of change, but at least she'd let them know they were all alive and well.

Daniel was in the driver's seat when she got back in after checking on Victory, who was chewing contentedly on some hay she had put in there for him earlier.

'You two ladies might wanna try and get some shut-eye on the next part of the drive. There isn't going to be much of a change to the scenery anyway. It'll be about three hours before we hit Mt Isa – just in time for a counter meal, I reckon.'

'Yeah, thanks, Dan. My eyelids feel like lead weights. I reckon I'll take your advice on that cat nap.' Sarah rubbed her eyes.

'Me too, mate. Slap me if I start snoring and drooling though!' Lily smiled. Daniel pulled back out onto the highway and drove towards Mt Isa. The girls were asleep in minutes.

*

They had been on the road for close to fourteen hours when Daniel pulled into the pub in Mt Isa. 'I'm starving, ladies, and drier than an Arab's fart. I could really sink my teeth into a big piece of rump,' he called, rubbing his rumbling stomach.

Lily yawned and sat up slowly, blinking. 'Me too. My mouth is watering just thinking about it.'

Sarah felt her belly growl too. 'Me three. I want mine still mooing on the plate – cooked for a few seconds each side and that's it. Any longer and you've killed the thing twice,' she said, opening the car door and stepping down from the truck. She'd been sitting for so long now she wondered if she'd ever get the feeling back in her bum cheeks.

Duke sat obediently in the back of the truck until Sarah told him he could get down. He ran up to the first tree he could find, directly under a huge floodlight in the pub's car park, and peed for what seemed like forever. Sarah hoped no one was watching.

'Poor bugger must have been busting,' Lily said, stretching her arms high up in the air. 'As a matter of fact I need to go too. I'll meet you two inside at the food counter, okay?'

'Okay, Lil. I just want to get Duke settled in the back with some food and check on Victory,' Sarah answered.

Daniel gave Lily a quick peck on the lips. 'I'll stay and help Sarah, beautiful.'

Victory was quite happy in the float. He was proving to be a great horse to travel with. He hadn't minded going in the horse trailer, and there was no kicking or mucking about. He actually seemed to enjoy it.

Sarah got Duke his dinner out of a can and put it in the back of the Cruiser along with a bowl of water. She whistled to him and in seconds he was digging into his food, back from joyfully sniffing around the car park.

'You keep guard out here, boy, and watch our stuff, okay? I'll bring you back some of my steak.' Sarah gave her loyal mate a pat as she headed off with Daniel to get some well-deserved dinner.

*

Lily was about to burst by the time she found the ladies' toilets. On her way to a cubicle she squeezed past a bunch of women dressed like they were ready for a night out on the town. They were checking out their reflections in the mirrors, hiking up their already short skirts and arranging their boobs for maximum cleavage. Lily quickly looked down, not wanting to catch their attention. They reeked of cheap perfume. As she passed, she couldn't help noticing the bright red nail polish on one of the girl's toes. While she sat on the loo she could hear them talking – there was no way she could avoid eavesdropping. The conversation sounded like an episode from *Days of our Lives* and Lily couldn't help but be a little curious.

'I know I shouldn't have done it in the first place, seeing I'm in a serious relationship. And I do feel kinda bad, but I *was* drunk, and fuck, he was good in bed. He banged me like a dunny door and I rode him like the bucking bronco he is!' said one of the girls in a high-pitched voice.

'Seriously? Oh my God, that's so hot!' said another.

'I think about doing it with him all the time now, I just can't help myself. Nobody knows, obviously, and if this got out, you know it'd all be over. But you are my besties, and I needed to be able to tell *somebody* all the juicy details!' She laughed drunkenly and her friends giggled along with her.

Lily waited until she heard the women leave before pulling up her jeans and flushing the loo. 'Sounds like she's conquered more pricks than a second-hand dartboard,' she muttered to herself.

*

Lily smiled when she spotted Sarah and Daniel already sitting at a table.

'Hey there, Lily, we've ordered for you. Hope you don't mind. You were taking ages – we thought you'd fallen down the loo. I was just about to send a search party in for you,' Sarah said as Lily pulled up a chair beside them.

'Sorry guys. It was all the bloody coffee. It took me ages to pee it all back out again!'

'My mouth is watering,' Sarah declared as she looked around the room, eyeing all the yummy-looking food people were eating.

The speakers blared to life as a woman's voice called out their number in a monotone. Daniel was up and out of his seat before the echo of the microphone had stopped.

'Come on you two, let's grab our dinner.'

They headed over to the counter where their steaks were waiting for collection. Each was a huge piece that hung over the edges of the plate.

'Shit, there's half a bloody cow on my plate. Awesome!' Daniel beamed.

They helped themselves to the salad bar and poured tomato sauce over their chips. Sarah was actually salivating by the time she got back to the table. They ate in silence, too busy enjoying their food to utter a word. Sarah collected the scraps off the plates and rolled them up in a serviette for Duke.

'You guys ready to head? We still have another two hours' driving.' Sarah downed the last of her light beer.

'I'm ready as ever. That was a great piece of steak.' Daniel stood up, undoing his belt a little.

'I'm going to crash as soon as my head hits the pillow tonight, even after my three-hour nap.' Lily yawned.

They lethargically wandered out to the Cruiser for the final leg. *Nearly there,* Sarah thought, as butterflies started in her belly. She couldn't wait to see her new home at Rosalee.

Lily and Daniel were asleep within ten minutes of leaving Mt Isa. Sarah flicked the radio on low for company, and hummed along. She finally hit dirt road and thought about all the stories she had heard about the min min lights. They were famous around these parts – there were even signs up on the side of the road warning people about them. *Talk about putting the wind up a person,* she thought. These mysterious lights appeared in the darkness and sometimes moved, and no one to this day had been able to really explain the phenomenon. They freaked Sarah out, and she was glad she had the two sleeping bodies in the car with her. There were so many different yarns about what they were and where they had originated from that you didn't really know who to believe.

She had been driving along the dirt track for about half an hour when she felt the steering wheel tug to the left. She sat bolt upright and gripped the wheel, her adrenaline rush making her feel acutely awake. It felt like she had a flat tyre and had lost control of the steering. The truck bounced and jerked, pulling over to the side of the road. It felt like driving on ice, and Sarah yelled out in fright, thinking of Victory in the float. Daniel and Lily snapped awake.

'It's all right, just calm down, Sarah,' Daniel said, clutching at his ribs. 'You've just hit a stretch of bull dust, that's all.'

'Bull *what*!' Sarah yelled, still struggling with the steering wheel. 'You better not be pulling my leg, Dan!'

'Just go with the flow, and you'll find you'll float right out of it. Keep your foot down on the accelerator about halfway, 'cause if you slow down too much it's even harder to drive through, but if you go too fast it will take control of the Cruiser,' Daniel explained, trying not to laugh at his sister's face as she concentrated hard on his instructions. She hunched forward like an old person trying to see out the windscreen, her knuckles white from gripping the steering wheel so tightly. Lily burst out laughing.

'What are you two buggers laughing at, then?' Sarah said, her face cracking into a grin. She was a country girl, that was true, but she hadn't ever driven out any further west than Charters Towers. This was her first lesson in the real Australian outback.

They drove on for another hour, chatting to each other to stay alert. The corrugations in the road were teeth-shattering, and on top of that the car was dodging cattle left, right and centre, so she had to drive with extreme caution.

It was close to eleven when they realised they were nearly there.

'Keep your eyes peeled for an old Toyota bonnet with "Rosalee Station" written on it,' Sarah said, barely able to contain her excitement.

'I can see something just up ahead. The headlights keep catching it when we hit the corrugations,' Lily replied.

'Yep, that's definitely it. Look at the big red arrow pointing the way to go – no road signs out here. You gotta love it!' Daniel laughed as the car swung past the sign and followed the dirt track for another ten kilometres or so before arriving at the front gates.

Sarah flashed her headlights to high beam, and within a minute she could see Brad walking towards the gates. She had to contain her urge to jump out of the car and kiss him. Brad smiled when he got close enough to see them, his pearly whites shining in the headlights. He opened the gates, directing them through with a cheeky grin. Sarah drove through slowly and stopped when Brad was level with the driver's window.

'Hi there. Wanna lift?'

'Don't mind if I do.' Brad leaned in the open window to give Sarah a kiss. Daniel and Lily moved to the back of the truck and Brad got in the front.

'How was the trip, babe?'

'It was long, but amazing to see how the countryside changes as you drive here.'

'Here, Sarah, take a left turn and you'll see the stables just ahead.' Brad pointed the way.

They got Victory settled into his new home, unhitching the horse float. Victory seemed pleased to be out of the trailer and in a wide open paddock.

Sarah drove on to the workers' cottage and parked her LandCruiser under a giant paperbark tree so it would shade all her stuff when the sun rose. She left her headlights on for a moment, studying the magnificent, papery layers of the tree standing powerfully in front of her. She jumped in fright as a ringtail possum scampered up the massive trunk, its eyes glowing eerily red in the beams of the headlights. Paperbarks were Sarah's favourite native tree, utterly striking to look at; she would admire its beauty more tomorrow.

'Bugger unpacking until morning,' she mumbled to Brad as she turned off the lights and cut the engine. She sat in the driver's seat for a few more seconds; gazing up at the infinite blanket of radiant stars filling the night sky with their brilliance. She shook her head in awe. She had never seen anything so beautiful.

In the distance Sarah could hear the generator clanking and sputtering, supplying the station with electricity. A quick glance in the back of the Cruiser caused her eyes to widen – there was a film of red dust covering every square inch, including Duke. He jumped down off the tray and Sarah gave him a loving scratch on the head.

'Come on, mate. Let's see our new home.'

Duke tipped his head as if to let Sarah know how much he was enjoying the attention. If he was a cat he would have purred as loud as the generator.

Sarah, Daniel, Lily and Brad headed for the workers' cottage with Duke in tow. He was sniffing the ground as he went, investigating all the new smells.

The outside of the large cottage was clean and simple. It was made from corrugated iron with a rustic Aussie charm. There was bougainvillea hugging every corner of it, the magnificent colours bright under the fluorescent light that lit up the cottage like an outback lighthouse. Millions of insects buzzed around, drawn to the lights, and geckos feasted on this endless buffet.

Once they set foot on the cool cement of the front patio they took off their boots, placing them near the other pairs thrown haphazardly about, and stepped inside. Sarah smiled: here she was, at Rosalee Station.

CHAPTER

6

Sunlight flooded the bedroom through the crack in the thick blackout curtains. It stirred Sarah out of her deep sleep and she stretched and yawned slowly, forgetting for a few moments where she was. It took her a second to get her bearings and then she smiled. She was lying beside Brad on a working cattle station in the heart of the Australian outback. What a dream come true! She rolled over to where Brad was sleeping and kissed him gently on the lips.

'Good morning,' Brad said sleepily.

Sarah was itching to get out of bed and discover the new place she was calling home. 'Would you like to make your lover a cuppa? I'd kill for a cup of tea and some Vegemite on toast, if it's not too much trouble,' she said, playfully poking him in the ribs.

'Sure thing,' Brad said, smiling as he commando rolled out of bed to ward off the tickling. 'We've got a big day ahead, showing you the ropes.'

As Brad headed into the hallway, Sarah got up, wearing one of Brad's T-shirts and boxers, and ripped open the curtains. The view took her breath away. It was not one of nature, but a naked guy walking on the cement path outside to the outside shower with a towel tossed over his shoulder. He was whistling away like he didn't have a care in the world. Sarah gasped. Before she had time to drop out of sight, the guy looked up and caught her looking out the window. She saw his lips shoot out, 'Shit!' as he covered his manhood and ran to the shower, his iridescent white arse glowing. She giggled to herself and tried to take in the view minus the nudity, but the shower and toilet block were in the way.

Just then the smell of toast reached her. She headed out towards the kitchen and found a much better view out the kitchen window. The land rolled in front of her like she was looking at a work of art. There was no end to the vast, flat, red plains. Dust floated in the air like it had an inherent right to be there and galahs flew about squawking to each other, enjoying the bliss of the morning sunlight. She could see the horse paddock too, and could just make out Victory with his head down, grazing. *Great*, she thought to herself. *Looks like he's settled in quite happily.*

Last night Brad had taken Victory to a paddock of his own instead of putting him in with the other horses. The gelding had been pleased to be out of the trailer, and Sarah had let him loose in the paddock for the night, since he had it to himself. No doubt he'd had a bit of a gallop around and checked out his surrounds.

'Brad, I just met one of the guys,' Sarah said, turning from the window, embarrassment making her blush.

'Oh, did you? That's great. Hope he was on his best behaviour,' Brad replied as he passed Sarah a piece of Vegemite toast.

'Well, um, he didn't really have the chance to introduce himself properly. I caught him walking butt-naked to the shower outside. Who does that in a house full of blokes?' Sarah asked as she felt her cheeks burn even brighter.

Brad burst out laughing. 'Oh, that's Liam. He's a bit of a character. Comes from Ireland but has lived here for about five years now, with his brother Patrick. I worked with them both last year. Shit, he's gonna be right embarrassed. Honestly, he's hilarious, Sarah, and he gets up to so much mischief. You two will get on like a house on fire.'

'Yeah, well, once we get over the fact I've seen him naked!'

Sarah and Brad did a quick tour of the cottage. Today was the workers' day off, so everyone was still in bed, apart from Liam, of course. There were six men, counting Brad, who worked on the station, and once you added Sarah herself, that meant seven bellies she would have to fill daily. *I can handle that,* she thought to herself. There was Stumpy, Patrick, Liam, Slim – who, Sarah gathered, was anything but – and a newcomer called Chris. Everyone except Chris had been working on the station every season for a while.

She could see straight away that the place was in need of a woman's touch, but it was not badly kept considering it was used mostly by men. There was the occasional jillaroo, but Brad had told her that single women staying in the cottage had caused too many punch-ups, so the station owners tried to keep any women in different sleeping quarters.

There were eight bedrooms centred round a huge lounge room with a massive box telly, which was right out of the eighties. Sarah was surprised it still worked. The floor was an incompatible mix of linos that looked to have been added at various points of the cottage's existence, with some bits looking quite new while other sections were nearly worn through to the cement flooring from all the foot traffic. Four mismatched couches, strewn with multicoloured cushions, were parked around the television and a massive coffee table made out of an old wagon wheel sat on a tired-looking rug. Sarah loved the homespun charm of it. Everything was a bit shabby, but cosy and inviting all the same.

The kitchen needed a good scrub-down, but it was actually a lot better than she'd expected. Brad told her that the owners had renovated it two years back as the cooks were complaining constantly about the shitty equipment.

'It's very impressive! I thought I'd be cooking in a kitchen from the dark ages. I'll be a happy little chef in here,' Sarah said, relieved. The kitchen opened out onto a huge back patio with shade cloth protecting the makeshift twelve-seater table. She gathered this was where they would be sharing all their meals. Party lights were strung up haphazardly around the edges of the shade cloth, and Sarah was sure the place had seen its fair share of booze-ups over the years.

'I'll go and see if Lily and Daniel are up so they can join us for some breakfast. Chuck on some more toast, would you?' Sarah padded off down the hall, enjoying the feeling of the cool lino on her bare feet.

She tapped on their bedroom door. 'Are you guys alive in there?'

'Alive and kicking, my little sister! We'll be out in a minute,' Daniel sung out.

'What's for breakfast, cook?' Lily asked cheekily a moment later as she cracked open the door.

'Brad's gonna make us a traditional Aussie breakfast – Vegemite on toast and a cup of Bushells tea. You better move your arses or you might miss out,' Sarah joked.

Sarah, Brad, Daniel and Lily were all sitting down at the table on the back patio, munching on their toast and laughing about Sarah's first encounter with bull dust, when Liam appeared and introduced himself to them all.

'Haven't I met you some place before?' he said, smiling as he shook Sarah's hand. She laughed and felt immediately relaxed in his company. Brad was right. Liam seemed like a really cool bloke.

One by one the men woke up and made their way into the kitchen to fill their empty bellies with toast, cereal and tea, joining the group at the table on the patio for a yarn. Duke, who'd spent the night on the porch, was jumping around like a toad in a sock with the excitement of it all. Stumpy got up first. He was the eldest of the lot and the boss of the jackaroos, with a weathered face that told a hundred stories of life in the saddle. His handshake was firm and genuine. Sarah could tell he was a man who said what he meant and meant what he said.

Slim was next up, and he was definitely the opposite of his nickname. He was a six-foot, beer-barrelled bloke with a huge face and freckly skin, his hair blazing ginger.

When he laughed, he warmed the place up like a fire on a cold night. He was closely followed out of bed by Patrick, Liam's brother, who was the spitting image of Liam with his shaggy brown hair and cheeky smile, like a naughty boy who'd been up to no good. Sarah warmed to all of them. Chris, the last one up, sat down at the table with a steaming cup of coffee, smiling awkwardly. He was handsome, Sarah thought, and he seemed friendly enough. But that was it. He *seemed* friendly, but there was something there that didn't feel genuine. Sarah shrugged off her vague feeling of distrust. After all, first impressions weren't always right.

Once breakfast was over, Sarah headed outside to start unloading the LandCruiser. She found herself grinning from ear to ear as she stepped onto the front porch. She took a deep breath, as if trying to breathe in the landscape that lay before her. There were red dust plains as far as the eye could see. Gidgee trees stood tall amongst patches of saltbush, while a flock of northern rosellas filled the skies with their rainbow of colours. She pulled on her boots and stepped out into the brilliant sunlight, feeling as though she'd finally set foot in the true outback. The atmosphere was still, uncomplicated, with a certain smell to it, a mixture of clean, fresh air with a hint of dust and dung. The huge paperbark tree was beckoning her and she walked over to run her hands over the peeling bark. Sarah's heart filled with joy as she realised that her new home was all that she had dreamt of.

Brad, Daniel and Lily pitched in to help unload the LandCruiser, and they got it done in half an hour. Sarah had tried to pack only essentials but it still felt like a lot. Her cookbooks were heavy, but a must – she wanted to provide decent meals for the men seeing as they had such a physically demanding job. Her favourite cookbook was just a notebook full of scribbled recipes she had gathered over the years from friends and family. It had some doozies in it that would knock the socks off even the fussiest of eaters – not that she expected to encounter fussy eaters out here.

'Who's up for a ride in the chopper this morning?' Brad said once they'd finished. 'The view from up there will blow your mind. One million acres to gaze at and about 20,000 head of cattle.' Three eager faces stared back at Brad, giving him his answer without having to utter a word.

'Righto, that's settled then! Firstly though, we'll all head up to meet the station owners. Judy will love the company. She could talk under wet cement with a mouthful of marbles. I think she gets a little lonely at times living all the way out here. She makes a wicked pumpkin scone, and normally has them on hand for anyone popping in.'

'I'm looking forward to meeting her. And it's going to be fantastic going for a flight with you!' Sarah squealed, barely able to contain her excitement.

They all piled into the LandCruiser, Daniel and Lily jumping up in the back with Duke.

'It's beautiful out here, Brad. It's amazing how such a vast space can be full of so much to look at. It just mesmerises you,' Sarah said dreamily. Weeping bottlebrush hung over the side of the dirt track that led to the homestead, their brilliant red flowers stark against the dusty backdrop. Colossal anthills were all over the place, the outback's version of skyscrapers, home to millions of workaholic ants that could pack a punch with one bite. They drove past a holding yard full of cattle, Sarah sniffing the air madly to catch the scent of them. The beasts bellowed loudly, kicking up billows of dust as they moved about. Next they drove past a huge shed full of machinery, new and old, before taking a turn down near a building that Brad said was the meat house, where the station butchered its cattle. Not far off to the right of the building was what looked like a professional bull riding area, chutes and all. Sarah felt her stomach lurch with excitement. 'What's that all about, then?'

'Oh, that's Matt's baby,' Brad said. 'The station owner's son. He uses that area to train his bucking bulls, and he also teaches young lads how to ride. You'll have to come down and watch him sometime. He's a brilliant bull rider.'

Sarah's eyebrows shot up, revealing how impressed she was. 'I'd love to watch someone training bulls. How bloody fantastic!'

They pulled up out the front of Judy and Steve Walsh's homestead, parking under the shade of a coolabah tree. A rustic timber fence bordered the massive, two-storey red-brick home, built to withstand the searing heat of the outback. The Colorbond roofing looked new, and there was a solar water-heating system on it. A swing chair hung in the shade of the front verandah, the perfect spot for relaxing with a cuppa. A wind chime sounded melodiously from near the front door. There was an enormous rainwater tank off to the side of the house; the size of it amazed Sarah. A windmill sat on the other side of the homestead, spinning lethargically in the morning sunlight as if trying to wake up.

But if the house was beautiful, the garden was even more so. It was like stepping from one planet to another when you walked down the path to the front door. Bougainvillea was in full bloom, in every shade imaginable, and the grass was greener than her lawn back home in Mareeba during the wet season. A thriving vegetable patch was visible off to the side of the house. It was like a tropical oasis in the middle of the harsh Australian outback, and gave you a warm, welcoming feeling before you even got inside.

Sarah was nervous about meeting her new boss and his wife. She wanted to make a good first impression. Judy and Steve had two children: Georgia, who was the same age as Sarah, and Matt, who was twenty-five. Georgia worked alongside her dad every day whilst Matt drove the semitrailer in and out of Mt Isa regularly to deliver cattle to the saleyards. He was away a fair bit, Brad had told her, but when he was home he bred stud bulls for bucking out at rodeos, and to sell for breeding.

Brad yelled out through the flyscreen door once they reached the front porch. Judy swiftly appeared in an apron covered in flour. 'Hello, you lot, you're just in time for some scones. Come in and make yourselves comfortable with Steve and Georgia out on the back verandah. But before you go anywhere, I must know – which one of you is Sarah?' Judy asked, wiping her hands on her apron.

Sarah stepped forward. 'Hi, it's so great to finally meet you, Judy. I'm really happy you guys have given me the job of cook. Thanks heaps.' Sarah reached out to shake Judy's hand, but Judy ignored her and leant in for a warm, welcoming and amazingly firm hug. It took Sarah by surprise, as Judy was petite, but when you looked a little closer, her hands showed years of hard work, and her kind brown eyes revealed a strength that came from years of living in the unforgiving outback. Sarah was overwhelmed by a sudden feeling that she and Judy were going to be in each other's lives for a long time. Shaking the feeling off, she quickly introduced Lily and Daniel, who were waiting patiently behind her. Judy gave them both one of her welcoming hugs.

'You have the most amazing garden,' Lily said, smiling.

'Thanks, Lily. I do love to garden. Mind you, I have to water a lot and Steve gets a bit cross with me. I tell him to zip his lip, though, because at least I don't want diamonds and pearls to keep me happy!' Judy answered with a cheeky grin. 'Now let's all head out the back so you can meet the larrikins of the household. Matt is away at the moment but you'll get to meet him tomorrow.'

Sarah took in as much as she could of the old homestead as she walked through it. There were black and white pictures of men riding bulls, showing days gone by, beautiful sunsets with cattle and dust in the foreground, and family photos adorning every wall. Old akubras were perched on hooks, and leather whips and saddles that had seen their days out mustering were now on show in corners of the house. A huge grandfather clock ticked away in the comfortable lounge room, commanding Sarah's attention with its antique beauty. Sarah presumed it must be a family heirloom. A large, black leather lounge held centre place amongst bookshelves filled to the brim with books.

Sarah was getting occasional wafts of the scones Judy had just baked, and her belly started rumbling in anticipation of the yummy mounds of golden yellow glories smothered in jam and cream. They were her favourite treat when she was a kid hanging around her mum's ankles, and nothing had changed since then.

Steve and Georgia were sitting with their feet resting up on the top rail of the verandah, pushing their chairs back to balance on the two back legs.

'Will you two buggers sit on those chairs properly?' Judy exclaimed, following Lily outside. 'You're going to go head over heels one day and get a right bruise on the back of your noggins!' Sarah smothered a smile as Steve and Georgia dropped their legs off the rail in unison and quickly but carefully lowered their chairs to the ground.

'Hey, guys, I'm Georgia. Happy to meet you,' Georgia said, standing to welcome them. Sarah noted how pretty she was while shaking her outstretched hand. Georgia had olive skin and jet black hair, pulled back in a tight ponytail with wisps floating around her face, and she was attractively curvy.

'You lot are just in time for smoko. You seem to time that well quite often, Brad,' Georgia teased. 'I think you're addicted to Mum's famous scones.'

'Oh no, you've caught on to my secret smoko plans,' Brad said, faking shock and smiling.

'Hi there, Sarah. Nice to finally meet you after all the stuff Brad has told me. Most of it's good, so don't worry,' Steve said, as he shook Sarah's hand like he was operating a jackhammer. 'We're rapt you've decided to come out here and feed our hungry mob. It was getting too much for Judy, so you're really helping us out.' Steve pushed more chairs over to the table on the porch for them all to sit down.

'I'm very happy to be here, Steve, so thanks for the opportunity. I'll make sure your workers are well looked after,' Sarah answered. She could not get over how much she felt like a part of their family already, and she'd only known them for ten minutes.

'Hey Brad, when Matt gets back home tomorrow, why don't we have a barbecue and a night of cards at the cottage so we can enjoy ourselves before the season really kicks off?' asked Georgia.

'Sounds like a plan to me, Georgia girl. You supply the beef and I'll supply the beer. Deal?' Brad answered.

'Deal. And you guys can meet Matt – and Brooke,' she continued, turning to Sarah, Daniel and Lily. 'Matt's bringing his missus back with him from Mt Isa – the city chick has finally decided to move out here.' Georgia rolled her eyes. 'Fat lot of help she's gonna be round here. She hates getting her hands dirty!'

'Well, we're always up for a party,' Daniel replied.

'Good. Party tomorrow night then,' Georgia said as she headed into the house to help her mum carry out the trays of scones and jugs of homemade lemonade.

*

Sarah slid into the chopper seat and pulled on her seatbelt, checking three times that it was firm and secure. She slipped the headphones and microphone over her head, watching anxiously as Brad prepared for their journey in the sky.

He checked everything carefully before he flicked a switch and the blades stirred into action. Sarah had always loved the noise they made, the powerful strength of the motor spewing out its energy through the immense force of the blades.

Stumpy had told her a bloodcurdling story about choppers that morning, explaining how he had got his nickname. When he was still a young lad, trying to break his way into the world of the jackaroo, he had somehow managed to slice off the top half of his left-hand fingers in a freak helicopter accident on a station. He said he could still feel the blades slicing through his fingers when he thought about it too much. Sarah shivered at the thought.

'It's time to hit the skies, Sarah.' Brad's voice boomed through the headphones, making her jump.

Sarah felt the chopper suddenly lift off the ground as if weightless, feeling her stomach lurch with the movement. She had been in a chopper a few times before with Brad, but it had been a while since the last time. She looked out the window, watching the homestead shrink quickly into the distance, her mouth dropping open in awe at the endless view that spread out before them. The ground below was a sea of red dirt, strewn with spinifex bushes and riddled with cracks, revealing the dryness of the earth beneath them. Far below kangaroos bounded this way and that, trying to escape the noise of the chopper. The terrain below looked completely treacherous to Sarah – she was glad to be viewing it from the safety of the chopper. Being stuck out there on foot would be a death sentence if you weren't bush savvy. Barbed-wired fencing stretched out for miles and miles, making Sarah admire the strength of the men that must have put them up with their bare hands. The occasional glimmer of a dam shone into her eyes, making her squint. Sarah watched a mob of cattle running away from the chopper, being swallowed by the clouds of red dust they kicked up behind them. She spotted the wheel of an old carriage sticking out of the ground. It lay buried under the years of life that had continued around it. Sarah wondered what happened to the people travelling in the carriage, many years before. It made her think about how immense the station was, and she felt a sudden surge of freedom. Brad pointed out areas below them, showing her the path they would be taking when they went on a seven-day muster across the station in a few months' time when Sarah would be camp cook. He explained how they would push the cattle along about twenty kilometres a day, putting them safely into a holding yard each night with food and water to let them rest their legs. They would then move camp the following morning and do it all over again, moving the cattle and putting them into the next holding yard, until they reached their final destination back at the homestead. Here the cattle would be loaded up and sent to the saleyards or the slaughterhouses. The younger ones would be tagged and sent back out to roam until the next muster.

'It's so amazing up here, Brad. I'm jealous you get this view every day. I pity the folk who live their lives in front of computers. They're missing out on all this.' Sarah waved her hands about, gesturing to the land beneath them.

'You're concentrating so hard on rounding the cattle up and working with the guys on the motorbikes and horses that you don't really get a chance to take it all in. You can come up with me tomorrow, if you want, and see what the mustering side of flying in a chopper is like,' Brad said as he turned the chopper back in the direction of the homestead.

A huge grin spread across Sarah's face. 'That sounds bloody fantastic! Count me in.'

*

Sarah let Duke come inside and sit out on the back patio. He had his very own spot out there now, so this was like his private bedroom, with an awesome view to boot. Sarah, Daniel, Lily and Brad gathered a few beers and a large packet of salt and vinegar chips and made themselves comfortable to enjoy the last few rays of the afternoon. Sarah gazed dreamily out at the horizon as the uninterrupted sunset filled the sky with a sea of spectacular colour. They were silent, other than the munching of chips, as they sat quietly admiring the sheer beauty of the scene as the sun slipped away and a clear sky full of stars took its rightful place.

Night time signalled dinner, and Sarah's belly started screaming for food. She and Lily went off to the kitchen to sort out some fodder while the men got the barbecue fired up. Slim, Stumpy, Liam, Patrick and Chris had joined them on the patio and were forming a rowdy crowd. The girls laid pieces of steak out on a tray and Lily took it out to the men. Sarah took on the duty of preparing a salad, whistling along happily to the tunes floating in from the stereo out the back. The Sunny Cowgirls were singing 'Dancing on the Darling' and she loved the song. It put her in a real party mood every time she heard it.

Taking a second to look up from the kitchen bench, Sarah drank in the scene that lay before her: a group of friends enjoying a night of food and laughter amongst the magnificence of the land sprawled out around them. She couldn't help but feel like the luckiest girl alive.

CHAPTER

7

Brad woke to his alarm at five a.m. He reached over to the bedside table and quickly switched it off so that it didn't wake Sarah – she looked so peaceful sleeping. Too many whiskies last night had left him with a dull throb behind his eyeballs and he groaned as he rolled out of bed. Slipping on a pair of work jeans and a T-shirt, he grabbed a pair of clean socks out of the clothes basket before he slipped quietly out the door.

'Good morning, guys. Ready for the big day ahead?' Brad asked as he wandered into the kitchen, rubbing his temples.

The men answered with grunts and groans as they stuffed pieces of toast into their mouths. Liam and Patrick were sipping coffee.

'You'd be able to stand ya spoon up in that bloody coffee by the smell of it, lads! I won't be able to keep up in the chopper after you down that much caffeine. You'll both be riding like you're in the Melbourne Cup!' Brad said, stirring them.

'Yeah, that's what all the women tell me,' Liam said, grinning like a Cheshire cat.

'Oh, pull the other one!' Brad laughed.

'Yeah, they say that too!' Liam threw back, and the whole room of guys erupted in laughter.

Stumpy put his cup in the sink to signal to the others it was time to head to work. 'Come on, you lot. We got ourselves some cattle to muster.' He picked up the packed lunch he had prepared that morning: Vegemite and cheese sandwiches, a packet of gingernut biscuits and a variety of different flavoured chips. Not really food fit for a king, but food all the same.

They stepped out into the cool morning air, enjoying it while they could. In an hour or so the temperatures would soar and the flies would stick to your skin like shit to a blanket. The flies were that brash out in the bush they would land on your eyelashes, refusing to budge, even when you swatted them like a maniac. They were an annoying part of the scenery, but the outback without flies would be like a lamington without coconut. It was just part and parcel of living in the Australian outback; even the flies out here had to be tougher than the city flies.

'Catch you lot out there. You got your walkie talkies turned on and ready for action?' Brad asked as he walked to his chopper.

'Rodger dodger,' Patrick answered in his strong Irish accent as he pulled on his well-worn boots.

Chris lagged behind the group as they went to get their horses, like he always did, puffing on his cigarette.

Slim tried to pull his jeans up under his belly, which was taking up a lot of space in his shirt. His buttons strained with every breath he took. He referred to his belly as the 'verandah over his toolshed', which always got a few laughs.

They saddled up in record time and headed towards the mob they would round up and bring in by tonight. The sun rose gloriously in front of them as they rode off towards the horizon in the sea of red dust from the horses' pounding hooves, their akubras perched high on their heads.

*

Sarah woke to the smell of bacon and eggs wafting into her bedroom. She stretched with the grace of a slinky cat and blinked a few times to allow her vision to clear, glancing at her watch. *Well, bugger me dead,* she thought to herself, *it's nearly nine a.m.* She heard a knock at the door. 'Come in if you're good-looking,' she sung out.

Lily peered through the door and smiled at Sarah, who had the wildest bed hair ever. It was like Sarah had stuck her finger in an electrical socket, and her crazy curls were the result.

'Good afternoon, Your Royal Highness. Are you gonna be joining the land of the living today? Daniel's been a real darling and cooked us a breakfast of bacon, eggs and baked beans. Real fart material,' Lily said, giggling.

Sarah threw her pillow in Lily's direction. 'Well, that's bad news for you two then, 'cause when I get a bad case of the arse burps my farts are right rippers!'

Lily ducked the incoming missile. 'You can say that again, Sarah. Poor Brad – he's gonna be stuck in the chopper with you in a few hours' time.'

Sarah threw another pillow, hitting Lily fair in the head.

Lily took a second to recover before picking the pillow up and heading for Sarah, who was now hiding under the sheets, screaming in mock terror. 'Right! It's on for young and old!'

Daniel appeared in the doorway just as one of the pillows exploded and the girls were covered in a sea of feathers. He burst out laughing at the sight of them.

Sarah blew a feather out of her mouth and turned to see her brother standing at the door, spatula in hand. Lily was giggling so much she had no strength in her legs to stand up. Tears of laughter were streaming down her face. The whole room looked like a bird had flown in the open window and hit the fan, succumbing to an instant and untimely death.

'Are you two all right there? Breakfast is ready and waiting when you've finished playing round like a pair of teenagers.'

Sarah rolled her bottom lip in mock sadness. 'Sorry Daniel. We got a bit carried away. Lily started it.'

'I think we know who started it, Miss Clarke!' Lily said.

Breakfast was so tasty Sarah almost picked up her plate to lick it clean, but she knew Daniel would slap her over the knuckles if she did that. He was a firm believer in good table manners, just like their dad. Neither Sarah nor Daniel had dared to move when they were kids at the dinner table. Until the last mouthful of food was eaten on everybody's plate, nobody would be excused from the table.

'What do you feel like doing for the next few hours? We can't go too far, 'cause Brad is coming back at lunch to take me up mustering with him,' Sarah said as she gazed out the kitchen window, devouring the view.

'How 'bout we go for a swim in the dam? It'll be nice to float around for a while,' Daniel suggested as he washed up the breakfast plates.

'That's a fantastic idea! Duke can tag along too. He'll love going for a dip.'

'I'm going to put my togs on then,' Lily said.

'Race ya!' Sarah said, whipping the tea towel at warp speed and slapping Lily on the backside.

The girls ran to get ready. Daniel smiled. The day had started well.

*

Sarah, Lily and Daniel made a beeline for the dam. Duke had jumped off the back of the Cruiser before they'd even had time to pile out. He was now swimming around in circles, barking at the splashes his paddling paws were making, creating a huge area of murky water around him. Lily squealed as her feet sunk into the soft, sludgy bottom of the dam.

'I hope there are no bloody snakes in here, girls!' Daniel teased.

Lily's face drained of colour. 'I'll walk on water if there is. They freak me out big time!'

'I think Duke would've scared them away with all his romping about, so don't worry, mate,' Sarah said. She knew snakes were one of Lily's biggest fears. When they were kids

Sarah had thrown a plastic snake on Lily as a joke, and Lily had completely lost the plot. She'd run around in circles screaming, too scared to touch the plastic predator hanging from her shoulders. Sarah thought it was hilarious but Lily had stormed off home in tears. She didn't talk to Sarah for days. Sarah realised then that Lily really had a hang-up about anything that slithered and hissed. She made a mental note to bring Daniel up to speed when Lily wasn't around.

It felt good to be splashing in the water. The sun was scorching hot, so hot it drained the energy out of them with every breath, even though it was only ten-thirty in the morning. The piercing rays had already heated the dam up, but it was still nice to be covered in water instead of sweat, dust and flies.

Sarah floated around on her back, giving Daniel and Lily some time together and enjoying the shade of the ghost gums at the edges of the dam. Their vivid white trunks glowed in the sunlight. Off in the distance, Sarah could hear the howling of dingoes, an eerie reminder of the hunters that called this land home, just as she did. The blue skies above filled momentarily with a mob of squawking cockatoos making their way to their next destination. A rare white fluffy cloud drifted past, giving Sarah the wonderful sense that there wasn't a care in the world.

*

'How goes it?' asked Brad as he walked into the cottage, kissing Sarah smack on the lips.

'Hey, babe. We hung out at the dam this morning and Duke caught himself some red claw. Not in the typical way, though. He came up yelping with one attached to his snout after chasing a rock down to the muddy depths below. Felt sorry for the poor bugger, but geez, it was funny!' Sarah giggled.

'That was until the beggar latched onto my finger when I was trying to get it off Duke,' added Daniel, inspecting the spot where the red claw had nipped his pinkie.

'Sounds like you had a fun morning, then. Good on you, guys. You ready, Sarah?' Brad paused, sculling a huge glass of water. 'We have to get back to where the men are before they finish their lunch and head to work again.' He sculled another one and then filled up his water bottle as Sarah said her goodbyes to Daniel and Lily.

Sarah was glad she'd followed Brad's advice and had a light lunch – she was already feeling nervous, and she hoped she wouldn't get sick. She felt the butterflies flapping around furiously as Brad manoeuvred the chopper into the air and around hills. At times he got so close to the ground Sarah swore she could have just stuck her hand right out and touched it. She watched over her shoulder, horrified, as the back propeller whipped up a massive cloud of dust after skimming the surface.

Stumpy spoke to Brad over the radio, telling him that a group of wayward cattle had gone off from the mob. Brad needed to get them back fast. Brad and Sarah had their eyes glued to the ground trying to spot them as Stumpy galloped off below them, his whip at the ready.

'There they are!' Brad boomed over the microphone. Sarah felt her stomach lurch as the chopper dropped down to the ground, heading straight for a large group of gidgee trees that the cows were huddled under. The smell of the fuel fumes pouring out of the chopper were making her queasy, and the dipping and diving was not helping one bit. She swallowed hard in an attempt to push her ham and cheese toastie back to where it was threatening to come up from. Meanwhile, Brad pulsed up and down in the air above the trees, trying to scare the cattle out towards the larger mob in the distance. All but one decided to heed the chopper's warning – a runaway bull took off in the opposite direction, kicking up clouds of dust. Brad swore as he lost sight of the bull for a split-second. Stumpy was on the ground, cracking his whip, trying to get the remaining cattle under control. The other men arrived at a gallop and circled the cattle like vultures, bringing the mob into a huddle while Brad held the chopper steady above them.

'I don't know where that bloody bull thinks he's off to. He sticks out like a country shithouse – there's nowhere to run and hide,' Brad muttered as he threw the chopper about vigorously in the air.

Sarah felt like she was on a fairground ride as Brad pushed the throttle forward to chase the bull. He pushed the chopper back up into the sky and flew over the top of the bull, dropping down with one swift movement so the chopper was facing the beast. The huge animal snorted and stomped his hoofs, defending his space. Sarah could not believe what she was seeing. This bull was ready to take on the chopper! Holy snapping duck shit, she thought to herself.

'Come on then, you bastard!' Brad yelled as he dropped the throttle even more and headed straight for the bull.

Sarah watched the big fella rethink his position quickly, then turn and run. They flew behind him, pushing him back towards the mob. Every time he tried to veer off Brad would dip and dive to each side, showing the bull where to go. Sarah was desperate to get out but she gritted her teeth and wore the nausea, taking sips from her bottle of water to settle her stomach. Brad didn't have time to take her back to the cottage until smoko, and the men would not think much of her if she interfered with the day's work. She forced herself to concentrate on the ground as the men began to push the cattle towards the yards, trotting at a nice pace now the rush was over. Brad hovered way above, keeping his eye out for any more wayward cattle. Sarah lent her eyes to the challenge, spotting the occasional cow that Brad would then push back towards the men on horseback. They crossed over rocky cliffs and deep valleys, searching for any movement amongst the scribbly gums. Water trickled through the deep crevices, bubbling up from natural springs deep underneath. It was a rare sight to see water out here, which made it all the more striking. Sarah saw a pack of dingoes drinking from a small watering hole, and wondered if they were the ones she had heard at the dam earlier. The ant hills out here seemed like palaces, even larger than the ones near the homestead. A wedge-tailed eagle rested on one of them, watching their strange metal bird in the sky. The weathered ground beneath rippled with the heat that rose from it. Even the air that forced its way around the cockpit was hot, so that Sarah and Brad were both dripping with sweat. All the elements of the bush were extreme, but Sarah couldn't help loving it, finding herself drawn to the spiritual timelessness of the vast untamed land. It was absolutely breathtaking, and made her feel so proud to be Australian.

*

At three o'clock the men let Brad know they were stopping for smoko. Sarah sighed with relief as the chopper headed back towards the landing pad near the homestead, silently applauding herself for having held on to her lunch.

Brad eased the machine down and gave her a quick kiss on the cheek. 'Have a nice arvo, gorgeous. I'll see you in a few hours. Georgia said to tell you she'll need a hand round five with all the food and getting the party set up, if that's okay with you.'

'No worries. I might take Victory for a ride and set him up in the main paddock before the men get back with their horses. At least that way he can settle in by himself for a few hours before contending with the others.' Sarah slid herself out of the seat and smiled when she felt her boots touch the earth below. She was as happy as a dog in a hub-cap factory to be out of the chopper and on solid ground.

Half an hour later she was trotting along on Victory, enjoying the scenery from the saddle. Victory had been happy to see her and seemed eager to go for a ride, which suited Sarah perfectly – she needed some time to herself. The last few days had been a whirlwind of travelling and settling into her new home. She wondered what her mum and dad would be up to right now. Probably in the packing shed, grinding away as usual. So far she'd only been able to speak to them for a few minutes to let them know she'd arrived safely. She'd give them a proper call at the end of the week.

Sarah spotted a huge bottle tree in the distance and gently motioned for Victory to pick up the pace, watching the trunk get bigger as they approached. Once beside it she was gobsmacked by its sheer size and couldn't help but slide out of the saddle and try to wrap her arms around it. Victory stood patiently as she tried to measure the width of the trunk with her arms like some tree-hugging hippy. It must have easily been two or three metres in circumference. Suddenly a thorny devil lizard scurried over her boot and she jumped in fright. They were the craziest-looking things, with intimidating spikes covering every inch of their bodies. She hopped back up in the saddle, the smells and sounds of the bush surrounding her as Victory gleefully clip-clopped beneath her.

Sarah was enjoying the peace so much that she got lost in her thoughts and completely forgot the time. When she remembered to check her watch it was nearly four-thirty. *Oh shit, I only have half an hour to get back and help Georgia,* she thought. She gave Victory a light tap in the ribs and instantly he threw his legs into a gracious gallop. Once back at the stables she gave him a good hose down, giggling at the way he tried to catch the water droplets with his lips, and settled him into his new paddock. 'Thanks for a fantastic ride, mate.'

Sarah went to grab Daniel and Lily from the cottage so they could all help Georgia out. Judy and Steve were coming along tonight, as well as Matt and his girlfriend. From a few comments the men had made about 'buckle bunnies', it was clear that they didn't like Matt's girlfriend much. But Sarah had decided she would make up her own mind.

Dusk was falling, awakening the stars in the night sky. Sarah carried a huge bowl of salad out to the table, already set with plates, cutlery and every sauce imaginable. The men had showered and dressed in their 'going to town' jeans and some of them had even gone to the effort of putting on aftershave. Georgia had gone home to get ready, leaving Sarah and Lily in charge of organising the barbie. The girls had found an old fridge in the storage shed, which now lay on its back, filled with cartons of beer in ice. The lid squeaked every few minutes as hardworking hands dug in, pulling out their next can of golden liquid. Sarah just hoped they could handle their liquor; they seemed to be drinking each beer in the blink of an eye. There were going to be some pretty sore heads tomorrow morning when they all got up at sparrow's fart. For now, though, the chatter was full of laughs as everybody relaxed and settled in for the night ahead.

'Which one of you lot wants to be in charge of throwing the snags and steak on the barbecue?' Sarah asked, breaking up the conversation about who had caught the biggest fish. She knew if she'd waited for the men to finish she would've been there all night.

'I don't mind doin' the cooking, mate.' Slim rubbed his big belly. 'I'm beginning to feel the twinges of major hunger comin' on. If I leave it to this lot we'll be eating charcoal, and I'll come dangerously close to being too thin.' He stood up to help, trying to pull his jeans up under his belly with no great success. Apparently he kept trying to go on a diet but food was his vice, and the odd sixpack was always great with dinner. Slim was a man that loved his meat, and thought that anybody who chose to be a vegetarian must have a few screws loose. 'I'll just grab another beer before I start cooking, though. I'm as dry as a bull's bum going up a windy hill backwards.'

There were a few chuckles as the men followed Slim over to the barbecue for moral support and to offer advice as to when he should be turning the meat. It was the same at every barbie Sarah had been to, and she guessed the tradition had been going on for decades.

'Brad and Dan, can you help carry the trays out for Slim? I have a huge bowl of onion too, so you might want to chuck that on first,' Sarah called, heading back to the kitchen where Lily was preparing her famous potato salad.

'Go on then, you two,' Liam said, smirking at Brad and Daniel. 'You've been summoned.'

'I wouldn't let Sarah hear you say that, mate. You might be eating shit on toast for breakfast otherwise,' Brad threw back at Liam. He didn't like Sarah bossing him around in front of his mates.

'Mmm, your favourite! Shit on toast!' Patrick said, playfully digging Liam in the ribs.

'Bugger off, you Irish twat!' Liam bellowed. He had always been massively ticklish, and Patrick knew it.

The two Irishmen wrestled each other to the ground. Stumpy stood off to the side of them all, buckled over in laughter at Liam and Patrick's antics. He was pushing sixty but he still had more guts and energy than most men half his age. Brad knew that Stumpy was normally the last one standing at the yearly welcoming-in party. He guessed tonight would probably be no different.

In the kitchen, Daniel wrapped his arms around Lily's waist and snuck a piece of potato out of the bowl. She slapped his hand, which sent the potato flying through the air and into her glass of Malibu and Coke. 'Gee whiz, I'm a good shot!' Daniel applauded himself as Lily picked up her glass and laughed.

'I'll have another now, barman, but this time without the chunk of potato!' Daniel smiled and did as he was told, taking a sip of his beer. His ribs were healing well, which meant he was able to cut back on the painkillers. It was good to enjoy a few beers without feeling the effects of the medication rubbing shoulders with the alcohol.

There was a holler from the doorway as Judy and Steve stuck their heads into the kitchen. Georgia was unsteadily balancing a massive glass bowl of trifle in one hand and a bottle of beer in the other. Judy had a huge basket of delicious-smelling homemade bread rolls and Steve was carrying a bowl of fried rice.

'My goodness, guys. There's enough food here to feed an army!' Sarah exclaimed, reaching out to save the bowl of trifle, which looked as though it was about to upend all over the floor. The bottom of the bowl was swimming in sherry-soaked sponge and Sarah's tastebuds went crazy in anticipation.

'Mum used half a bottle of sherry in that, so watch out!' Georgia said, as if reading Sarah's thoughts.

Steve put his bowl down on the kitchen bench, his nose leading him outside to the sizzling meat and the safety of the testosterone-surrounded barbecue.

'Matt and Brooke will be here in an hour or so,' Judy said. 'They left Mt Isa a little later than expected. Let's make sure we keep a couple of plates of food for them. Brooke still hadn't finished packing, even though she's had weeks to do it. That girl needs to learn that the world doesn't revolve around her.' There was a hint of annoyance in Judy's voice.

'Maybe you and Dad want to make her feel welcome, Mum, but I don't. I can't bloody stand her, that fake blonde hair and annoying voice.' Georgia scowled. 'She's afraid to break a fingernail – she'll be as handy as lips on a chicken out here. I'm glad they'll be living in the granny flat and not in the house with us.'

'Now, Georgia, please try to be nice to her for Matt's sake. He's smitten with her, and it'll only cause arguments if you start pushing Brooke's buttons,' Judy said pleadingly.

Georgia rolled her eyes. 'Sure, Mum.' She looked in Sarah and Lily's direction, changing the subject. 'Thanks for all your help today, ladies. Mum and I would've been snowed under otherwise.'

'No worries,' Lily said. 'I've really enjoyed cooking today.'

A haze of smoke wafted into the kitchen from the back porch.

'We better go out and check the men haven't forgotten about the meat. Smells like the snags might be burnt to a crisp,' Judy said, sniffing the air comically.

Slim liked to think he was the barbecue king but he always got roped into chatting and ended up forgetting the task at hand. The sausages were usually still edible once you piled the tomato sauce on top of them.

Once the meat had been rescued, it was time to eat. They all filled their plates from the spread that lay before them. Afterwards they lounged back on the plastic chairs strewn around the patio, enjoying the afterglow of good food and telling yarns about cattle and life in general. Duke loved getting all the scraps left on the plates as well as the pieces of meat that weren't going to be eaten. He curled up on his bed in the corner of the patio, contented.

'It's a dog's life,' Sarah muttered to Brad as she looked in Duke's direction. Brad didn't answer, biting distractedly on his fingernails. He had been out of sorts all night. Sarah noticed his eyes were red-raw and realised he was probably exhausted from the day. She decided not to make a big deal of it. When Brad was tired he was a right grump, and she didn't feel like having an argument with him tonight.

Suddenly Adam Harvey came on the stereo and Lily turned it up full blast. 'Come on, you lot! Let's party! Woohoo!' She started dancing around the patio, pulling people to their feet. They'd all drunk enough not to worry about dancing around like idiots, and soon everyone was up and bootscooting to the music. The speakers belted out one country tune after another and they all sang along. Even Judy and Steve joined in.

Everybody was too busy dancing and having fun to notice Matt and Brooke wander in. Matt smiled as he took in the scene. Liam and Slim were flapping their arms around like a pair of headless chooks while their legs seemed to have a mind of their own. Stumpy had clearly had a few too many, and was swaying slightly as he did circles around everyone, amazingly staying upright. Patrick was trying to linedance with Georgia but both of them kept banging into each other, and tears ran down their faces from laughing. Judy and Steve were spinning and jiving like there was no tomorrow.

Matt noticed Brad swaying with a beautiful chick, who must be his girlfriend. He didn't know the other two with them but they were laughing and spinning each other around at a speed that made him dizzy just watching. Yes, they were certainly having a good time, and he was slightly pissed at Brooke that she had made them late. He enjoyed spending time with the boys but she always seemed to find a way to divert his attention away from his mates and back onto her, making him miss out on any fun they might have been having. He would have to make a stop to that sooner rather than later seeing she was now going to be living with him. He had to have some time to himself with his mates. Brooke wasn't so controlling when he had first met her, she had been the complete opposite, but recently she had dug her nails into him, so to speak, and liked to know what he was doing at all times and with whom. He couldn't understand why; he was the most loyal boyfriend any woman could ask for.

Brooke stood with her arms folded, staring at the dancers, an unreadable look on her face. She watched as a few of the gyrating mob decided to have a break and wandered from the dance floor in search of drinks. Smiling, she reached out her hand to Sarah, who was the first off the dance floor.

'Hi, I'm Brooke. You must be Sarah. I've been looking forward to meeting you.'

Sarah took in the girl standing before her. She was attractive in her own way. She had shoulder-length, bleached white-blonde hair and a huge smile with pearly white teeth. Her fingernails and toenails were painted red to match her lips and she had a short dress on. Sarah wouldn't have been caught dead looking like her, but Brooke was clearly being as welcoming and friendly as she could be. That had to count for something.

'Nice to meet you too, Brooke. I'm sure we'll be seeing a lot of each other now we've both moved out here, hey?'

'Yeah, I guess we will,' Brooke replied.

Sarah turned to Matt, who was standing beside Brooke. He gave her a piercing look from intense brown eyes and held out his hand, shaking hers with a strong, firm grip. She saw he had a tattoo on his forearm, just visible beyond the cuff of his sleeve. It looked like a set of bull's horns curving up his muscular arm. As their hands touched, Sarah felt an electric current run between them, and she quickly pulled her hand away. She found herself staring at Matt. He had short, almost shaved brown hair, deep chocolate-brown eyes and a smile that brought out a dimple on his chin. He was tall, tanned and broad-shouldered, and Sarah couldn't help gazing at him for a second longer than she should have. Nobody else seemed to notice, though – they were too busy chatting and catching their breath after the boogie on the makeshift dance floor.

'Hey, Sarah. I'm Matt. How's life for you on Rosalee so far? I hope you're settling in okay and the boys are treating you well?' Matt shuffled on the spot, gazing back at Sarah, and she couldn't help wondering whether he'd felt the same sensation as her.

'Yeah, they're making me feel right at home. I'll officially start tomorrow night when I cook them all a roast.' Sarah felt strangely nervous and couldn't stop talking. 'Mind you, I'm not just going to be tied to the kitchen. I've told your mum and dad I'm happy to give them a hand round the place as well. So, any work you can throw my way I'll gladly do. I want to learn all I can about station life.'

Matt raised his eyebrows. 'You might've set yourself up for some hard labour there. Dad's not one to say no to an eager extra hand. And, you know, no matter how many people we have working out here, there are never enough hours in the day, so any help will be appreciated.' Matt looked up to see Judy carrying two plates of food over to the table. 'Ah, Mum's brought out our dinner. I'm bloody starved! We'll catch up a bit later, hey, Sarah?'

Still shaken from their handshake, Sarah smiled and let him go. As she turned back to join the party animals she bumped into Lily and Daniel, who were having a good old snog.

'Get a room, you two!' Sarah said. The couple parted and Lily staggered when Daniel took his arms from her waist.

'Think I better take this one to bed. She seems to have lost all sense of balance,' Daniel said.

'I can hold my own, Danny boy. I'll give you an arm wrestle if you like!' Lily slurred in between hiccups.

'Nah, it's bedtime for you, princess.' Daniel grabbed Lily and picked her up, kicking and laughing, throwing her over his shoulder. He kissed Sarah on the cheek. 'See you in the morning, sis.'

'Sweet dreams, you two.' Sarah watched them both head towards the direction of the patio door, stopping briefly so Lily could introduce herself to Matt and Brooke from over Daniel's shoulder.

Sarah looked around the patio for Brad but he was nowhere to be seen. She wandered off into the darkness, hoping to find him so she could tell him she was going to bed too. She was feeling pretty drunk. Finally she found Brad sitting in a clump of emu bushes behind the shower block with a cigarette hanging from his lips. He was gazing into space, blowing smoke rings into the air. Then the sharp tang of marijuana hit her nostrils and Sarah felt surprise and anger rush up into her throat. *He's smoking pot!* she screamed in her head. *I can't believe this. He knows what happened to my dad. He knows how that hurt my family.* Brad's actions felt like a punch in the face. Sarah realised that she was rooted to the spot. Finally she found the strength to move, hurt and anger boiling within her. She walked over to Brad whose eyes widened in shock at her presence. He tried to stub the joint out under his boot, swatting the air around him in an attempt to get rid of the smell, but it was too late.

Sarah shook her head at him in disbelief. 'What are you *doing*, Brad? You said you hated that shit!'

Brad threw his hands up in the air, realising it was no use pretending.

'How long has this been going on?' Sarah demanded.

'I dunno. A while. It's not exactly your business, is it?'

'Not my business? I'm your *girlfriend*, Brad! Don't I have a right to know?'

'What can I say, Sarah? I like smoking pot. I really don't know why you have to get so worked up about it. Don't you think it's time you got over the past and stopped being such a pain in the arse about it all.'

Sarah stared at him, stunned beyond words by the cynical stranger in front of her.

'Maybe if you tried some you might even get over your hang-up and understand why I like it so much,' Brad went on.

'Well, Brad, I'm *not* going to be trying it, so you can just shove it where it fits!' Sarah said, finding her voice as she turned on her heel. Her head was in turmoil – she was too drunk to talk to Brad now, and way too emotional.

'Fine! Have it your way, Miss Goody Two Shoes!' Brad yelled after her, and Sarah just about burst into tears. She could feel her blood boiling – how long had he really been hiding this from her? The whole time they'd been together? 'What in the hell am I gonna do about this?' she mumbled to herself as tears threatened to run down her cheeks. The light spilled from the patio outside, and she took a deep breath before stepping back into the party. Everyone was back on the dance floor having a whale of a time – even Brooke was dancing, swinging around with Chris while Georgia danced with Matt. Sarah made a quick dash for the back door, scurrying towards the privacy of her bedroom before her emotions erupted for all to see.

She lay in bed for hours with tears streaming down her face, listening to the sounds of the party winding down. Eventually, the snores of the drunken men filled the house like thunderbolts. Brad didn't come back to the room, but she refused to worry about him. He'd probably passed out in the emu bushes, seeing as he was so stoned, oblivious to her pain. Anger and sadness churned inside her as she pondered the question over and over again: could she ever love a man who was into pot? She *did* love Brad – but how could she ever look at him in the same way? Sarah tried to tell herself that they could still make it work – maybe tomorrow things would seem better – but somehow she knew it was over. She finally fell into a restless sleep, nightmares gripping her mind and taking her to places she didn't want to go.

CHAPTER
9

It was five in the morning when Sarah felt herself jolt awake. She sat bolt upright, covered in sweat, as the memory of last night's exchange between her and Brad hit her like a freight train. It didn't matter whether she was drunk or sober, the thought of Brad being a pot smoker still made her sick to her stomach.

Her head was pounding and she could feel a killer hangover lurking, but there was no time for moping about – she had to talk to Brad before he went to work. Waiting the whole day would just kill her. She crawled out of bed to make herself a cuppa, hoping it would clear the haziness from her head. She had to be thinking straight before she saw Brad, or she'd say things she didn't mean and it would end in an all-out war. As furious and upset as she was, she didn't want that.

Sarah flicked on the kettle and leant on the kitchen bench, waiting for it to boil, as she gazed out the window.

The house was silent, except for the soft shuffle of feet behind closed bedroom doors. She was startled suddenly as Brad stormed past her with his towel over his shoulder, heading for the outside shower. He'd slept on the couch, apparently. Sarah was amazed that he didn't even try to talk to her, as if she was the one in the wrong. She braced herself to face him, and followed him to the shower. She tried knocking on the hardwood door and calling his name, but Brad ignored her, singing loudly under the trickling water. Sarah was too tired for his nonsense. She shoved the door open.

'Bloody hell, Sarah, can you give me a minute here? Can't you see I'm busy?'

'I don't know if you deserve a minute, Brad. Why are you treating *me* like dirt when *you* are the one who's been hiding your pot smoking from me?' Sarah could feel tears squeezing from her eyes, burning her cheeks, and a lump in her throat the size of a tennis ball. She was scared it was going to cut off her airway if she didn't release it soon.

'Please, Sarah. Just let it go, will you? You're making a big deal over nothing. You need to get off your high horse and realise it's not my fault your dad went to prison.'

'Don't you mention my dad, Bradley Williams! This is about *you*, and you need to decide what's important in your life – me or the pot!' Sarah yelled, her emotions getting the better of her.

Brad lost his temper and yelled back in her face. 'Fine, Sarah! If you want to give me an ultimatum then I'll take the pot, okay?' He grabbed his towel and wrapped it around his waist, his face twisted in anger. 'There, are you satisfied now? I'm not joking. And if you can't handle it, why don't you just pack your bags and go home?' He pushed past Sarah and headed back to the cottage.

Sarah dropped to the ground, hugging her knees into her chest and gasping in shock. She could feel her heart splitting down the middle, and the pain was choking her. Her mind spun with images of all the happy times with Brad. It made her feel physically ill. She didn't know how long she'd been sitting there when she felt somebody trying to help her up. Sarah wiped her face and looked up to see Lily struggling to lift her off the floor. Lily was saying something, but it just wasn't registering. It felt like the end of the world.

*

Sarah was sitting on the couch, sandwiched between Lily and Daniel with Duke at her feet. He kept placing his paw on Sarah's knee in support. Sarah hadn't seen Brad since he left her at the shower block. Although she had so many questions for him she knew that, no matter what his answers were, she could never be with him again.

She had thrown up twice already from the emotions thundering inside her and was now sipping on an extra sweet cup of tea that Lily had gently placed in her shaking hands. Her mind was slowly clearing and she had rediscovered her anger, but it was tinged with a deep sorrow. Brad had told her to pack her bags and leave, as simply as that, as if he didn't care for her at all. She was snapped out of her thoughts as Daniel put his arm around her, his face dark with anger.

'I'm going to knock him to the ground and kick him in the guts. Then I'm going to rip his balls off and shove them down his throat like he deserves, the dirty rotten mongrel. It goes to show you never really know anybody as well as you think you do.' Daniel's leg jiggled up and down with impatience to get at Brad, and Sarah placed her hand on it lightly to stop it from moving.

'Daniel, I'm a big girl now, and I want to fight my own battles. I know you're just trying to protect me, and I love you for that, but all that will happen is you'll end up in jail for assault.'

'What're you going to do now, matey?' Lily asked, her big brown eyes full of sympathy. 'Do you want to come home with me and Daniel?'

Sarah shook her head. 'No *way* am I letting that bastard chase me away from a dream I've had for as long as I can remember. I'm here to stay. He can be the one to leave if he wants it that way.' Sarah marvelled at the strength in her voice. An hour ago she couldn't even stand on her own two feet, but now she was digging her heels into the ground, ready to defend herself and fight for what was right. She could feel the Clarke determination pumping through her veins. She wasn't going to walk out on Rosalee; not now, not yet. It already meant too much to her.

'Will you talk to Judy about it? Maybe you could live in the women's quarters? The only thing is you'll still have to cook for Brad, and that will be a bit hard.'

'Yeah, once I calm down I think I'll go have a yak with Judy. I think that's the only option I have. Oh, Lily, he's broken my heart into little pieces.' With that Sarah let the tears flood her eyes once again and roll down her cheeks. She couldn't get a handle on the way she was feeling – one moment she was full of determination, then she was bursting into tears again. A range of emotions, from utter despair and heartache to fierce rage, swept through her in waves.

'Are you sure about staying, sis? Lily and I have to head back home soon and I'll be worried about you after all of this.'

'I'm absolutely positive. I'm not going back home with my tail between my legs, Daniel, I'm just not. I know I'll get through this and enjoy my time out here. I just know I can't live under the same roof as Brad!'

'You're a determined sheila when you want to be, hey? Just remember where your home is, and that we're all there for you when you need us. Seriously, I can't promise not to give Brad a good smack around the chops after the way he's treated you, but I promise I'll at least try not to.' Daniel gave Sarah a little wink.

Lily wrapped her arms around Sarah and gave her a big hug. 'I love you, mate, and I'm here for you any time of the day or night. I know this is going to be hard for you, but I also know you're a very strong chicky babe, and you'll get through it in the end. I'm so proud of your determination, babe. You deserve much better than Brad.'

'Thanks for your support, guys. I'm so glad you're here.' Sarah sniffed as she stood up. She looked around at the dozens of tissues at her feet and decided she'd shed enough tears over Brad for now. She had to start thinking about preparing the roast dinner for tonight, as well as the homemade apple pie. There was a lot of baking to do too, so the men had a decent assortment of goodies for smokos. She also had tomorrow's lunch to prepare – it always had to be done the night before as the mornings were too busy. Plus there was the grocery list to write so that Judy could ring and order it from Woolies. She clapped her hands together and stood up, taking a good deep breath.

'Rightio, guys. I have a lot of cooking ahead of me today, as well as a good old scrub-down of the kitchen. Come on, Duke, my mate, I'll give you a treat this morning. You can have a bowl of fresh meat instead of your usual dry bikkies, hey?' Sarah leant down and gave Duke a hug around the neck. He was her loyal friend and one who was always there for her.

'Tell us what you want us to do and we'll gladly help.' Lily stood up, a smile appearing on her face.

'Great, I'd appreciate a hand.' Not for the first time, Sarah was filled with happiness at the thought of having Lily and Daniel there for the next couple of days. Some familiar faces would help her through the worst of it, and then she could deal with it on her own – if Judy let her stay on.

They headed into the kitchen and Daniel turned on the radio to distract them all. Sarah smiled, recognising 'The Rising Sun' by Jimmy Barnes. She and Lily had danced their butts off to this tune on many an occasion. As Sarah stood watching, Daniel and Lily swung each other around the kitchen, grabbing the salt and pepper shakers to use as microphones as they sang along. Sarah grinned to herself and, for the first time that day, felt like things were going to be all right.

CHAPTER

10

Daniel was the first to stop dancing, his eyes catching sight of the thick, black smoke filling the sky out the kitchen window. It was billowing into the blue so quickly that it looked like someone was tipping black ink out of the heavens.

Sarah knew immediately that something bad had happened under the blanket of black smoke. It didn't look like a bush fire. The smoke had an intensity to it that usually only came from an explosion. She knew instinctively that somebody would be badly hurt, if not dead, with smoke like that.

'Holy shit! We better head over to Judy and Steve's and see what in the hell has happened!' Sarah said anxiously as she started hurriedly for the door. Lily and Daniel ran after her.

Duke jumped up in the front of the LandCruiser with Sarah as Lily and Daniel hurled themselves in the back.

Sarah hit the accelerator and threw a storm of stones and dust out behind the truck as she sped off towards the homestead going twenty to the dozen.

When she pulled up it was absolute mayhem. Slim, Stumpy and Chris were running around yelling orders at each other while throwing things in the back of Steve's ute. Their horses stood under the shade of a wattle tree, sweat dripping off them, drinking eagerly from a bucket of water. Georgia and Steve were packing what looked like medical equipment into the front of the ute while shouting at each other to hurry up. Judy was standing on the verandah crying into the phone. Nobody had noticed Sarah, Daniel and Lily arrive. Sarah scanned the area for Brad. He wasn't anywhere to be seen.

Judy was the first to see them and ran in Sarah's direction with her arms outstretched. Sarah's heart dropped to the floor. It had to be Brad. The world started to spin beneath her feet. She wanted to run to Judy, but she felt like her feet were weighed down with cement. Judy reached Sarah and hugged her in close.

'What's happened, Judy? We don't know anything except that there's a huge ball of black smoke out there,' Daniel said, glancing to the sky, which was turning blacker with each passing second.

Judy's face changed and she took a few deep breaths. She stood back from Sarah, still holding her hands, and was clearly searching for the right words. Sarah could feel Judy's hands trembling as they held her own.

'Brad crashed the chopper. He was flying a bit too low and the blades clipped a tree, bringing the chopper down on its side. Stumpy saw it all happen, and he and the boys raced over to Brad to help. The chopper had already caught on fire by the time they got there. Liam and Patrick have quite bad burns to their arms from dragging Brad out. He's unconscious but still breathing, and I've just called the flying doctors. Once they arrive we'll have a better idea of his condition. Matt and Brooke have already gone out there. Steve and Georgia are heading out now, and you can jump in the back of the ute and go with them. I was going to come over and tell you as soon as I could. I only found out ten minutes ago myself when Stumpy and Chris came tearing over on the horses to tell us. Our two-way radio has been playing up lately and they couldn't get through to us, so they rode over as fast as the horses would carry them.' She paused and looked deep into Sarah's eyes. 'I'm so sorry, Sarah, to be the bearer of bad news.'

Sarah's face had drained of all colour and her mouth was so dry she didn't think she'd be able to speak. Her mind was on loop, replaying the scene Judy had described, and she felt like she was in the middle of some nightmare.

Before she knew what had happened, Sarah collapsed into Lily's arms, tears flooding her face. Daniel rubbed Sarah's back while her whole body shuddered with sobs.

Steve shouted over to the group from the ute, 'We're going now. Are you lot coming? Jump up in the back, quickly!'

Sarah lifted her head and gave him a nod. She whistled for Duke to stay put with Judy. He let out a whine but sat down on top of Judy's feet in his eagerness to do the right thing. It was enough to lift Sarah's heart up off the floor and give her courage for what lay ahead.

Sarah, Lily and Daniel ran over to join Slim, Stumpy and Chris, who were already in the back of the ute. Once they were all safely in, Steve planted his foot and headed in the direction of the billowing cloud of black smoke.

Slim rubbed Sarah on the shoulder. 'He's gonna be okay, mate. He's in a bit of a state now, so try and stay strong when you see him, but at least he's alive. I was too far away from the crash to get to him quick enough. I'm sorry, mate.'

Sarah just nodded in reply. She didn't trust herself to speak. She needed time to take in what was happening.

Stumpy smiled weakly at her. It was clear he didn't know what to say but his eyes told a thousand words. His face was covered in black soot and his left arm had ugly-looking burns on it. His shirt was torn all the way down the front, leaving his grazed and bloody chest bare. He sat against the back of the ute and hung his head in his hands. Sarah wrapped her arm around his shoulder.

'Thanks for helping Brad, Stumpy. I know you would have done your best to stop him from getting hurt.' Up close she could see just how bad his arm was and she winced at the thought of how painful it must be.

'I tried so hard to pull him loose, mate, but his legs were jammed in there and I think … I think they broke when the three of us finally pulled him free. He was screaming for us to get him out 'cause the chopper was going to blow. He had fuel leaking all over him. His feet were on fire when we got him out. I tried my hardest, mate, I really did. I'm so sorry I didn't get to him quicker.' Stumpy was not a man to show his emotions but he had tears running down his weathered, filthy face. The shock of it all looked like it was beginning to hit him hard and Sarah tried to hold in the tears that were threatening to appear yet again.

'You did what you had to do, Stumpy. He wouldn't be alive at all if you hadn't been there to drag him out. Be proud of what you've done for him and don't beat yourself up over not having done more. He's lucky to have you as a mate.'

'Thanks, Sarah,' was all Stumpy could muster. They sat there in silence for the rest of the trip.

*

Brad was lying under a tree on a blanket that Matt had laid out for him. He was conscious now, and screaming in pain. Wet towels wrapped with ice were lying on his burns. Liam and Patrick had wet towels draped across their arms. Sarah could see Brooke sitting beside Brad, crying as she held a towel to his head.

Matt looked over in her direction as she climbed off the back of the ute and the compassion in his eyes enveloped her. He was kneeling beside Brad, trying to soothe him. Brooke stood to one side, giving Sarah room.

Sarah ran to Brad's side, and the reality of the accident came crashing down on her properly. Brad's face was badly swollen, with shards of broken glass sticking out below his left eye. There was blood oozing from cuts all over his body. His right leg was lying at an unnatural angle. He looked like he had been tumbled around by a group of angry bulls.

Sarah fell to the ground and touched Brad gently on the hand. She was filled with a wave of compassion and love. Despite what had happened between them, she loved Brad, and to see him in such pain was agonising. She prayed silently that he would be okay. Brad looked up at her and tried to grip her hand as another wave of pain came crashing down on his bent, bloodied and broken body. He screamed out in agony, and it was all Sarah could do to stop herself from screaming with him.

She stole a glance at his legs and quickly looked away; Brad's boots had melted on to his feet. It was a horrific sight. Steve and Georgia were busy attending to some of Brad's smaller wounds with their medical kit, while the rest of the mustering crew stood back and gave them some space. Sarah quietly wondered if Brad was even going to make it to the hospital.

Thirty long minutes later, the flying doctors' plane came into view. Relief flooded through Sarah as she watched the doctor and nurse come running. Within minutes the doctor had given Brad strong painkillers and was getting him loaded onto the plane to be taken to the Mt Isa hospital. It looked like Brad had two broken legs, quite severe head injuries and suspected internal bleeding. The burns to his feet could not be properly assessed until his boots were removed. Meanwhile, the nurse had dressed Liam, Patrick and Stumpy's burns and told them all to take it easy over the next few days.

The shocked group stood near the smoking wreck of the chopper and watched the plane take off. The fire in the chopper was slowly burning itself out and there was nothing more to be done for the time being.

The sun was just setting when Steve's ute pulled up out the front of the homestead. The exhausted and smoke-blackened group sat silently in the back. Judy came running out to hear how Brad was, and insisted that they all stay for dinner. Sarah thought she might never be hungry again, but couldn't bring herself to say no to Judy, who was only trying to help. Duke ran to Sarah's side and rested his head against her thigh. He gazed up at her like he knew exactly what she'd been through. She scratched him behind the ears and told him it was all going to be okay. She just needed to believe that herself.

CHAPTER

11

The next four days went by in a blur. Questions flashed through Sarah's head day and night, and she found herself wondering whether Brad might've crashed because he was upset about their fight, or whether it was just a horrible accident. She tried to banish these questions from her mind, but they wouldn't go away. She knew she shouldn't blame herself, but it didn't make the accident any easier to come to grips with.

Judy had insisted she stay on as cook, much to her relief. Sarah had wrestled with her conscience, wondering how much to tell Judy and the men about what happened the morning of the accident. Finally she settled on telling them that she and Brad had decided to break up the night of the party. She couldn't bring herself to tell anyone about Brad smoking pot. It felt like she'd be kicking him when he was down.

Sarah had been ringing the hospital twice a day to see how Brad was going. Amazingly, he'd suffered no internal bleeding but had two broken legs and a shattered cheekbone. As expected, his feet were badly burnt, but given time they would mend with minimal scarring. Apparently the thick work socks Brad had worn underneath his boots had saved his feet from irreparable damage – just. It could be quite some time before he'd work again, though.

Lily and Daniel were leaving tomorrow, and Sarah knew it was going to be hard being at the station on her own. She reminded herself that she wouldn't be alone. Over the last few days, she'd got to know Georgia more, and realised she was a great chick. And Judy had been checking in on Sarah throughout each day, making sure she was doing okay. Sarah knew she'd have support when she needed it.

The phone rang just as the men were leaving for work. Sarah dried her hands on the tea towel she had tucked in the top of her jeans and picked it up.

'Sarah, love, it's Dad. Your mum wanted to ring and see how you're coping. She's been having sleepless nights worrying about you out there after all that's happened.'

Sarah couldn't help but smile a little, knowing that Jack was really talking about himself. 'I'm doing okay, Dad. I'm a Clarke, remember – we don't quit when the going gets tough.'

'I'm glad to hear that you're all right, love. Have you heard any more on how Brad's doing?'

Sarah could hear the tension in Jack's voice. Her parents were the only people, apart from Daniel and Lily, who knew that Brad had been smoking pot. Jack had just about blown the phone to pieces when he heard.

'Yeah, he's going to be okay. All in all he's a lucky man. I'm going to see him tomorrow after I drop Daniel and Lily at the airport in Mt Isa. I'm still angry at him for hiding it all from me, but I really want to see him.'

'You're doing the right thing, love. But don't let him off the hook just because you feel sorry for him – remember, a leopard doesn't change his spots,' Jack answered seriously. 'I'm proud of you, Sarah, deciding to stay out there and follow your dreams. Give us a call tomorrow to let us know how you go, okay?'

'Okay, Dad. Love you.' Sarah was gobsmacked to hear her father say he was proud of her, and her heart ached to reach out and give him a hug. But his words confirmed her decision for her – staying at Rosalee was the best thing for her to do.

CHAPTER

12

Daniel threw the bags in the back of the LandCruiser as Lily said her goodbyes to Duke, who was sulking on the porch. He knew he wouldn't be coming with them. Sarah gave Duke a quick farewell rub under the chops. He tried one last time to win her over with his sad eyes, then wandered over to his rug with his tail between his legs. Sarah knew he'd be over it by the time she left the driveway.

The last twenty-four hours had been a frenzy of sorting and cleaning as Sarah packed Brad's clothes to take to the hospital. She was desperate to spend some time with Victory, but there had been too much to do. She'd mentioned to some of the men that she was looking forward to a day out riding soon, and they'd invited her to come mustering with them when she was back. She had accepted with enthusiasm.

Sarah, Daniel and Lily chatted quietly on the way to Mt Isa about the tumultuous events of the last week. Sarah was nervous about seeing Brad, but she knew her mind was made up. Her heart was broken, but her feelings for Brad had changed the morning of their terrible fight. That wasn't going to make it any easier to see him in such pain in hospital.

*

Sarah sat in the car park of the hospital for ten minutes, doing some deep breathing to calm herself down. She'd just said a tearful farewell at the airport to Lily and Daniel, and now she was facing another round of emotional turmoil. All the sadness she'd felt the morning of the fight was resurfacing, and Sarah didn't want to break down in front of Brad. She finally plucked up enough courage to step out of the security of her LandCruiser and walk towards the hospital, Brad's bag of personal items thrown over her shoulder, her boots clip-clopping on the bitumen. She dusted her jeans off before she stepped through the automatic doors, and as she asked at the front counter for Brad's room number, she noticed her voice was quivering a little.

She took note of the floor and room number and stepped into the lift. Sarah hated hospitals. Unless she was going to the maternity ward to see a cute bundle of new life she detested coming anywhere near them. The smell of disinfectant in the corridors made her throat feel like it was going to seal over.

Reaching Brad's room, she tapped lightly on the door, and without waiting for a response walked in. Sitting in the chair beside Brad was Matt. Sarah felt her belly do a 360, and she tried to regain her composure quickly before Matt noticed. He had a weird effect on her.

'Hey, Sarah. I was in town with a load of cattle so I stopped in to check on Brad,' Matt said, holding Sarah's gaze.

Sarah quickly found her voice and gave him a smile. 'That was thoughtful of you, Matt. Has he woken up while you've been here?'

Matt shook his head. 'Nah, not yet. I was hoping he'd come to but I think they have him pretty bombed out for the pain.' He stood up and placed his hat on his head. 'I reckon you should wake him, Sarah. He'd probably like to see a familiar face. I'll take off now, anyway, as I have to get back and do a few things on the station before dark. Tell him I said g'day. I'll see you back there, mate.' He gave her a quick smile and a nod and left before Sarah could say a word.

Sarah came closer to the bed. Brad looked better than she'd thought he would, apart from the drip in his arm and the cuts and bruises on his cheekbone. He mumbled something under his breath and his eyelids flickered open.

'Hey, Brad. How're you going?' she whispered as she leant closer.

He smiled weakly. 'As well as to be expected, I guess.'

Sarah sat down beside him. 'I'm so sorry about the fight we had, Brad. I've been killing myself thinking I might be partly to blame for the crash.'

'I'm sorry too, Sarah. But the accident had nothing to do with you. I shouldn't have been smoking the night before – I was tired and hungover and I stuffed up.' Brad took a sip of water from the cup on his bedside table.

Sarah breathed a sigh of relief. She felt absolved by his words, and a weight lifted from her shoulders.

Brad continued, 'It's just, I dunno, I would be lying if I said I was going to stop smoking pot. Do you think you can look past it? I'll make sure I don't smoke around you.'

Sarah paused. 'I'm deeply sorry about your accident and the pain you must be going through, but that doesn't change the way I feel. I can't be with a man who takes drugs. I know it's really bad timing to be telling you this, but I think we both know it would never work. We need to let go now, otherwise we'll ruin a brilliant friendship too.'

Brad closed his eyes and Sarah felt her heart sink. She rushed on. 'These are your things from the cottage. I think I've packed everything for you. I spoke to your sister yesterday, and she'll be arriving late tonight to be with you. Your mum will be here tomorrow morning, so you'll have support here. I just can't be the one for you, Brad. Under different circumstances you know I would've been, but I think we need some space.'

There was a long pause. 'We just weren't meant to be, hey?' Brad's voice cracked a little. 'I hope we can remain mates. You look after yourself out there on the station, and keep in touch, okay?'

Sarah squeezed his hand. 'I promise I'll keep in touch.'

Brad smiled sleepily in response as his eyelids fought to stay open. He was drifting off again. As Sarah let go of his hand she realised this was the end of the road for her and Bradley Williams. All the emotions she'd been pushing down rushed up with full force. Almost gasping for air, she got out of the building as fast as she could. She held it together just long enough to make it back to the car, where her emotions erupted. She sat in the driver's seat, sobbing her heart out by herself. She cried for what seemed like hours, until her tears dried up and she could no longer cry. A quick glance in the rear-view mirror showed her a face that looked like it'd been stung by a thousand bees. It was time to get a hold of herself.

She popped a CD into the stereo, turned it up full blast and hit the road. Before long she found herself singing her heart out. By the time she arrived at the station gates two hours later, she felt a hundred times better than she had at the hospital. The stillness of the outback was just what she needed to clear her mind.

Duke ran up to the door of the LandCruiser as she pulled in and she smiled down at her loyal pal. 'I'm home, mate. And I'm here to stay.'

CHAPTER

13

The alarm on Sarah's mobile sang out merrily and she rolled over to slap it off. Four-thirty a.m. and time to start the day. It had been almost three weeks since the chopper accident, and Sarah was slowly getting into the routine at Rosalee. It was still a weird feeling waking up in what had been Brad's room but it was definitely her space now. There were photos of her family up on the walls and her prized country music collection was displayed on the rickety timber shelf she'd found abandoned behind the shed. Thanks to trusty Mr Sheen it had emerged from layers of dust with a rustic charm that Sarah loved. Old furniture had a certain character about it that new furniture just didn't have. Judy had given her a nice doona set as a welcoming gift last week, with matching curtains that she'd made herself. Sarah had only got around to decorating the room with them yesterday and she loved the rich, deep red colours of them. It wasn't exactly the Hilton, but it was comfortable. She took a few moments to breathe in the new day peeking in at her from behind the curtains before bounding out of bed to start her morning. After breakfast there was not a dirty plate in sight, and Sarah hadn't even started the washing up. The men had polished off the food in a matter of minutes, leaving their plates scraped clean.

'That was a breakfast fit for a king!' Stumpy said whilst licking the last of the tasty meal off his knife and fork, a habit Sarah was not too fond of.

Patrick leant back in his chair and smiled like a bear who'd found the honey pot. 'Can I put my order in for the same again tomorrow, or is that too cheeky?'

'Thanks, guys. I hope you like your lunches. I've packed you some homemade blueberry muffins and a chocolate cake, along with my famous egg, zucchini and bacon pie. Have yet to meet somebody that doesn't like it.'

Slim was rubbing his belly with satisfaction written across his large round face. 'I'm as full as a bull's arse in the middle of spring but I'm looking forward to lunch already, mate. You're a great cook. I'll have to be careful or I'll lose this fine figure of mine!'

'Yeah, you look like you need a good feed, Slim!' Liam laughed.

Chris drained the last of the coffee from his cup and rubbed his red eyes. Sarah had noticed how quiet he had been all morning.

'Looks like you had a late one, Chris. What were you doing till all hours of the morning? I heard you come in after we'd all hit the sack. Bit of a night owl, hey?'

Chris shifted uncomfortably in his seat. 'Just taking in the night sky, and before I knew it I'd fallen asleep. I woke up at two a.m. with bloody meat ants crawling all over me!'

The men laughed, but Sarah noticed an inexplicable look of relief cross Chris's face.

She made sure everything was packed in the esky for smokos and lunch, along with plenty of water to wet the men's chops. Stumpy gave her a hand.

'Matt's been doing a brilliant job of flying the chopper guys, don't ya reckon?' he said. Matt had taken over chopper duties since the accident until a replacement could be found.

Sarah felt a surge of emotion at the mention of the chopper. Stumpy put his arm over Sarah's shoulder.

'Sorry, mate. I didn't think before I mentioned the chopper.'

'No worries, Stumpy. I'll be fine.' Sarah had to bite her lip to stop it from quivering. Thinking of Brad and the chopper accident still gave her nightmares, and she doubted she would ever be able to step foot in a chopper again.

Sarah watched out the kitchen window as the men rode away on their horses. The sun was rising on the horizon, making the whole sky glow like it was made from liquid gold, the men's akubras casting shadows across their faces as the dust stirred lazily around them.

It was a beautiful morning to get out and about with Duke. Sarah hadn't had a lot of time for him lately, and felt bad for the poor bugger. Last week Matt had mentioned that there was some good-sized red claw in one of the dams, along with barramundi. A fishing excursion was just what she and Duke needed. She'd drop by the homestead and get directions.

Sarah walked out to the LandCruiser and whistled for Duke to join her in the front. He jumped in with such eagerness that he slid across the seat and slammed into Sarah.

'Keen to go then, boy!' Sarah said, laughing as she revved the truck to life, a puff of black diesel fumes flying out the exhaust. As she drove past Matt's rodeo ground, she pulled over for a moment. Leaving the Cruiser idling away, she nosed around, admiring the set-up that Matt had built himself. She was impressed by his obvious passion for rodeo. Over the past few weeks she'd seen a bit more of Matt around the cottage – he often popped in after work to share a beer with the men. She'd sat down with them once or twice, but had been keeping out of Matt's way. Was she afraid she might feel something she wasn't ready for? Meanwhile, Sarah hadn't seen much of Brooke at all, considering they lived on the same station. She didn't seem to be out and about much, and Sarah wondered what she did all day. She found it odd that Brooke didn't help him out. Gently shutting the gate to the chute she'd been inspecting, Sarah headed back to the car before Duke chewed his way through her Tupperware container and ate the delectable goodie inside.

Judy was pleased to see Sarah when she opened the front door of the homestead, giving her a warm kiss on the cheek. Sarah produced the container from behind her back and proudly presented an orange cake to Judy. 'From one cook to another. I made it with your oranges so I thought you might like some with a cuppa. I could use some girly conversation after being surrounded by blokes these past few weeks.'

'Thanks, love! I bet the cake's divine. Come in and bring Duke with you. He can sit out on the back porch with us. Make yourself at home while I fetch us a pot of tea.'

'Did you hear that, mate? You've been invited to join the ladies for some cake and tea,' Sarah told Duke in a posh voice.

Judy fussed about in the kitchen, talking to Sarah through the window that looked onto the back verandah. 'Have you heard any more updates on Brad, love?'

'Yeah, I spoke to his sister a couple of days ago. He's back in Mareeba with his parents now, which is a lot better than being stuck in hospital. The burns still have a way to go, but his legs are on the mend.'

'That's wonderful news! And how are you doing?' Sarah could hear the compassion in Judy's voice and she was reminded of her mum. She felt a sudden pang of homesickness.

'I'm floating along quite well, I guess. I think, deep down, I always knew Brad and I weren't meant to be, but I just didn't want to admit it. The move out here made me realise that. I just feel like I'm right where I'm meant to be for now, and it is a really comfortable feeling.'

Judy joined Sarah out the back, placing a bowl of mince down for Duke. 'There you go, boy, plenty to go around. Dig in.' Duke wolfed it down in two seconds flat and Judy laughed.

'You'd think I never fed him,' Sarah said, rolling her eyes and smirking at her best mate as he licked the last of the mince off his chops.

Judy pulled a chair out and sat down facing Sarah, reaching across the table to grab Sarah's hand. 'Oh, I'm so happy you're enjoying it out here. You're a tough woman, hanging round after all that you've been through. Cut out for this dusty old country, I reckon, without a doubt!'

For the next hour the two women sat and talked about station life. Sarah realised how much she'd been missing female company. Just as she was about to leave Matt came strolling out to the porch.

'G'day, you two gasbaggers! Have you saved some cake for me? It looks bloody good.'

'Sarah made that from our very own orange tree. It's lovely. I'm hoping to steal the recipe off her,' Judy said with a wink in Sarah's direction.

Sarah couldn't help but gaze just that little bit too long at Matt as he smiled and gave her a wink, the tattoo on his forearm clearly visible. She had butterflies in her belly. What was wrong with her? Until this moment she hadn't allowed herself to register how much she was attracted to Matt. As he turned to grab a piece of cake from Judy, she noticed another tattoo snaking out of his collar and up the back of his neck, and for a dangerous second she visualised herself running her fingers down it and below his shirt. When he turned to brush his hands off the railing of the verandah, she took in his arse. *Stop! He's in a relationship!* she told herself. But it wasn't breaking the law to admire a handsome man, she thought dreamily.

'Hey, Matt, I was wondering if you could tell me the best place to drop my line in. I was thinking of going fishing this arvo but I don't know where to go, and I'm afraid I might get a bit lost.'

Matt wiped the crumbs off his lips. 'Tell you what – I'll give you a shout when I'm free, and I'll show you the best places to fish. It's not very often I get a few hours spare, but for fishing I'll make the time. I'll challenge you to see who can catch the biggest barra!'

'I'd love that!' Sarah said, trying to quell her excitement. 'Bring Brooke along too so I can get to know her a little better.'

'Nah, Brooke hates fishing. She doesn't like to get the smell of the bait on her fingers. She reckons it doesn't wash off for days.' Matt's brow furrowed slightly. 'Anyway, I better chuff off. I've gotta go muster in the chopper this afternoon. Oh, by the way, Sarah, I've been meaning to ask, do you know anyone who can fly a chopper? I'm up to my armpits with work and it'd be a godsend if there was someone who could fly for me.'

A broad grin spread across Sarah's face as an idea suddenly came to mind. 'Yeah, I reckon I do, Matt.'

CHAPTER
14

Tiny flecks of blue paint all over her face, Sarah sat down on the upturned bucket in the middle of the lounge room. The furniture was draped in plastic sheeting and there was a lot to clean up, but Sarah was pleased with herself. She'd managed to paint the whole cottage in just over a week. It was satisfying to sit back and see how good the place looked. Last week she'd replaced the brown 70s curtains with brightly patterned handmade ones, and she'd made new cushion covers for the couch to match the curtains, courtesy of Judy's sewing machine. Yesterday morning she'd spent hours going through all the bits and bobs in the storage shed, finding old saddles, whips, spurs and saddle bags, which she had polished up and parked in designated spots around the cottage, giving it a real country feel. She'd even found an old brass lamp, which now sat in pride of place beside the telly. The place had a country charm now, like the land it rested upon; the changes had brought out the substance and character it had all along. It just needed a little primping to uncover it.

Sarah glanced at Duke sitting beside her; he had blobs of paint amongst his normally black and white coat. She had a giggle at the state of him – it looked like he'd been to the hairdresser's for a botched blue rinse. *Better clean up,* she thought, absently rubbing the blisters on her fingers and glancing at her watch. The mail plane was due any minute.

The whirr of the Cessna filled the skies just as Sarah finished getting the paint off her face. She ran out the front door and jumped on the quad Stumpy had parked under the paperbark tree and took off towards the landing strip with Duke in tow.

Sarah waved as she saw a familiar face through the plane's windscreen. Jimmy grinned back widely at her as the plane finally came to a halt.

'Jimmy!' Sarah shouted. Her bull-riding mate from Mareeba had arrived, ready to take up the post as chopper pilot.

He almost fell out of the plane, his lanky legs taking three steps at a time as he bounded down the stairs to greet her. He hit the dirt with a thud and coughed comically as red dust rose and filled his nostrils, swiping at the air to add to his show.

'Sarah, great to see you!' Jimmy gave her a huge hug.

'You too, Jimmy! So glad you could take the job. Matt, the owner's son, has been flat out. It's gonna be great having you out here for the rest of the season.'

'Happy to help out. I love a bit of mustering.'

Stan the mailman emerged from the Cessna with a sack of mail thrown over his shoulder. 'How goes it, Sarah?'

Sarah clobbered a fly that had landed on her arm. 'Yeah, great, Stan. Thanks for bringing Jimmy out for us, hey, we appreciate it.'

'Made the trip a lot more enjoyable with this bloke sitting beside me. I haven't laughed so much in years!' Stan threw his thumb in Jimmy's direction. 'Do you mind taking this to the homestead for me? I have to get a shift on. I've got loads to deliver today. Anyone would think it was Christmas!'

'No worries, Stan. Catch you next week.' Sarah took the bag from him.

Sarah and Jimmy watched as Stan got back in and revved the Cessna to life, waving as he flew off into the yonder.

Back at the cottage, Jimmy dropped his bag on the comfy-looking bed in his new bedroom and looked around the bright airy space. 'This place is tops, Sarah!'

'I've been working hard to get it looking good for you. Take your time and settle in – I'll be out in the kitchen. We're having a big barbie for you tonight and I've got to prepare the feast.'

Sarah popped Johnny Cash on the kitchen CD player and sang along with his husky country voice as she chopped up the cabbage for the coleslaw, Duke howling beside her. She was so engrossed in the task at hand that she nearly hit the ceiling when Jimmy tapped her on the shoulder. 'Oh shit, Jimmy. You scared the bejesus outta me!' she said, clutching her chest.

'Sorry, mate. Didn't mean to surprise you. No wonder you didn't hear me come in. Are you practising for *Australian Idol* or something?'

'I warn you now that I tend to sing when I'm cooking. It makes it all the more fun!' Sarah giggled.

'Well that's the main thing – you're enjoying yourself. Now, do you want me to give you a hand? I don't mind.'

'I wouldn't say no, mate. Thanks. You can start by peeling all the leader prawns I have in the sink. I'm gonna pop them on skewers and marinate them for the barbecue later. Slim tends to think he's the king of the barbie. You gotta watch him, though, as he tends to yak too much and forget about it. You end up with twice-killed steaks.'

Jimmy grinned. 'Sounds like a right laugh. Rightio, chef. I'm your humble kitchen hand.' He started peeling the massive sea creatures.

So what have I missed out on back home, Jimmy?'

'You know Mareeba. Not much happens in a year, let alone a month. Apart from Brad coming back and recovering well, there's nothing to tell. By the sounds of things your life has been more exciting out here.'

Sarah nodded. 'You got that right, mate. So much happened in that first week here, it was pretty full on. Since then things have quietened down. It's getting better every day. I love the work, and the men are great – you'll love them.'

Sarah couldn't help but smile as she gave Jimmy a description of each of the workers. She had grown close to all of them – other than Chris, who kept to himself, making it quite obvious that he preferred it that way.

The sun was setting when Sarah carried the last of the salads out to the patio table. Jimmy was now chatting away to the men, who were standing around with beers in hand as Slim guarded his station at the billowing barbecue. Sarah heard Matt's voice behind her, saying a quick g'day to everyone, and felt her cheeks flush and her belly fill with butterflies. Telling herself to calm down, she took a deep breath and turned around.

'Hi, Matt. Just in time for dinner. Where's Brooke?'

'Hey, Sarah. Brooke's not coming tonight. She reckons she's crook. She looked all right to me, though. I reckon there's something on the telly she wants to watch and she's spinning me yarns.' Matt's face showed a flash of annoyance. 'By the way, we're motorbike mustering tomorrow. I'm gonna be taking the quad if you wanna hop on the back and come along.'

Sarah felt like doing a tap dance on the spot but she controlled the urge. 'I'd *love* to come if you don't mind me tagging along. That'd be brilliant!'

'I thought you'd jump at the chance.' Matt smiled, the dimple in his chin visible.

Matt wished Brooke showed as much interest in station work as Sarah. The only thing she seemed to be interested in these days was herself. Come to think of it, maybe she'd always been a bit like that. He pushed the thought out of his mind. He didn't want to think about Brooke now, not while he was enjoying Sarah's company. There was something about her that made Matt smile. He found himself keeping an eye out for her when he came to the cottage, listening out for her laugh and hoping to catch a glimpse of her curly blonde hair. He snapped out of his thoughts as Sarah dragged Jimmy towards him. 'This is our new chopper pilot, Jimmy Turner!'

'Nice to meet you,' said Jimmy, stretching out his hand for a handshake. 'I've heard about you from the blokes I ride rodeo with. They say you're a top bull rider.'

Matt blushed slightly, returning the handshake. 'Nice to meet you, mate. Thanks for coming out here to help us out.'

'I'd love to get some bull riding lessons from you if you have any time one day. The buggers keep tossing me off before the eight seconds!'

'Of course I'll give you some lessons. Towards the end of the mustering season, when things slow down a bit.'

Jimmy was visibly chuffed. 'Fan-bloody-tastic!'

'Dinner's served!' Slim bellowed out from behind the smokescreen at the barbecue.

'Sounds like our cue to dig in!' Sarah rubbed her stomach with glee.

CHAPTER
15

Sarah had breakfast well under way before her alarm sang out at four-thirty a.m. The smell of bacon and eggs wafted through the cottage as she hummed to herself in the kitchen. She'd barely been able to sleep she was so keyed up at the thought of motorbike mustering. What more could a girl ask for? Adventures in the outback *and* being chaperoned by a hunky man in jeans and a cowboy hat.

The stars still shone in the sky above her as she and the men ate their breakfast on the patio. The sun was still busy warming the masses on the other side of the planet.

'You can't sit still, girl,' Stumpy observed, smirking. 'It's like you've got bloody ants in your pants!'

Sarah grinned as she finished the last of her bacon. 'I've never been mustering in the saddle, let alone on a bike, so it's gonna be a day full of new experiences. I can't wait.'

Slim chuckled. 'It'll be interesting to see if you still feel
the same tonight, mate – when your bum is sore and you've
got dust in places you never dreamed possible!'

*

The motorbikes roared to life, echoing in the silence of the
clear, cool morning. The sun was just beginning to rise,
sending golden light bouncing off the red dust. Matt sat on
his quad and leant forward so Sarah could slide in behind
him, and Sarah felt the electricity between them as soon
as their bodies touched. Matt smelled of leather, soap and
deodorant, with an underlying scent that was all his own. He
smelt good enough to eat. She didn't want to crowd him too
much, so held herself a little away from his body. Being this
close to him had already made her tense with excitement.

'Slide in a bit closer, Sarah. It'll be safer if you hang onto
me. I promise I won't bite!' Matt grinned as he looked back
at her, squinting in the rising sun, pulling his akubra down
a little more.

Oh, please do, Sarah thought. She moved closer to him
so that her body sat snugly against his, feeling her breasts
pressing against his muscular back. As she wrapped her
arms around his waist, she felt his abs under her hands.
Matt reached back and touched her on the leg, causing her
to start. 'You good to go, mate?'

'Right as rain!'

'Let's head,' Matt called, addressing the five men in front
of him. They were off. Sarah loved feeling the wind whip
across her body as they rode through the outback. There

was a sudden roar above them and she held on to her hat as she watched Jimmy fly overhead. The downward pressure from the chopper's blades threw dust up around the quads, making Sarah feel like she was in a tumble dryer filled with a tonne of dirt. She covered her mouth and nose in an attempt to avoid sucking up half the countryside before they'd even begun. Slim had been right. The dust was going to be a firm part of her by the end of the day.

Sarah felt goosebumps run up her spine as they spotted the first of the cattle way off in the distance, gathered under a massive gum tree. Jimmy flew close by overhead again, edging the mob out slowly towards the men. Sarah watched carefully as he switched positions, hovering dangerously close to the swaying treetop as he kept the cattle together. Dust surrounded the chopper as Jimmy worked his magic, coaxing the cattle into a steady pace towards the motorbikes. The cruisy atmosphere of the ride out changed in the blink of an eye as the men rode out wide on their bikes, pushing the bellowing cows in the direction of the yards where they were to be branded and drafted.

'See that one? We'll try and get him,' Matt yelled over the noise of the engines and the cattle. Sarah looked to where he was pointing and saw a micky bull that was trying to break away from the mob, causing upheaval at the back of the pack. She hung on for dear life as Matt went full throttle towards the wayward beast. Her adrenaline levels peaked as the bike hit a dip in the rocky terrain and flew through the air, but gravity swiftly pulled it back down. As the quad hit the earth Sarah let out an involuntary squeal of delight. Her hat flew off and toppled in the air behind her like it was attached to an acrobat but she let it go, her arms wrapped tightly around Matt's waist.

Matt got past the bull rapidly and, with a quick turn of the quad, positioned the bike directly in front of the snorting, aggressive beast. Sarah held the gaze of the temperamental animal, terrified of what its next move was going to be. Time seemed to slow as the stand-off lengthened. She felt her body suddenly tense as the micky snorted viciously, deciding to charge the bike. Matt quickly rubbed her thigh, as if to say he'd take care of her. A heatwave flooded through Sarah, but she barely had time to register it before Matt threw the bike into reverse. Sarah could hear shouting in the background as the men tried to distract the bull and stop it from charging them, and the bike screamed hysterically as they went full throttle backwards. Just when it seemed like the bull was almost on top of them, the chopper swooped in, sending up clouds of dust. It hovered centimetres above the ground, separating Sarah and Matt from the bull. Even so, it took close to a minute before the bull decided to return to the mob, and another couple for Sarah's pulse to return to normal.

Less than ten minutes later the micky made another dash for freedom, this time running for a patch of scrub, causing the mob to break as well. Matt was once again hot on the bull's heels, Sarah clinging to him with all her might. She felt the bike skid to a halt as they reached the edge of the scrub, and watched in complete disbelief as Matt bounded from the quad and ran on foot after the bull. Sarah screamed as the bull swung around and charged Matt, and she wanted to jump from the bike and save him but was frozen to the spot. The men had come to Matt's rescue, though, and were closing in from the rear while Matt danced around in front of the bull like a rodeo clown, eventually getting a firm grip on the beast's tail and throwing it off balance. Sarah watched in amazement as the one-tonne animal fell to the ground. The men piled on top of it and soon the bull was being shepherded back to the mob. Sarah let out an enormous breath she hadn't even realised she'd been holding.

Matt dusted off his jeans nonchalantly and leant down to pick up his hat from where it had fallen on the red earth. He slid it on his head with a casual grace and gave Sarah a cheeky wink. As he got back on the quad, she felt her body ache with desire, and had to fight the urge to slip her hand under his shirt. *He's spoken for,* she told herself. But that didn't stop her body responding to him in a way she had never before experienced.

After lunch they spent the afternoon in the yards. Sarah worked the crush with Matt, branding the young cattle, whilst the rest of the men drafted. With the sun beating down relentlessly it was extremely strenuous work, but Sarah enjoyed every second of it – not least because of Matt. By the end of it, though, she was exhausted.

Walking back to the quad after everything was finished, she took a big slug from her water bottle and passed it to Matt. He accepted with enthusiasm, letting the water splash over his face and down his tanned throat. 'Thanks, mate. I needed that. I must say I'm mighty impressed with your efforts today. You can certainly pull your own weight.'

Sarah blushed, and was glad for the red dirt that covered her face. 'I've really enjoyed today. I love getting out and getting my hands dirty.'

'I wish Brooke would take a page outta your book, Sarah. She bloody thinks dirt is gonna kill her.'

'Some people just aren't cut out for the bush, I s'pose.' Sarah shrugged, looked at Matt and instantly realised she'd put her foot in it. She felt her heart tug as Matt's gaze became distant, emotion filling his deep brown eyes.

'Oh, shit, I'm sorry, Matt. I didn't mean to — I just meant —'

Matt interrupted, still looking away from her. 'I know you're right, Sarah. I guess, ah … I just keep holding on to what we used to be, not what we are now. I can't believe I'm telling you all of this. Sorry.'

Sarah's heart melted, and she desperately wanted to hug Matt, but didn't want to embarrass him. Instead she gave him a friendly slap on the back. 'Hey, mate. Don't apologise. I'm all ears, anytime you feel like getting it off your chest.'

Matt looked at her. 'That means a hell of a lot.' He smiled, and Sarah couldn't help but smile back.

*

Over a dinner of heated-up leftovers the phone rang loudly, demanding attention. Sarah was the first to jump up.

'Lily! Oh my God! It's so good to hear your voice.'

'Hey, Sarah! Likewise, mate. It feels like you've been gone for a year, not a month!'

'I know. Hey, guess what? I went mustering today and had an absolute blast! Matt caught a bull with his bare hands.'

'Ooooh, do I detect a change in tone there? Not falling for the cowboy, are you, Sarah? Just remember he's taken, my friend. But it doesn't hurt to have a bit of a perve, hey?'

'Yeah, I know he's taken, Lil, but I'm not sure it's going too well,' Sarah said, dropping her voice to a whisper. 'His relationship with Brooke is sounding a little rocky. He opened up a bit today and told me a few things that made me think it wasn't going to last too long. But I can't hang out waiting for that, I know. I've just gotta get on with things.'

'If it's distraction you're after, I'm your woman. What would you say to another visit from Dan and me?'

Sarah squealed with delight. 'Lily, that's fantastic! I'd love to have you guys come back out again. How long for?'

'Only a couple of nights, but it's better than not at all, hey? Greg's coming to Rosalee in a couple of months to buy some bulls from Matt, and he's asked Daniel and me to come along.'

'I'll be counting down the weeks till you get here! So how's everyone else there?'

'How about they tell you themselves? I'm at your parents' place and everyone wants to speak to you,' Lily replied.

Sarah hung up the phone half an hour later, feeling high with happiness. Any pangs of homesickness she had were eased. Jack had basically hogged the phone, not letting Maggie get a word in edgeways until she finally tickled him so he would let go of the receiver.

While Sarah dried the dinner dishes – the men had kindly washed up – she daydreamed about all the things she could get up to with Daniel and Lily on their visit. Putting the last piece of cutlery in the drawer, Sarah let out a long contented sigh and switched off the light to the kitchen. She was ready to hit the sack.

CHAPTER

16

A kookaburra laughed noisily, distracting Sarah momentarily from her task. She wiped the sweat off from her forehead and wished the flies would lay off for a bit. They just wouldn't go away, no matter how much she threw her hands around in the air. It was nearly midday and her belly was growling like a lion, but she concentrated on the job at hand. She and Matt were trying to fix the water pump at the main dam. It sent a fresh supply of water to the paddock for Matt's prized bucking bulls and had kicked the bucket overnight. In this heat, leaving the bulls without water would be as bad as sticking them in a paddock full of king brown snakes.

Matt was leaning over a huge puddle of muddy water, doing up the last of the screws on the pump. It had been a couple of weeks since they'd been motorbike mustering, but she had barely stopped thinking about him since. The longer he bent down over the pump, the longer she was able to admire his arse, but the muddy puddle presented an irresistible temptation. Sarah gave Matt's arse a shove, and he lost his balance and started to fall. But as he did, he turned and grabbed hold of her Bonds singlet, pulling her down with him. Sarah barely had time to be surprised before they both fell to the ground and rolled about in the puddle, laughing and wrestling until she could no longer see for the mud caked over her eyes. She flopped onto her back and lay there, trying to catch her breath. Matt sprawled out beside her, stinking of the stale, muddy water.

'Geez, Matt, I love the aftershave you've put on today. It's enough to drive a girl wild!' She cheekily sniffed the air, her white teeth gleaming through her muddied grin.

'You don't smell too bad yourself, Sarah,' Matt said, sitting up on an elbow and pushing himself closer to her. 'What's the name of your perfume? La Stink, the pure smell of the muddy earth?'

Sarah rolled to her feet, and Matt started laughing. She touched her hair and realised her blonde curls were caked to her head. Looking down she could see that every inch of her was covered in drying, stinky mud. She put her hands on her hips.

'What's so funny?' she said, trying to keep a straight face. 'Don't I look ready for a night out on the town?'

'We both look like we're dressed to impress!' Matt sat up and tried to wipe the mud from his arms. 'I reckon we better wash this stuff off before we even think of getting back into the truck.' He chuckled.

'Race you!' Sarah said, running for the dam. Within seconds Matt was running behind her. Ripping off her boots and jeans, Sarah ran into the cool, fresh water in her singlet and undies. Matt hopped on the spot comically as he removed his boots and jeans, then followed her into the water in his jocks and T-shirt.

Sarah floated around on the top of the water, enjoying the serenity that the dam provided. It was ringed with massive paperbarks that shaded them from the harshness of the sun. All that could be heard was a gentle breeze shifting the leaves, and the birds calling out to each other from the trees. It felt indescribably good to get the sweat and mud off her skin.

Matt was the first to speak. 'Are you looking forward to mustering tomorrow? I bet Victory'll have fun.'

'I can't wait, Matt. It hasn't been long since I went mustering last and I'm getting withdrawal symptoms! And this time will be different because I'll be on horseback.'

They were floating gradually closer together, and suddenly Matt's leg brushed against Sarah's thigh underwater. She felt electricity race through her, like Matt had just flicked on a light switch in her body. Her mind filled with images of his body, the taste of his skin and the feel of his lips pressing against her own. It was becoming an obsession. Matt was in her dreams every night, kissing and caressing her, bringing her to euphoria with his touch. She always woke with a sense of disappointment. She wanted to stay asleep; dreamland was the only place she could touch him.

Matt's husky voice snapped her out of her fantasies. 'We better head back to the homestead, Sarah. I'm gonna chew my own arm off soon I'm that hungry.'

'Sounds like a plan to me. I'm famished.'

*

Sarah scoffed a sausage roll that she had just nuked in the microwave. She was too hungry to wait for it to cook in the oven. It was foul and burnt the top of her mouth, but filled the gap in her belly all the same. Duke danced around her feet, happy his master was home from her morning at work. She fell to the floor and gave him a hug, play-wrestling with him, giggling as he licked her face. She was still on a high from her morning with Matt.

'Come on then, Duke, we gotta get dinner sorted.'

Duke barked, like he knew exactly what Sarah was saying. She laughed and rubbed him under the chops.

CHAPTER

17

With a steaming cup of tea in her hand, Sarah parked herself at the patio table, enjoying the splendour of yet another beautiful outback day unfolding in front of her eyes. In the short time before dawn it felt as though the earth was coming alive, preparing for the new day ahead, and it filled Sarah with a sense of pure bliss. She had made it her morning ritual to sit here with a hot cuppa, before the men had risen from their beds. It gave her time to gather her thoughts for the day. She gazed up at the stars above that were slowly dissolving into the lightening sky, making way for endless blue.

Gulping down the last of her tea, Sarah heard movement in the cottage. She had breakfast to cook and then lunches to pack before saddling up Victory and joining the men for a full day of dust, flies, cattle and sweltering heat.

Chris came out of his bedroom and into the kitchen while they were all eating breakfast, looking like hell and clutching his belly. 'I ain't gonna be able to work today, guys. I feel like I'm coming down with something.'

Stumpy gave him the once-over. 'You do look like shit, Chris. I'd rather you stay here than work when you're liable to make mistakes. Maybe you should try to get to bed early one of these nights – it might be what's wrong with you!'

Chris didn't even bother to answer, heading back to his room and slamming the door behind him. Raised eyebrows were exchanged around the table.

'Gee whiz. Someone got out of the wrong side of the bed today,' Sarah said, surprised.

'Yeah, well, he's his own worst enemy. I hear him coming in at all hours of the night. God knows what he's doing out there in the dark, and to be honest I don't wanna know. I need him on the ball when he's at work, though, and he's just not,' Stumpy said with crumpled brows.

'I agree with you, boss. I'm sick of having to pick up his slack at work,' Slim said.

'One of these nights I'm gonna follow him and see what he's up to,' Patrick said casually.

Sarah shook her head. 'Seriously? Do you really want to know? Count me outta that one, Patrick. I ain't no detective. I'll leave the mystery solving to you.'

'Just call me Sherlock Holmes,' Patrick said, trying to do a posh English accent. They cracked up laughing.

*

Victory could barely stand still once Sarah was in the saddle. He was following her lead, as always, but with an added spring in his step. He held his head high as Sarah took in the scenery. She felt goosebumps travel up her spine when she saw the chopper fly overhead, remembering the motorbike mustering, and wondered what the day held in store. It looked like she was slowly getting over her fear of the chopper. She might even be able to go for a flight with Jimmy one of these days. Maybe it had something to do with Brad's recovery. He was doing well in Mareeba and getting around on crutches, according to his mum.

There were always adventures to be had when mustering. Sarah couldn't help grinning at the thought. Her heartbeat sped up a little as she watched Matt riding in front of her, his muscular arm lazily holding the reins of his horse. It was getting harder with each passing day to hide her feelings for him.

After an hour at a steady pace they reached the area where they would be working for the morning. The cattle needed to be rounded up and pushed into the yards for branding and sorting. Some would be going to the saleyards, and others would be let back out to roam and fatten up some more for the next muster. Not quite sure of what she should be doing, Sarah decided to hang back with Victory and watch the men work the cattle, eager to learn their ways.

She felt as though she was part of a real-life outback adventure film, but instead of John Wayne and Clint Eastwood, the stars were real men. She watched in awe as Jimmy hovered above the men and horses in the chopper, pushing the cattle in the right direction. Two hundred head of cattle rushed about in a scene of wild exhilaration, creating thick clouds of dust, and at some points Sarah struggled to see the men amongst the red. The cattle rarely laid eyes on humans other than at mustering time. Some bellowed loudly, expressing their unhappiness at being so rudely torn away from their daily rituals, while rival bulls went head to head like they were opponents in the ring. Cows mooed noisily in the throng for their lost calves, making Sarah want to run into the midst of the turmoil and find their babies for them. Mustering was a massive change of pace for the herd, who spent most of their days roaming about looking for the next bit of fodder to graze upon.

As she watched, an unruly beast with horns big enough to kill an elephant decided to try and break free from the mob. Straightaway Matt came galloping in from the side, his roo-hide stockwhip cracking into the air with a sound like a gunshot. His horse turned on a three-penny bit to head off the incoming bull. Sarah admired how sure-footed Matt's horse was, at the same time unable to stop from noticing how sexy Matt was as he cracked the whip powerfully. Stumpy rode in from the opposite side and the bull snorted, clearly undecided about charging the two men and their horses. Luckily it gave up on the idea and headed back to join the adrenaline-charged mob.

With her eyes on the bull, Sarah was taken by surprise when a large cow rushed by her after breaking free. She felt Victory take off before she had time to pull him back. He got past the cow in no time and spun round at full gallop to face it. Sarah barely had time to register what he was doing before she felt herself start to slip in the saddle. Instinctively she wrapped her arms around his neck and grabbed handfuls of his mane. Her quick response was the only thing that saved her from hitting the dirt below face-first. As Victory and the cow were facing each other off, she had a few seconds to regain her composure, securing her boots in the stirrups and grabbing control of the reins. The cow backed up, lowing defiantly, and then turned with a dismissive flick of its tail. Sarah proudly gave Victory a rub on the head. 'Good boy! You could've warned me first, though, buddy, but I suppose it's in your blood to muster.'

'Thanks, Sarah!' Slim hollered. 'You've got yourself a good horse there, mate. You can tell he's done that a few times before!'

Sarah grinned. She was still pumping from the rush of chasing the cow. She would have to come out more often and get some experience mustering. With Victory beneath her, she knew she had a good teacher to show her the way it was done.

Eventually the cattle seemed to calm down and one of the older cows came out the front of the mob and took the lead, clearly remembering where they were going, and that in the saleyards there would be water and food. Occasionally a cow would still try and break ranks with one last desperate bid for freedom, only to be pushed back. Sarah felt her confidence grow as she had a few goes bringing the wayward cattle back into the mob, glancing up to see Matt lifting his hat and nodding at her from the other side of the mob with an impressed look on his face.

It was lunchtime when they finally reached the saleyards, and Sarah could feel her belly rumbling like mad. For lunch she'd made some homemade pumpkin scones and jam, fruitcake she'd whipped up the night before and plenty of chicken and coleslaw sandwiches. After eating her fill, Sarah was ready for a nap. Her bones were already aching and she knew she'd be sore tonight. She found a shady place under a tree and settled down, swatting at the flies that clung to every bead of sweat on her body. Swearing under her breath, she pulled her hat down so she could at least rest without them all over her face. Within seconds she was asleep.

*

A sudden icy sensation shocked Sarah awake, and she gasped in surprise.

Liam stood in front of her, beaming proudly. 'Now that's how you wake a sleeping princess!'

'You're a turd, Liam!' Sarah growled, still trying to figure out if she was angry or amused. 'I'll get you back when you least expect it, mate!'

'There'll be plenty of time for that later. We have heaps of work to do, and the clock is ticking!' Liam called as he headed for the mob of cattle huddling in the yard.

Sarah spent the afternoon by Matt's side, helping him brand the cattle as they went through the crush. Within half an hour her shirt was clinging to her body with sweat, hugging every curve. She pushed on throughout the day, working hard, trying to ignore the screaming aches and pains in her body. She firmly set her mind on the task at hand in a bid to distract herself from the pain. By four o'clock, the skin on her hands had acquired deep splits that were beginning to bleed, and her body felt like it had aged a hundred years from all the sun exposure. Her back had started to throb unrelentingly and she knew it was only her determination driving her on. She did her best to keep smiling, trying not to let Matt see she was hurting. Occasionally he'd look up at her and smile, nodding admiringly at the way she handled the conditions.

For his part, Matt was amazed at how hard Sarah worked, and with a smile on her face the whole time. He was learning to ignore the strange whisperings at the back of his mind – the urge to touch her, to feel her sweet lips against his, to taste her softness. He couldn't cheat on Brooke. The thought of Brooke sent his thoughts wandering back to last night, and he felt his anger rise as he remembered the fight they'd had. He'd asked her if she wanted to come mustering, and she'd refused. She didn't want to help out on the station at all – it was a man's job, according to her, and she wasn't about to start ruining her skin out in the sun every day. She had not even spoken to him this morning, like it was his fault that she chose to drive herself to boredom by spending her time on the couch watching soaps all day long. Something had to give, but he just didn't know what – or how.

By six p.m. the team were happy with their efforts, and decided to retire before they had to ride home in the dark. The work had been done with professional precision, and Sarah was amazed by how much she'd learnt over the course of the day. She hosed Victory down while the men did the same for their own horses, and got him settled for the night before heading home for a shower. Sarah stood under the meagre flow in the shower block, washing the dust from her sun-kissed skin and massaging her aching arms gently. It had been an incredible day, and she'd discovered that mustering was addictive. She could only hope there'd be another chance for her to go soon.

*

Matt headed back to the granny flat at the homestead, exhausted and filthy. He hoped Brooke might've made some dinner, but doubted it. *She hasn't done it yet, so why start now?* he grumbled to himself as he stepped through the back door. Brooke was where she normally was, on the couch, watching reruns of *Days of Our Lives,* chocolate wrappers and dirty cups strewn about the coffee table in front of her. Matt felt his temper flare.

'Hi, Brooke. Hard at work, I see.'

'Sure am, Matt!' she answered sarcastically, her eyes remaining glued to the telly.

'All right, Brooke. I've had enough of this crap. I haven't done anything wrong, other than go off to do an honest day's work.'

Brooke let out a sigh. 'I'm bored to death in this hole of a place! You're never home, always too busy off gallivanting around the countryside. I'm sure there's not *that* much to do around here!'

'Well, Brooke, if you bothered coming out with me for a day you might *see* just how much there is to do round here. What do you want me to do? I have a station to run, and I can't leave it all to Dad and Georgia. I'm a cattleman through and through, and I'm not going to change.'

'I don't think you should *expect* me to kill myself out there in the heat. It's not a place for a woman to be working.'

Matt felt his temper begin to rise. 'Sarah doesn't seem to have a problem with it. And she's a woman, through and through.' He regretted the words as soon as they left his lips. It was the wrong thing to say.

'I wouldn't want to be like Sarah! And what do you mean by a woman through and through? You barely even know her! Or do you?'

Matt quickly changed the topic. 'Tell you what. Next week I'm going mustering for the whole week. You're welcome to come with me if you like. Who knows, you might even enjoy it?'

Something unreadable flickered in Brooke's eyes. She softened, smiling gently at Matt. 'I'm sorry. I just miss having you around, that's all. Let me think about the mustering, okay?'

Matt gave her a nod and headed to the bathroom for a shower. His mind was in turmoil. He did care for Brooke, but he just wasn't sure how much he really loved her any more. *I'll give it another few weeks,* he thought to himself. *I'll give her one more chance to prove herself out here.*

CHAPTER
18

The Toyota that Sarah was driving was packed to the rafters. The men had each put in one bag of personal belongings, plus there were swags, fuel, cooking equipment, water and plenty of food. Sarah had Lee Kernaghan keeping her company in the CD player and she hummed along happily as she dodged cattle, which were parked in the middle of the road, refusing to move like stubborn teenagers who didn't want to get out of bed in the morning. It was only five a.m. but she'd already been bumping along the uneven dirt road for close to two hours, following the men on their horses. They'd passed through five gates so far and crossed more cattle grids than she could count, but she knew there would still be quite a few to go. The massive ruts in the dirt track were big enough to swallow her tyres whole, and she had to be careful not to slip into any of them – it would put the team way behind schedule if they had to dig the truck out of a ditch. Despite this, Sarah was living a country girl's dream. The full moon hovered above her, filling the land with its brilliant luminosity, and Sarah could see for miles and miles across the wide open plain. It was nice to have the men in front of her, their hats on in preparation for the imminent sunrise. While the moon was still visible, it sent silvery light bouncing off their silhouettes, creating a beautiful image that Sarah captured with a click of her camera.

The trip to the first camp for the week's mustering would take Sarah and the men five hours. Jimmy was the only lucky one still back in bed – it would take him just an hour or so to get there in the chopper. A little pang of disappointment shot through Sarah at the knowledge that she wouldn't be joining them out in the saddle this time. Her job was to drive the support vehicle, and it was with sadness that she'd left Victory back in the stables. She could swear he was sulking when she said goodbye, his bottom lip drooping at the thought of not going with them all. It was as bad as leaving a child home when you were off to the rodeo. They had left extra early as Matt wanted to get to the first camp with time to spare so the men could help Sarah set up before heading out to muster the cattle.

By eight o'clock, the sun had well and truly risen, and the group had reached their first destination, a rustic old cattleyard in the middle of nowhere. Sarah just had time to whip up some breakfast before the men left for the day. She set off with Stumpy to find some firewood so they could get the barbecue ready to go. Sarah was surprised at how easy it was to set up camp. It basically involved finding a shaded spot and tossing your swag underneath. The only priority was setting up the camp kitchen. When Sarah and Stumpy returned with arms full of timber, she smiled at the effort the blokes had put in to making the camp comfortable while she was gone. A hammock had been strung between two golden wattle trees so she at least had somewhere shady during the heat of the day where she could lie back and read. It was all she was going to able to do on the long and lonely days she would be at the camp on her own while they were out mustering. Sarah had packed a couple of good books and was looking forward to a bit of rest and relaxation.

Matt stoked up the fire while Sarah filled the billy with water from the drums she'd brought in the back of the Toyota. Once she was done, she hung the billy on a stick and balanced it, somewhat precariously, from two open-ended branches that Liam had pushed into the ground on either side of the fire. While the water boiled she unpacked the box of tin cups, plates and cutlery, placing it all on a wobbly foldout table that Patrick had set up for her. The battery-operated esky was in prime position on the back of the truck, and Sarah grabbed some eggs and bacon from its icy coolness. By the time she returned with tongs in hand, the barbecue plate Matt had set up was red hot and ready to go.

Sarah noticed Matt watching her as she kneeled in the dust beside the campfire, cooking breakfast. She wondered how he was feeling about Brooke. They hadn't spoken about Brooke since that candid moment motorbike mustering, but she knew he was disappointed Brooke hadn't come on the mustering trip. She'd decided to spend the week back in Mt Isa catching up with friends instead. She really didn't have any interest in station life, it seemed, and Sarah wondered how a girl like Brooke had ended up with a guy like Matt.

She watched the men saddle up and waved to them on their horses as they headed out for the day's work. Jimmy had joined them halfway through breakfast, his chopper nearly blowing the camp away when he landed smack down beside them. Now, his chopper was the only way she could tell where the men were – she caught occasional glimpses of it in the air in the distance. She started to tidy up the breakfast plates, washing them in a small tub she had brought along, deciding to let them drip dry on a tea towel on top of the table.

Sarah found herself pottering around the camp for the next few hours, trying to pass the time. She walked through the cattleyard and cleared the scum off the top of the concrete water tank. She found a few large rocks, which she rolled along the ground to rest near the fire so the men didn't have to sit on their heels whilst eating. She watched a flock of white cockatoos land on the rails of the cattleyard. They announced their presence loudly and took turns dipping in the coolness of the water tank as if it were a day spa for birds. Sarah tried to get close to them so she could take a photo, finding comfort in their liveliness. The barren land that was to be her home for the next week seemed bereft of life. The birds didn't take kindly to her approach and flew off into the distance, squawking like a pack of loonies. Deciding there was not much else she could do for now, Sarah plopped herself into the hammock with a book.

*

A loud bang startled Sarah awake. She sat bolt upright, forgetting she was in a hammock and finding herself upended on the ground below with a thump. What the hell was that noise? It had sounded like a gunshot. Her senses were screaming, her eyes searching for the source of the noise. It took a few moments to locate the cause, and when she did, she doubled over in laughter. A can of baked beans had fallen off the card table and rolled into the hot coals of the fire. Once the metal had heated, the can had exploded, and baked beans had spewed everywhere. The gooey tomato sauce dripped from every imaginable place – the bullbar of the truck, the esky, the swags – like the skies had opened and rained baked beans from above. *Only out here could something like this happen,* she giggled to herself while she cleaned it all up.

She glanced at her watch for the first time since falling asleep and just about died. *Shit,* she thought, *it's nearly four o'clock.* She must have nodded off for a few hours. Thank God that the baked beans had woken her up. She began prepping dinner rapidly – tonight it was hamburgers, made with her secret recipe, followed by fresh damper with loads of butter and oozy golden syrup. He mouth watered at the very thought of it. Sarah mixed the dough up for the damper and wrapped it in alfoil before placing it to the side, ready to be slid into the camp oven later on.

The men appeared just as the sun was setting, a huge mob of cattle in tow. Sarah watched them ride in perfect formation around the cattle, who were eager to get to the water in the cattleyard. She ran over to open the gates before the mob arrived, keen to help out and eager for company as soon as possible. She was incredibly happy to see the men's dust-covered faces grinning at her beneath their hats as they walked the cattle into the yard. It had been a lonesome day without them around to give her jip.

Matt slid down off his horse and walked over to Sarah as she shut the gates behind the mob. 'How was your day, mate? Hope it wasn't too boring.'

Sarah swatted at a fly that was hanging off her eyelash like it was a bungy cord. 'Nah, I had a good day. It even rained baked beans this afternoon.'

The men laughed till they cried as Sarah explained the baked beans incident. She was delighted to add a bit of sparkle to their day. The damper had turned out even better than she'd hoped, and between them they devoured every last bite, more than one person finding the need to undo the top button of their jeans afterwards.

'Well, I'm heading yonder to give birth to a brown bear,' Slim said, standing and stretching.

'Just make sure you put your belt round the right turd when you're finished!' Liam laughed.

Slim shook his head and chuckled as he headed off into the scrub to do his business.

After cleaning up dinner and yarning around the fire, it was time to hit the sack. Sarah slid into her swag, shivering at the freezing temperature, a total contrast to the heat of the day. The way the outback went from one extreme to the other always amazed her. A curlew called eerily in the distance, filling the quiet night with its calls; it sounded more like a woman screaming than a harmless bird. Sarah felt the hair stand up on her neck. She called goodnight to the men, tucked in their swags around the campfire. A staggered chorus of goodnights sung back at Sarah from various points, and then there was no sound but the low crackle of the embers in the fire. Sarah lay awake for a while longer, staring at the sky above her. It was filled with more stars than she had ever known existed. She fell asleep while silently trying to name them, nodding off at the Southern Cross.

CHAPTER
19

The silence was almost deafening, with only the whisper of wind blowing across the dusty plains. Sarah felt like she spent more time swatting flies in the outback than doing almost anything else. She swiped lazily at one as it landed on her singlet, which was stuck to her body with sweat. Her clothes would definitely need a good wash at the station, even though she had handwashed them in soapy water yesterday and dried them on the bull bar. As she sat there swatting away, a kangaroo bounded through the camp, knocking over everything in its way. Sarah smiled to herself, enjoying the distraction. She hoped she could shake the low mood she had woken up in this morning.

It had been six days in the outback filled with monotonous daily rituals, and she was beginning to feel a little loopy from the daily solitude. The high of the first few days' droving soon diminished when she took in the full impact of spending days alone in the middle of nowhere. She had moved camp every day as the men edged closer to the main holding yards back at the homestead, packing up on her own once the men had left and unpacking at the new camp in wait for their arrival home at sunset, but this only killed so much time. She had listened to every song on her iPod at least twice and had read both books she had brought along within three days, leaving her twiddling her thumbs to pass the time. She was tired of lying in the hammock and had spent most of the last couple of days in search of a puddle of muddy water where she could rinse herself off, always wondering afterwards if she stank more instead of less. Her packet of wet wipes had become more valuable to her than gold – on the days she couldn't find somewhere to bathe, she pulled a couple out of the packet as though they were made of finest silk, and luxuriated in a quick wipe-down. She was craving a long, hot shower and would have given an arm or leg for a can of creaming soda. Water and tea were beginning to dull her tastebuds, and she yearned for something fizzy, icy cold and sweet to trickle down her forever-dry throat. She rolled her eyes at herself –she rarely drank soft drink back in the land of the living, but out here, when you couldn't get something, it haunted you until you thought you were going to go nuts.

The positive side of all this solitude was that she'd had time to think about her life and the direction it was heading. There were no distractions – no electricity for the likes of a television or stereo, no friends to visit or phone calls to make. Just Sarah and her thoughts. And she found those thoughts always drifted to Matt.

After lunch and an afternoon nap, Sarah got stuck into preparing dinner. She was making a big pot of curried beef tonight and some homemade campfire bread to dip into the juices. As she kneaded the bread, she reminded herself that she'd be back at Rosalee in less than twenty-four hours, and the thought cheered her no end.

The noisy bellowing of the cattle, followed by the thunderous thudding of their hoofs hitting the ground, was the first sign that the men were close to camp. The chopper appeared above her and landed off to the side, sending a cloud of dust in Sarah's direction. It stayed suspended over her for a good few minutes before settling over the camp, covering everything in sight. 'Thanks a lot, Jimmy,' Sarah muttered as she squinted off into the distance, trying to catch a glimpse of the men as they rode in. The sun was setting behind them, casting long shadows on the ground and darkening their faces, making it hard for Sarah to pick out who was who. Their broad silhouettes in akubras rode in the fiery red sunset, dust riding from their horses' hoofs. Even though she'd seen it before, she felt her heart lighten at the beautiful sight.

Jimmy sauntered into the camp before the others, whistling happily like always. His jeans were nearly black from the amount of dirt caked on them. He looked in desperate need of a good hose-down; mind you, Sarah thought, they were probably all in need of it.

'Hey, cook. How's it hanging?'

'Well, if you haven't noticed, Jimmy, I don't really have anything to hang, being a sheila and all, but I'm great now you blokes are back, if that's what you were asking,' Sarah answered with a cheeky grin.

Jimmy laughed. 'Always the kidder!' He sniffed the air like a dog on a scent. 'Cor, dinner smells fantastic.'

'Thanks. Believe me when I say that I've been slaving over it most of the afternoon. It ain't so easy when you haven't got a kitchen but I secretly like not having to clean down all the bench tops at the end of the night!'

'That's the spirit. You gotta look on the bright side, hey!' Jimmy pulled his towel from the tree branch it was hanging from. 'I'm off to find a puddle to bathe in. If I'm not back in an hour send a search party.'

'Right you are!' Sarah called as she watched him disappear behind the chopper.

She checked to make sure the curry was simmering away nicely in the camp oven before heading over to open the gates for the rest of the men, as she'd done every night. Matt lifted his hat to her as he came into view. 'How's tricks, mate?'

Sarah took in his handsome face as he got down off his horse. 'Much better now you guys are back. It's lonely out here sometimes. I feel like I could talk for a million years to anyone willing to listen.'

'I know it can be tough, mate. I hope this trip hasn't made you shy away from station life,' Matt said gently, moving closer.

'No way. I still love it. Spending a bit of time with my own thoughts has been interesting, though. I feel like it's helped me get my life into perspective a bit.'

'It's always good to have some peace and quiet to think. I've been doing a lot of that myself.' Matt shot Sarah a look but she couldn't read it.

Slim trotted over and slid off his ride. 'Hey, Sarah! I'm looking forward to your fine cooking tonight. Look at me – I'm fading away to a shadow after all this hard work!'

Sarah was happy to see him but wished he hadn't interrupted her conversation with Matt. She felt like he had been on the verge of telling her something important.

Liam, Patrick and Chris sauntered over after making sure the cattle were all tucked away safely for the night in the yards.

'Do I have time for a nice long hot shower?' Patrick asked cheekily.

'No probs, go for it. I'll just heat your grub up in the microwave if it gets cold,' Sarah answered with a giggle.

Chris took his hat off and tried running his hands through his sweat-soaked and dusty hair, but didn't get very far. 'Friggin' hot out there today. I could drink a swimming pool, I reckon.'

After a week living in the same camp, Sarah still hadn't quite figured Chris out. He'd certainly been in better sorts this week, compared to his hissy fit before the last muster. He seemed less grumpy and better rested – probably because he wasn't wandering about half the night.

Before dinner the men all headed into the falling darkness with torches and towels to have a quick rinse in the small pool of water that Sarah had found earlier. It was the cleanest she had come across the whole trip, but stale-smelling all the same. By the time the men had returned, marginally cleaner than before, Sarah had dinner on the foldout table, ready for them to help themselves. She was pleased to see all of them went back for seconds.

Once they'd finished eating, Sarah boiled the billy and made everyone a cuppa. They sat around the campfire, mugs in hand, scaring each other with ghost tales.

Stumpy spoke with a hushed voice. 'And then the slimy creature grabbed him by the ankles and pulled him from his swag, blood dripping from its fangs. He struggled with all his might to get free, but the creature had its claws buried deep within the skin of his legs. The whole camp heard the man's bloodcurdling screams as he was dragged into the blackness of the night, never to be seen again!'

Stumpy finished the story by shining a torch beam on his face and pulling a ghastly expression, sending chills up Sarah's spine. She'd found the first few stories amusing, but after that she began to feel really unsettled. The tales were getting hairier and scarier, told in graphic detail. 'Shit, guys, I'm gonna be too afraid to sleep tonight if we don't stop scaring each other's pants off!'

Matt gave her a grin. 'You can pull your swag up beside mine if you like. I'll make sure the boogie man doesn't get you.'

A dingo howled in the background, adding to the already sinister atmosphere. Sarah felt her skin prickle with goosebumps, and she was tuned in to every little sound in the darkness beyond the fire.

'I think I'm gonna take you up on that offer, Matt.'

Matt dragged his swag over next to hers, and Sarah's fear instantly abated. She snuggled into her swag. 'Thanks for being my knight in shining armour.'

'I don't know about that, but hey, no worries, Sarah,' Matt said, sliding into his swag and yawning.

Sarah closed her heavy eyelids, feeling the warmth of Matt's swag through hers. 'Well, night then, Matt.'

'Night, Sarah. Sweet dreams.' Matt's husky voice caressed her ears in the silence of the night. A boobook owl hooted in the tree above them, calling to its mate. Sarah smiled to herself as its mate called back, then drifted off to sleep.

*

When Sarah woke, the moonlight was kissing Matt's face as he slept beside her. He was pressed up against her swag, and his bare arm was draped over her. She found herself fighting the urge to leave it there, but she knew it would look bad if any of the others woke up and saw it. Reluctantly, she lifted Matt's arm gently and placed it slowly down on his chest, hoping not to wake him, and smiling when she succeeded without him even stirring. She squinted at her watch, trying to make out the time, eager to catch a bit more sleep before the new day. She finally saw that it was four-thirty, which only gave her another half-hour of sleep. *Oh well, better than nothing,* she thought.

She drifted off back to sleep, only to be woken again by Slim letting a massive fart loose. He sleepily pronounced that his arse was the alarm clock, sending them all into muffled fits of laughter in their swags.

*

Sarah was delighted. After sitting on her own doing nothing for six days, she was finally able to get involved. She idled slowly in the Toyota behind the men on horseback, dreaming about a hot shower, as they moved the cattle towards their final destination. Her attention was caught by a calf struggling at the back of the mob, its legs wobbling around like mad. As she watched it collapsed under a tree. She wound down her window. 'Hey, Stumpy! You wanna put that calf in here, mate? Looks like it's not doing too well out there.'

'Good idea, Sarah,' he called back. 'Just give me a minute.'

Matt had heard the conversation. 'You keep going, Stumpy. I'll look after it, buddy.'

Stumpy nodded and continued on. Sarah pulled over and watched Matt as he scrambled with the exhausted calf, trying to get his arms around it. It fought for a few seconds before deciding it wasn't worth the effort, allowing Matt to pick it up and carry it over to the Toyota. She jumped out of the driver's seat and ran round to open the passenger door.

'Nice of you to offer to take it in here,' Matt said, out of breath as he got the calf settled on the floor. It immediately tried to clamber onto the seat, foamy saliva dripping from its mouth.

'I couldn't bear to watch it struggling. Better to have it in here slobbering all over me than collapsing out there.'

Matt smiled at her in a way that made her heart melt. 'You just keep on surprising me, Miss Clarke.'

'All in a day's work,' was all she could come up with as he shut the door and walked back to his horse, his jeans clinging to his divine butt.

Sarah turned her eyes back to the road. She spoke to the calf like it was a long-lost friend as she drove the rest of the way towards the homestead.

'Well, my friend, I'll let you in on a little secret: I'm really falling for Matt, big time. He's gorgeous and such a deep thinker, and I love that in a bloke. He makes me feel so good when I'm around him, too, always telling me what a great job I'm doing. I really wanted to kiss him this morning when I woke up and he was asleep beside me in his swag. I'm not sure, but I reckon he might like me too. There's something in the way he smiles at me.'

The calf's big, wet eyes looked up at her in bemusement and she tried her best to keep it calm, giving it an occasional scratch behind its oversized, floppy ears, laughing at the absurdity of her having a heart-to-heart with a calf.

It was a slow journey and Sarah's legs were starting to ache as the procession neared the last gate. She was itching to get out of the Toyota and on to solid ground. When they finally arrived at the yards, Steve and Georgia were there to meet them. Georgia ran to the truck, her eyes widening when she saw the calf with its head on Sarah's lap.

'Gee, Sarah, fancy picking up a hitchhiking calf on the way!' Georgia helped her lift the calf from the passenger seat as the men yarded the cattle they had mustered.

'Yeah, well, crazy things happen out there, Georgia!' Sarah laughed.

She bagged the first shower, and sighed with pleasure as she turned on the taps and soothing warm water poured over her filthy skin. She gazed at the concrete floor, watching the water running off her body in brown rivulets before disappearing down the drain. She used half a bottle of shampoo washing her long hair three times, then shaved the Amazon jungle from her legs before sticking some conditioner on her ringlets, which had started to turn into dreads after a week in the bush.

While the water trickled over her, Sarah reflected over the last few months. She couldn't believe how much her life had changed in the little time she had been at Rosalee but she felt stronger and more focused because of it. She lived on a massive cattle station, had a group of great mates, had learnt how to muster cattle and discovered why people in the outback loved it with a passion – it was simply the breathtaking beauty of it all. She had conquered so many of the things she had dreamt about. Except for one – Matthew Walsh. Was she ever going to conquer him, or would he forever be an untouchable desire?

CHAPTER

20

The air brakes on Greg's truck groaned outside the gates of Rosalee. Sarah squealed in delight. The men were sitting in the lounge room enjoying their day off watching Westerns, the air conditioner whirring at top speed. She flew past them, trying to pull her boots on at the same time, tripping over her own feet as she went. 'Slow down, mate, or you're gonna do yourself an injury!' Stumpy called, laughing.

'I can't, Stumpy! I'm too excited! They're finally here!' Sarah called back as she ran out the flyscreen door and towards the front gates. It had been three weeks since she got back from the muster, and she'd been counting down the days until Greg, Lily and Daniel arrived from Mareeba. She waved like a lunatic when the truck came into view, and felt happy tears burning her eyes as she saw Lily waving frantically back to her from the cab.

Sarah swung open the gates and ran over to the door of the truck, still waving. The door opened and Lily slid over the top of Daniel and jumped down out of the cab, her arms outstretched, ready for a hardcore hug.

'Sarah! It's so good to see you, mate! I've missed you!'

Sarah wrapped her arms around Lily. 'I've missed you too, Lil! I'm so glad you're here. It's been months!'

Daniel got down from the cab before Greg drove the truck through the gates. Once the girls had disentangled themselves Daniel picked Sarah up off the ground and spun her around, a huge smile cracking his face. 'Great to see you, sis. The farm hasn't been the same without you. Just a shame I couldn't pack Mum and Dad in my suitcase.'

'Daniel, it's great to see you! How was the trip?'

'It was a really good drive, actually. Greg knows how to keep you entertained. He has a DVD player and everything up there.'

'No way! Wish I'd thought of that when we drove out here!' Sarah said. 'Speaking of Greg, I better go and say g'day to the old bugger.'

Greg sauntered over from where he'd parked the truck, stretching his legs. 'Now, now. I may have a body of an older man, but I have a mind as sharp as a twenty-year-old's.' He reached out his arms and gave Sarah a big hug. 'How's station life treating you?'

'I love it. There's always so much to do and I learn something new every day. The Walshes – they're the owners – have made me feel like part of the family.'

Greg lit a cigarette and blew a smoke ring, his weather-beaten face creasing as he spoke. 'I just knew you'd love it out here, Sarah. I reckon it's in your blood to be a cattle

woman and you've picked one of the best families around
to learn from.'

'You got that right! Hey, who's up for some lunch?' Sarah
said, realising her own stomach was rumbling. 'I bet you're
all hungry, especially you, Daniel!'

Daniel grinned sheepishly. His sister knew him well.

Over lunch there was a loud rap at the door. 'Anyone
home?' Matt called. Sarah was the only one without a
mouthful of food. 'Yeah, out the back, Matt!' She felt her
heart flutter; knowing that she was about to see him sent
her stomach plunging.

She hadn't seen Matt much recently – he'd been spending
time up at the homestead or in Mt Isa, driving the cattle
to and fro, and had been too busy with other jobs on the
station to help out with the mustering. She'd crossed paths
with him a few times in the last couple of weeks, but he
was always with Brooke, and she found those conversations
awkward. She couldn't shake the feeling that Brooke didn't
like her. Maybe she'd done something to offend her? The
guys had told her that Brooke and Matt were trying to work
things out, so she figured that might explain why Matt wasn't
around much. Apparently Brooke had come back from her
week in Mt Isa a changed woman, keen to help out when
she could. Sarah had felt her heart sink at the news, and then
kicked herself for even thinking that there might have been
a chance for her and Matt. She tried to be happy for him –
he deserved to be happy; she just wished it was with her.

Matt grinned from ear to ear when he spotted Greg at
the table, and stretched his hand out for a firm handshake.

'Greg, mate! It's been too long. Great to see you here. And I see Sarah is feeding you up on her fine tucker.'

'She's a bloody top cook, Matt. I've never had a bacon and egg burger taste so good!' Greg grinned, tomato sauce still stuck to his chin. Sarah smothered a smile at the sight of him.

Patrick put the last bite of burger in his mouth. 'Tell me about it! With Sarah as cook, I reckon I put weight on when I was out droving when normally I lose weight out there.'

Slim looked down at his rotund belly. 'Yeah, and look at what she's done to me. I've lost my ribs somewhere.'

'I reckon I could find them.' Liam poked Slim with the handle of his fork.

Sarah started to feel her face going red. 'Oh, come on you lot! It's not that hard to make a burger.'

Lily let out a burp and quickly covered her mouth. 'Oops! Pardon.' Sarah laughed at her innocent expression.

Matt pulled up a chair so it was facing backwards and planted his butt down like he was straddling a horse, his muscular forearms resting on the back of the chair, tattoo showing. 'I have an idea, guys. I reckon we have ourselves a mini rodeo here tomorrow, seeing as we've got the weekend off. What do you reckon?'

Jimmy was so excited he jumped up without warning, and his chair flew out behind him, barely missing Duke and landing with a crash on the patio floor. 'Bloody oath, Matt! What a corker of an idea! Can I ride?'

'Of course you can. I was hoping you would. I thought maybe you'd like to give it a bash too, Daniel, if your ribs can handle it,' Matt said, eyebrows raised.

'Count me in!' Daniel replied eagerly.

'I reckon I'd like to give it a go too,' Liam said.

'Me too!' Patrick said, clapping his hands in the air.

'Oh shit. Does this mean I have to as well?' Slim asked, fear written across his face.

'Of course not, Slim! You can help me out at the chutes,' Matt replied. He directed his gaze towards Liam and Patrick. 'Since neither of you have ridden before, why don't you start with something simple? I'll need one of you to be the rodeo clown and one of you to work the eight-second blower for me.'

'No worries. I'll be the rodeo clown!' Patrick said, grinning.

'And that leaves me to play with my blower – oops, I mean do the blower!' Liam joked.

Sarah rolled her eyes and grinned. 'You need to get your mind out of the gutter, Liam!'

Matt slapped his hand on his leg. 'Great! It's a done deal. We'll do it tomorrow arvo.' He stood up. 'You wanna come and have a look at the bulls when you're finished, Greg?'

'My word I do, mate. Maybe tomorrow we can buck out the ones I like so I can see how they perform in the arena.'

'No worries. Come find me at the homestead when you're ready. The missus is cooking me lunch.'

Stumpy raised his eyebrows. 'Gee whiz, Matt. That's a change. Good to hear, buddy.'

'Tell me about it!' Matt called back over his shoulder.

Sarah felt deflated. She quickly stood from the table, not wanting the others to notice her sudden change of mood, and picked up a few plates to take into the kitchen.

Lily followed suit and followed Sarah. 'You okay?'

Sarah rinsed the plates and cutlery off under the tap, shooting Lily a wry glance from under her brows. 'Boy, Lily. I can't hide anything from you, mate, can I? I'm okay. I just, I … um … I've really got to know Matt well in the last couple of months out here, and I really like him – a lot. More than as a mate, if you get my drift.'

Lily put her hand on Sarah's shoulder. 'Oh, mate. Can anyone blame you? He's a nice bloke and gorgeous to boot. Try not to let it get you down, though. Life always has a way of working out for the best.'

'I know, Lily. It's just … I wish things could be different.' Sarah smiled weakly.

'Dan and I will take your mind off it! Let's have some fun!' Lily grabbed Sarah by the hands and started spinning her around in the kitchen. Sarah giggled. Lily always knew how to make her feel better.

*

By midnight, Lily and Sarah were still raring to go, while the men were heading off to bed. Daniel gave both girls a kiss and joined the men in the general exodus, leaving the girls to spend a bit of time together. Sarah and Lily had danced like a pair of drunken teenagers in the lounge room to a country music greatest hits CD until they couldn't stand any longer, falling in a laughing, gibbering heap on the floor, tears rolling down their faces. 'I haven't had this much fun in ages,' Sarah slurred between hiccups, red wine staining her lips bright red, her wild blonde hair all over her face.

Lily wiped the tears from her face, trying to catch her breath. 'Me neither! When are you gonna come home, buddy? I miss this.'

'I'll be home for Christmas, Lil. And then I'll figure out whether I want to come back here for another season or not.'

Lily clapped her hands with glee. 'Yay! Home for Christmas! And then I'll convince you to stay.'

'We'll see, Lil. Hey, I'm so pleased for you and Dan. You both seem so happy!'

Lily smiled warmly. 'We're head over heels for each other. I never thought I could feel so in love, but I do. We're even talking about moving in together.'

'Oh my goodness, that's great, Lil!' Sarah felt tears prick her eyes and she tried to quickly wipe them away.

'Oh mate, what's wrong?' Lily wrapped her arm around Sarah's shoulder.

Sarah sniffled. 'It's just I wish I could be with the man I'm head over heels in love with, but that will probably never happen. Oh, what am I going to do, Lil? It's driving me insane not being able to touch him.'

'I don't know what to tell you. You have to let things take their course and believe in your heart that if you are meant to be together, fate will somehow find a way.'

'Yeah, you're probably right. It's just so damn hard seeing him with Brooke. She doesn't deserve him!'

Sarah flopped back on the rug, slightly dazed. She was beginning to feel a little sick from all the booze and the room had begun to spin. 'I think I better go to bed. I'm not feeling too good.'

Lily lay down beside Sarah. 'Me neither. Can't handle my red wine like I used to. Shall we carry each other to bed? I don't think I'll be able to walk on my own.'

The two girls helped each other up off the floor, cackling like a pair of chooks as they staggered around. It took three attempts before they made it up, leaning on each other for support. They wobbled their way down the hall, looking like a pair of penguins, sniggering quietly at the snores coming from the men's rooms.

'This is my stop, Sarah,' Lily announced as she fell against the guest bedroom door.

'Night, my bestest friend!' Sarah whispered, before sliding her way unsteadily down the hallway wall to her bedroom. She stumbled into the dark room and fell flat on her face on the bed, asleep before her head had even hit the pillow.

*

Jimmy fidgeted tensely while Greg, Slim and Matt loaded the first bull into the chutes for the day. It was a whopping one tonne beast, looking very unhappy to have been pulled from his paddock.

'God, Jimmy. Anyone would think you've got ants in your pants!' Daniel said as he buckled up his chaps.

'Strewth, Daniel, I can't help it! Have you seen the size of this bugger?' The whites of Jimmy's eyes were growing larger by the second.

Daniel gave him a slap on the back. 'You'll be right, Jimmy. Patrick's out there doing clown duties and I'm sure he'll look after you when you hit the dirt.'

Jimmy nodded, clearly unconvinced. He looked over at the small huddle of onlookers. Lily and Sarah waved to him eagerly from their foldout chairs, and he gave them a quick wave back, lifting his hat for good measure.

'This is exciting, isn't it, girls?' Judy chortled as she set up a foldout table next to them, stacking it high with baked goodies. She gave Steve a quick, playful slap on the wrist as he nicked a lamington.

Georgia laughed. 'Pass us one while you're at it, please, Dad!'

Steve looked apprehensively at Judy.

'Oh go for it, you silly old duffer. The food's here for eating, not for looking at!' Judy said, hand on her hip.

Steve grinned lovingly at his wife and wrapped an arm around her waist.

'Will you two get a room?' Liam called cheekily from his front-row foldout chair.

'I should be so lucky,' Steve replied mischievously.

'*Dad!* Going visual! I really don't want to picture it!' Georgia pulled a face.

Sarah watched Brooke as she headed in their direction from the homestead, clutching a bright pink folding chair.

'Here comes the missus,' Lily whispered.

'I spotted her a mile away. That chair is hurting my eyes it's that bloody bright!' Sarah pretended to shield her eyes.

Brooke parked her chair in between Chris and Liam, saying a fleeting hello to Sarah and Lily over her shoulder.

'Hey, Brooke. There's room here if you like,' Sarah said, moving her chair over so Brooke could sit next to her. Being friends with Brooke was not exactly her idea of fun, but she told herself to get over it. After all, Brooke had made an effort, and so should she.

Brooke waved her red fingernails in the air like she was swatting at flies. 'Nah. I'm right here, but thanks anyway.'

Sarah was taken aback but recovered quickly and smiled broadly. 'No worries. You've got front row there with Liam and Chris anyway.'

'Do we smell or something?' Lily hissed at Sarah.

Sarah smothered her grin by shoving a bite of lamington in her mouth. 'Ssh, Lily.'

Her attention was drawn to the rodeo, where Patrick had walked out comically and was now standing in the centre of the ring, wearing a pair of bright shorts and an even brighter shirt. He also had on an odd pair of footy socks pulled right up to his knees. The girls had helped him paint his face with make-up this morning in an attempt to make him look more like a clown. He had somehow managed to get half of the lipstick up the left side of his face, making him look even more ridiculous. He smiled mischievously at the audience, lifting his akubra and revealing a bright orange wig.

'The rodeo is about to begin!' He ran to position, ready for the incoming bucking bull.

Slim flung open the gate and the first bull came bounding out, snorting and bucking like a demon. Jimmy was clamped on its back, clinging to the rope, his arm flinging about like it was broken. Liam counted down the eight seconds for the spectators from the front row. Jimmy was bucked off at five seconds, landing on the ground heavily, dust surrounding him for a few seconds. Patrick immediately ran in from the side and diverted the bull's attention as Jimmy scrambled to safety. Sarah cheered his effort along with everyone else, genuinely impressed.

She pulled her akubra off and swatted at the flies, cooling her face at the same time. Her singlet was stuck to her back and she wriggled in her seat, trying to free it from her skin. With Lily's gentle nudging, she had opted to wear denim shorts, which were a refreshing change from her normal attire of jeans. She felt good in them, too, and she wondered whether she'd imagined the double-take Matt had given her when he saw her earlier.

Patrick ran to the rails and grabbed a water bottle from Liam, taking a quick guzzle. 'Daniel's up next, ladies.'

Lily clapped and wolf whistled. 'Go you good thang!'

The gate burst open and Daniel came out, hanging on for dear life as the bull tried its hardest to buck him off. Daniel's body swayed with every shuddering kick, like a feather in the breeze; his perfect form would've put most bull riders to shame. Liam honked the blower at the eight-second mark and Daniel jumped from the bull, landing firmly on his feet before making a break towards the rails. Patrick danced and weaved about, directing the bull towards the ring exit, trying to avoid its massive horns. Once safe, Daniel dismounted the railing and threw his hat up in the air, bowing to the lively audience.

Sarah and Lily squealed madly, cheering him for his brilliant ride. Brooke shot a sideways glance at them, and Sarah saw a tight, fake smile on her face before she turned back and whispered something to Chris. What was her problem? Sarah had to bite her lip – it wouldn't pay to say anything she might later regret.

Matt walked out in the ring next, asking Liam to go behind the chutes and help Greg. Sarah shot a look at Lily and beamed like a lovesick teenager. Lily leant over and whispered in her ear, 'This is only going to make you fall for him more, Sarah. A sexy man riding a grinding, gyrating beast – what woman could resist!'

Sarah's gaze was transfixed on the ring, waiting for Matt to appear. She could just see the top of his head behind the chutes, and she saw him nod, high up on the bull's back, letting Slim know he was ready to go. Slim swung the gate open and the bull came out, bucking like there was no tomorrow, creating clouds of hovering dust above the ring. Matt was moving his body in perfect rhythm with the bull, one hand on the rope, the other up in the air to balance himself, anticipating the bucking animal's next move with precision. Sarah couldn't take her eyes off him – it was man versus beast in the most dangerous sport around, and Matt made it look easy. The eight seconds ticked by brutally as Sarah held her breath, watching on in awe as the bull spun in circles, its aggression palpable. Liam yelled from the chutes that Matt had reached the eight seconds and the crowd stood, clapping and cheering, but Matt stayed glued to the bull, seemingly determined to outdo the eight-second glory. Sarah began counting under her breath, adding the extra seconds to his already dazzling ride.

At ten seconds Matt released the rope from his hand and jumped from the bull, running directly for Sarah as he dodged the charges the bull was aiming at him, scarcely missing a bull's horn fair up the date. With her heart in her mouth, Sarah looked over at Brooke. She wasn't even watching. Instead she was deep in conversation with Chris. Sarah's brow furrowed as she pulled her gaze back to Matt, who was now throwing himself over the rail as the bull head butted the fence directly in front of Sarah and Lily. The girls jumped back with fright, almost knocking over their chairs. Even though there was no way the bull could get to them it was still very confronting to have it snorting and kicking only a metre away.

'Good ride, Matt!' Sarah gasped.

Matt found his feet and stood up. 'Thanks, mate. I just wanted to see how long I could last on the bugger. He's a corker, isn't he?'

Lily clapped her hands. 'You boys know how to entertain a crowd.'

Matt gave a little mock bow. 'That's what I aim to do. Please you guys.'

Judy gave Matt a quick slap on the thigh. 'Don't scare me like that again, my boy! Eight seconds is plenty long enough for me to hold my breath!'

They watched as Patrick, Liam and Slim jumped around like farts in a bottle, trying to get the irate bull out of the arena. Georgia laughed as Slim and Liam ran full pelt for the exit then threw themselves over the rail as the bull passed through the exit gate, Patrick slamming it shut behind it then collapsing on the ground to catch his breath.

Matt turned to Brooke, who hadn't said a word yet. Sarah knew she'd missed most of Matt's performance anyway.

'What did you think of the ride?'

Brooke looked a little lost for words, then clapped her hands softly. 'Brilliant, Matt! Just brilliant!'

Matt gave her an angry look and marched off to the back of the chutes.

Judy hadn't only baked, she'd cooked lunch as well. Soon everyone's plates were groaning with food as they sat in the shade beside the ring, now quiet and still.

'What time are you guys heading off in the morning?' Sarah asked sadly as she crunched on a piece of pork crackling.

'I reckon we'll hit the road around six in the morning. Matt's meeting me down the yards at five so we can load up the bulls I've bought, and then we'll be on our way,' Greg replied.

'I can't believe how fast the weekend has gone!' Lily sighed, shoving a spoonful of peas in her mouth.

'Time flies when you're having fun!' Liam said wryly.

'Tell me about it. It feels like you guys only just got here, and now you have to go again,' Sarah protested.

'Hey, where's Chris?' Stumpy asked, chomping on a mouthful of roast potato.

'He reckons he's not hungry. I don't get that bloke. Sometimes he's nice as pie and other times he doesn't wanna know you,' Patrick said.

'Well, he's missing out on a good feed!' Jimmy dipped his bread in the thick gravy.

Three hours later everyone had moved back to the cottage and the stereo was pumping with Brooks and Dunn. Daniel had the tomato sauce bottle and was using it as a microphone, and the girls leant in and sang along with him. Slim, Jimmy and Greg were doing the best rendition of the chicken dance Sarah had ever seen, and every time she looked at them, she cracked up laughing. True to form, Stumpy was dancing like Peter Garrett on the sidelines. Patrick was swinging Georgia around the patio, bumping into Duke, who was barking and dancing along with them. Sarah had noticed something between those two, but wondered if they'd ever do anything about it.

Suddenly Sarah heard a crash behind her, and found Lily lying on the floor in fits of laughter with a potplant on top of her. Daniel lay next to her with his shorts around his ankles, chuckling like crazy. Liam stood behind them, beaming like a naughty child. 'I dakked him!'

Sarah buckled over in laughter just as Matt walked out onto the patio with a beer in hand.

'God, look at you lot. Looks like I've missed out on a ripsnorter of a party.'

Sarah tried unsuccessfully to regain her composure before giving up and falling to the floor, laughing. 'Where've you been? We missed you. I missed you.' She was shocked to hear the words come out of her mouth.

Matt smiled down at her. 'Here, give me your hand, princess, and I'll help you up.'

Sarah gazed back at him, warmed by his answer, and reached out her hand. He took it, never taking his eyes off her face, and helped her up.

Once on her feet she looked around for Brooke. 'Where's your missus?'

Matt shook his head. 'Don't ask. She and I had a massive argument and she's stormed off somewhere. I'm really over it all at the moment.'

'I thought you guys were doing better lately.'

'Yeah, well, me too, Sarah. But enough about my dramas. Do you wanna dance?' He didn't wait for a reply. Before Sarah knew it, he'd grabbed her hand and was pulling her out to the middle of the patio. They pushed in between the others and Matt slipped his arm around her waist. Most of the time he kept her at arm's length, but every so often he'd bring her close, and electricity would shoot through her feet as his body brushed against hers. They laughed and twirled, bootscooted and waltzed their way through song after song, with Lily and Daniel joining them.

By one a.m. only Sarah and Matt were left standing. Everybody else had made their way to bed, drunk as skunks and in need of some shut-eye.

'I better be off, Sarah,' Matt said, holding her hand. 'Thanks for a fun night, mate. I've had a blast dancing with you.'

Sarah couldn't get a word out. She was completely focused on the sensation of Matt's hand in her hand.

'Hey, do you wanna go drown some worms tomorrow?' Matt asked.

Sarah turned her head to the side. 'Huh?'

'Go fishing, Sarah; you know, like dangle a line. Sorry, sometimes my slang can confuse people.' Matt laughed.

'Oh! I'd love to. 'Bout time, too. I asked you about that months ago!'

'Come meet me at the homestead around eight if you like.' Matt leant in and for one heart-stopping moment, Sarah thought he was going to kiss her on the lips. But instead he brushed his lips against her cheek briefly, gave her a quick smile and was gone.

Sarah's cheek felt on fire. She gently placed her hand on it and grinned.

CHAPTER

21

Dawn drew near as the sun peeked over the horizon. Sarah grabbed Daniel and Lily and gave them both a massive hug. Greg tooted his horn outside. 'I'm gonna miss you!'

Lily wiped her tear-streaked face. 'I'll miss you too, babe. See you back home soon, hey?'

Sarah nodded. 'You sure will, mate.'

Lily leant in and whispered in Sarah's ear. 'And remember what I said about Matt: if it's meant to be it *will* happen.'

'I hope it does, Lil,' Sarah whispered back.

Daniel picked Sarah up off the ground and gave her a huge squeeze. 'Love ya, sis. Take care.'

'Love you too, bro!'

She waved them off, tears dripping down her face and spotting her pyjamas. She watched them drive away until the taillights had vanished into the vastness of the outback.

*

Sarah, Matt and Duke piled into the LandCruiser as Judy waved from the front verandah of the homestead. Matt was sitting next to Sarah, and as she turned a corner his leg pressed against Sarah's thigh. His touch instantly sent waves of heat through her body. It was like she was leaning on a radiator, and it was going to burn a hole right through her jeans. She quickly moved her leg, scared he would somehow sense her feelings…

Matt took his akubra off and put it on the dash. 'So, how'd ya feel this morning? I've got a wee bit of a hangover, myself.'

Sarah kept her eyes on the dirt track ahead of them. The memory of dancing with him and his goodnight kiss was still overwhelming, and she knew it would show in her face. 'I've not pulled up too bad. Got a bit of a headache, but nothing a few litres of water won't fix. How are things between you and Brooke this morning?'

'She slept in the spare room last night and she's still there, so probably not that great by the looks of things,' Matt replied, staring out the window.

'It'll all work out. Don't worry, Matt.' Sarah turned to look at him but he was still gazing out the window. 'Now, where in the hell am I going? I need your directions before we end up in Alice Springs!'

'Sorry, mate. I forgot you don't know your way around as well as I do.' Matt turned back to Sarah. His voice this morning was even huskier, like warm whisky on a cold winter's evening.

Sarah followed Matt's directions, glad she was in her trusty Cruiser given the state of the dirt track they were taking. More than once, her head hit the roof as the tyres dropped into huge crevices on the track. It really did feel like an outback adventure. Duke had his head hanging out the passenger-side window with his tongue flapping around in the breeze, panting happily.

Even though she'd been on Rosalee for months, Sarah was still amazed at how far they had to drive. The station was simply massive, and dotted with cattle grids that they rumbled over on their way to the fishing spot. For some strange reason the grids made Duke bark like a madman, and each time they crossed one Matt and Sarah cracked up laughing at Duke's frantic barking.

By the time Sarah finally saw the glistening water of the northern dam ahead, she'd driven through four gates and across countless grids, but the long trip was worth it. The dam was like a huge diamond encrusted in a sea of red earth. There were trees growing around every inch of the water's edge as though clustering around a campfire, and the water was clean and cool.

She parked the LandCruiser up beneath a huge old jacaranda tree that was in full purple-flowering glory. It looked stunning against the red dirt terrain. Duke was so excited to have arrived he jumped out the window and was in the water before Sarah even had time to turn the motor off. She yelled after him, 'You're gonna scare all the fish off, Duke, you maniac! Get your bum back here now!'

Duke obeyed his master and came running back, wet and ready to shake all the water off him. Matt and Sarah had just stepped out of the truck, and took cover behind their arms as Duke shook enthusiastically and wet them both. Pleased with himself, he then marched underneath the truck for a morning nap. 'Geez, you have a hard life, Duke!' Sarah said, laughing and rolling her eyes.

She'd packed all the necessary equipment for a successful catch. One of the tricks she had used since she was a young girl was to pack an old sock full of dry dog food and place it inside the red claw pot. It worked a treat. She'd checked three times to make sure she'd packed her lucky fishing line, which had never failed her in her fishing trips with her family. She was hoping she'd catch enough to give the boys a feed of seafood tonight.

Matt started grabbing all the fishing gear out of the back of the LandCruiser. 'What's with the socks?' he asked, confusion written across his face.

Sarah smiled proudly. 'That's my secret recipe for catching a shitload of red claw. You just wait.'

Matt raised his eyebrows provocatively. 'We'll soon see, mighty fisherlady!'

'Yes, you will! Chuck my tackle box over and I'll set our rods up.'

Matt slid the box over. 'Tell you what, Sarah Clarke. You and I could become good fishing buddies. I've never seen a sheila come so prepared! I'm well impressed.'

The two set off towards the bank of the dam. Matt seemed to know exactly where the best spot was, and Sarah followed, taking in the nice curves of his butt in his Wrangler jeans. She couldn't help herself.

'So do you have a name for this dam?' Sarah asked as they dropped the pots in and sat down.

'It's called Ned Kelly dam – my grandfather was a fan of Ned Kelly.'

'I like that; it's a very Aussie name.' Sarah paused and looked around, taking in the peaceful surroundings. 'Ah, this is exactly what I needed. I love fishing. It's the most fun you can have with your pants on.' Sarah felt a blush rise on her neck at her words, but Matt didn't appear to notice.

'Yeah, I agree. I wouldn't be dead for quids right now,' he answered.

'I can't believe I've been at Rosalee for nearly four months now. Time has flown by.'

'Crazy, hey? Life can pass you by if you aren't careful. I reckon you just have to live life to the fullest. Do what it is that makes you happy because you only get one chance at it. Working and living on the land is what makes me happy, Sarah. I could never see myself doing anything else. It makes me the man I am, and I love the peace and serenity of it all.'

Sarah smiled in response, a deep, genuine smile that brought out her sparkling green eyes. At that moment, with her curly blonde hair dancing in the breeze and that smile on her face, she'd never looked more beautiful.

As Sarah put the bait on her rod, Matt thought about how Brooke would squirm at the idea of doing such a thing. And unlike Brooke, Sarah was a hard worker, and obviously had been all her life – her body was fit and athletic. She was always willing to help, no matter how dirty or labour-intensive the job, and she did it with a smile. But what was the point in thinking like this? he wondered. He was with Brooke, and he wasn't a cheater, no matter what he felt for

Sarah. But what was happening with Brooke, anyhow? He couldn't shake the niggling feeling that there was something going on that he didn't know about.

Sarah kept an eye on the red claw pots, and as promised, she pulled out at least six red claw every time she brought the pots up from their muddy hollow below. By the end of the morning they had nearly forty red claw. On top of that, Sarah had caught two barramundi big enough to feed the lot for dinner tonight. Matt had only caught one small barra that he had decided to throw back for next time.

Once they were satisfied with their catch for the day they packed up and headed for the truck. This time Duke sat next to Sarah, and Matt got in the passenger side. Sarah turned the key in the ignition but nothing happened. There was not even a spark of life coming from beneath the bonnet.

'Shit, Matt. The bloody truck won't start.'

'Don't stress. I'll hop out and have a Captain Cook at it. You got any tools?' Matt asked as he jumped out of the truck and lifted the bonnet.

'Yeah, there's a toolbox behind my seat.'

'Excellent. I'll have us up and running in no time. Piece of piss!' Matt called from under the bonnet.

*

Three hours later Sarah had resigned herself to sitting in the shade of the trees with Duke whilst Matt poked and prodded his way through the motor, still trying to figure out what was wrong. She had tried to help but felt like she was just getting in the way.

Matt looked up for a moment and Sarah burst out laughing. His face was covered in black grease, the only white showing the whites of his eyes. She tried to stop laughing but every time she'd look up, the sight would set her off again. His comical facial expression made it even more hilarious. 'What's so funny?' he asked, throwing his hands up in the air.

Sarah pulled herself together enough to speak. 'I think you should have a look in the side mirror, Matt, and then you might get what I'm laughing at.'

Matt peered in the mirror and immediately cracked up. Laughing, he ran towards Sarah with his hands outstretched, ready to cover her in black grease. Sarah jumped up screaming and ran towards the safety of the water. A quick glance over her shoulder told her Matt was almost on her, and she jumped in jeans and all in her haste to get away from the incoming grease attack. Matt ploughed in straight after her, boots and all, and lunged for her in the water. She ducked, and they splashed around like a pair of schoolkids, Sarah trying to avoid Matt's blackened hands. Finally, out of breath, they both fell back into the water.

'Truce!' Sarah said, before closing her eyes and letting herself float on the cool water. It was nice to enjoy the silence and refreshing feel of the water.

Matt floated near her, the temptation to touch her incredibly strong. He sat up abruptly, giving his wet hair a quick ruffle with his hand. 'I better go and get this truck going, mate.'

Sarah waved him off, deciding she was enjoying the water too much to get out just yet. It was the hottest part of the day, with the sun beating down in full force, and the water was a much better place to be than back on land. She watched Matt dry off in the sun, her eyes following him back to the truck, where he started to work on the motor again. She sighed inwardly. If only things were different.

By the time she dragged herself out of the dam her skin was looking a bit prune-like. A few minutes standing in the sun soon fixed that, though. 'How's it going?' she called to Matt.

'I think I've finally found the problem. It looks like a few of the pipes going to the fuel pump are cracked. I can do a bit of a bodge job now to get us home, but we'll have to order some new ones to be flown in on the mail plane with Stan next week. Give me ten minutes and I reckon we'll be on our way. Brooke's going to be right pissed off with me. It's nearly three o'clock, and Dad and I are going shooting tonight, so I won't have spent much time with her at all today. I'm already in the shit as it is.'

'I'm so sorry the truck broke down, Matt. Brooke will understand, though – it wasn't your fault.'

'Oh, don't be sorry, mate. I've really enjoyed fishing with you. We'll have to do it again when we get the chance. I'll even challenge you to a fishing comp to see who can catch the biggest barra!'

'Deal!'

Sarah watched over his shoulder while Matt connected the battery leads back up. She stepped forward to help him close the bonnet, tripping over a tree branch as she did so. He reached out and caught her, but she was already off balance and pulled him down with her, both of them falling to the ground in a heap. Sarah giggled and looked up at Matt, her blonde curls framing her face as she lay in his arms on the dusty ground. He smiled at her, and their eyes locked together.

And then something happened that Sarah had only dreamt of: Matt leant over gently and touched his lips to hers. The passion of the moment almost overcame her as she felt the heat of his body, and she ached for him. Sarah closed her eyes and felt her body come alive; she parted her lips and explored his warm mouth with her tongue. He responded, kissing her more firmly as he pressed himself against her. Tingles ran down her spine, the exhilaration of the moment taking her breath away. And then just as quickly as it had started, it was over.

Matt pulled back. 'I'm sorry, Sarah. I shouldn't have done that.'

Sarah tried to catch her breath, the electricity still jolting through her body. 'No, Matt, I —'

'No, Sarah. It was wrong of me. I'm with Brooke. Cheating goes against everything I believe in.' And with that Matt gently shifted his body away from Sarah and stood up, leaving Sarah lying on the ground.

She sat up quickly and tried to gather her emotions, feeling vaguely foolish. A few minutes ago she was living a dream, and now she was filled with panic at the thought of having ruined any chance of being with him. Matt's sudden change of mood made it clear that he believed what he'd said. What had just happened between them was a massive mistake. She took a deep breath and stood up, taking her time to walk over to the driver's side door. Matt was already sitting inside, staring out the window, with Duke planted firmly in the middle. Sarah started the LandCruiser and they made the trek back to the homestead without a word uttered between them.

The minute Sarah pulled up at the homestead, she knew things were bad. Brooke was tearing towards the truck like an incoming cyclone, anger contorting her face. Matt opened the passenger door and stepped out. Sarah went to speak but Matt walked away from the LandCruiser with a simple wave of his hand. The silence between them was deafening. Sarah watched as Matt headed towards Brooke and the storm that was about to shower down on him. Sarah caught Brooke's eye for a split second before she drove off, and if looks could kill she would have been dead.

CHAPTER
22

Matt concentrated on looking straight ahead out the windscreen of his truck, trying his best to push the confusion from his head. What a bloody afternoon. It had started when Sarah dropped him off at the homestead and Brooke had been storming towards him like a lunatic. He had felt the darkness of Brooke's energy surround him like thick smoke when she got close enough to scream in his face. He was embarrassed that Sarah saw it all unfolding as she drove away.

'Where the hell have you been, Matt? Your mum said you went fishing early this morning and were supposed to be back before lunch. I've been worried sick! And to make matters worse you pull up with a bloody worker, who as far as I'm concerned is a cheap floozy out to win you over! How do you think this looks to me?'

She'd burst into noisy tears, but instead of feeling compassion Matt had been filled with anger. He couldn't believe Brooke would call Sarah a floozy. He hadn't trusted himself to say anything, so ignored Brooke and kept walking in the direction of the granny flat. Brooke ran after him ranting and raving about how selfish and uncaring he was, telling him he only thought about himself. She went for dig after dig in a bid to get him to react.

'If I know you've been out with that slut again I'll pack my things and leave you, Matt!'

That had been the final straw. Matt couldn't take Brooke speaking about Sarah that way any longer. He'd turned to face Brooke and lashed out.

'You don't even know her, Brooke, so don't talk about her like that. She's had a couple of really hard knocks since she's been out here, and I thought I'd show her a place she could go and fish when she wanted some time out. The LandCruiser broke down, and I've just spent the last few hours trying to fix it. I'm sick of you always assuming the worst, and telling me what I can and can't do all the time. I'll spend my time with who I choose, and if you don't like it, then too bloody bad, go ahead Brooke, leave! It'll be your loss anyway.' Matt threw his hands around in the air in frustration. 'Talking to you is like pissing in the wind. I've got to get ready – I have to help Dad shoot pigs tonight.'

Brooke's face had dropped and Matt noticed her shaking, whether with rage or shock he didn't know. Did she imagine he'd drop to his knees and beg her forgiveness?

'Oh, that's just great,' Brooke said, finding her venom. 'So you can go around with other girls and I'll just have to deal with it, hey? And now you're going shooting, so I'll have to sit here alone tonight again. I thought I came before everybody else, but obviously I'm the last priority around here!'

She'd brushed angrily past Matt and into the house. Matt was happy to see her go. More than happy – he suddenly realised he had to get away from her. He followed her into the house and headed straight to the bedroom, where he pulled his overnight bag from the wardrobe and started stuffing clothes in it. His dad would just have to understand him skipping shooting tonight – he wasn't in the mood.

Brooke came flying in and stared at him. 'What do you think you're doing?'

'I'm going to Mt Isa for a few nights. I need some time to think,' Matt replied without looking at her.

Brooke had tried to grab the bag out of his hands, but Matt pushed her roughly off. 'Just leave me be before I say things I'll regret!'

She finally backed off, then marched out of the room and into the spare bedroom, slamming the door behind her. Matt had zipped up his bag and headed over to tell his parents that he was going away for a few days. And then he'd hit the road.

He found himself reflecting on the first couple of years with Brooke, when everything was great. She'd been easygoing, fun, and happy to help out on the station. Then she made some new friends at the beauty course, started to change the way she dressed, and worried about her appearance a lot more. Over the past year he had watched her slowly change into a person he felt he didn't know any more. The only things she seemed to give a shit about now were her make-up and her hair.

He'd hoped that asking her to move out on the station might bring back the girl he'd fallen in love with, but she was only getting worse. She'd become distant and selfish, and unless things went exactly the way she wanted she would get moody and not talk to him for days. She'd also lost interest in coming with him to Mt Isa, despite having friends there. She preferred to stay on the station while Matt drove the cattle back and forth. From time to time he'd wondered what she got up to while he was away, and suspicions were stirring in his mind. Something just wasn't feeling right, and that was *before* he'd kissed Sarah. But there was too much turmoil going around in his mind and his heart right now to deal with it all.

He rolled the images of kissing Sarah over in his mind, savouring them illicitly, before swearing at himself. He had to stop thinking like this. He'd ruined any chance he'd ever had of being with Sarah. No woman, especially not her, would want to be with a man who had proved himself capable of cheating. He knew he had to tell Brooke about what had happened – it would be wrong not to – but with the savage welcome home he'd received he hadn't been able to. It could wait a couple of days.

*

Sarah had tears pouring down her face when she pulled up outside the cottage. She still found Matt's reaction to the kiss hard to comprehend. She was terrified that she'd not only ruined any chance she'd ever had of being with him, but had ruined their friendship. The connection she felt with Matt was stronger than any she'd ever felt with a man before, and she couldn't ignore it. She knew he felt the same – it was there in the passion of his kiss. But why had he pulled away so abruptly? And ignored her so coldly, like he was angry with her? She wondered what was going to happen now. It would be impossible for them to be around each other after what had just taken place.

Sarah wiped her tears away and tried to compose herself. She took a deep breath, mentally packing away all her emotions. The men weren't home yet but she had to get dinner happening, and she didn't want the men to notice she'd been crying. She would have plenty of time to mull over her thoughts when she went to bed tonight. 'Come on, Duke. Let's go and get this food on the barbecue, buddy. I want to have it all ready for the men when they walk in the door.'

The only word Duke really took note of coming out of his master's mouth was *food*, and that was enough for him. Together he and Sarah headed to the house with the red claw and fish, Duke turning circles in his excitement. An hour later Patrick stuck his head into the kitchen, the first through the door. His face lit up like a Christmas tree as he smelt the amazing aroma coming from Sarah's pots and pans.

'It smells like we have a feast of seafood for dinner!'

'You little ripper!' Slim and Stumpy said in unison, sticking their heads in behind him.

Sarah put on the happiest voice she could muster. 'Hey, you lot, there's a surprise for dinner tonight. I caught us some barra and red claw today at the dam, and I've done a few bits and bobs to go with it. You reckon you can handle that?'

'She's weaving her way to my heart through my stomach!' Liam said, his eyes widening in anticipation.

'I'm allergic to seafood,' Chris said, the last to come in, and the only downcast face amongst the sea of happy ones.

'Oh well, beans on toast for you then,' Patrick quickly joked.

Sarah was genuinely upset. The thought that one of the men might be allergic to seafood had not even crossed her mind. 'Oh, no. Sorry, Chris. I can make you something else. What would you like, mate?'

'Forget it,' Chris snapped. 'I'll make myself something later.'

'Hey, man. Lighten up,' Stumpy said, with a warning tone in his voice.

Chris muttered something under his breath and walked out of the kitchen.

'Looks like I royally stuffed up. Oh well. I *did* offer to make him something else.' Sarah lifted her hands up in the air in defeat.

'Don't worry about him. He's been complaining all bloody day. Maybe he should try getting more sleep rather than gallivanting around all night doing whatever it is he gets up to. He's been as useful as a chocolate teapot today,' said Patrick. 'We're all chuffed that you've done this for us, Sarah. You're a champ!' He grabbed Sarah in a warm hug.

'I'll leave a can of beans out for him with some bread, so he can't say I didn't feed him tonight,' said Sarah, still not sure what to make of Chris's reaction. 'Now do you blokes want to have a shower before dinner? You all smell a little fresh.' Sarah playfully swiped the air and screwed up her nose.

'You're the boss of the kitchen, mate, and if you want us all showered and smelling like roses before we eat, then that's what you'll get. Your wish is our command!' Stumpy smiled.

'I bags the first shower!' Liam ran to grab his towel.

Sarah felt her spirits lifting. The guys always put her in a good mood with their cheery banter, and she was glad she'd gone out of her way to treat them. They'd been so wonderful to her, and she wanted to repay them for their kindness. From the looks on their faces as they gazed at the food, she was repaying them plenty.

They showered in record time and were soon seated at the table ready to enjoy the buffet of food. Sarah had made a huge garden salad, a potato salad, baked fish stuffed with garlic and lemon, red claw done in garlic butter, boiled red claw, homemade seafood sauce to dip it all into and some garlic bread, and there were plenty of beers to wash it all down with. The group sat back like beached whales after it was all finished, but there was still no sign of Chris.

*

Matt sat at the bar, his head hung low from the weight he was carrying in his heart. He was on his seventh whisky on the rocks and he knew he would have to hit the sack soon, before he fell off his bar stool. He couldn't stop thinking about Sarah. The kiss at the dam had sent feelings flooding through him that were incredibly powerful. The look in her eyes when he had left her lying on the ground cut him deep, but he hadn't known what else to do. Even though it was just a kiss, he'd known he wanted it to be more, and given half a chance he would've let himself go. But he had to end it with Brooke – the fact that he was deeply unhappy in his relationship was no excuse for what he'd done. He knew it was going to break Brooke's heart, but he had to tell her about the kiss. He sculled the last of his whisky, crunching the remnants of the ice between his teeth as he put the glass down. The alcohol felt like thick liquid oozing through his body and he desperately needed to lie down.

Matt tossed and turned under the sheets in the hotel room, the turmoil in his heart making him unable to sleep. Finally he fell into a restless sleep, and Sarah appeared before him. She was standing in front of him, kissing him gently down the throat, whispering in his ear that she loved him. He threw her back in his arms and kissed her hard on the lips, his desire for her ripping at his core, making him want to taste her all over. She tore at his shirt, the buttons falling by the wayside as she exposed his broad chest. He slowly unzipped her jeans and slid them down her slim, tanned legs, kissing her as he went, all the way down to her toes. He hooked her underpants under his fingers and slid them down slowly, but before he could explore she reached for his face and pulled him gently back up to her. She caressed his lips with her mouth, running her tongue over his. He could taste her sweetness. He slowly unbuttoned her shirt and when he reached her flat belly he licked it, running his tongue around her belly button. Slipping her lace bra off, he cupped her full breasts in his hands and lowered his mouth to them, letting his warm breath wash over her nipples, teasing her, licking and sucking them. She moaned in pleasure. He picked her up and placed her on the bed, barely able to contain his desire. She looked deeply into his eyes and he knew she wanted to feel him inside her. He pulled down his jeans and stood in front of her, his longing for her obvious. She sat up and licked down his shaft and over the tip of his erect penis, causing him to groan in delight. He felt his legs go weak. He needed her, wanted her and craved her. He pushed her gently back on the bed and slowly entered her, sighing in pleasure. His body tingled and pulsed from head to toe as he felt her warmth envelop him.

And then with no warning, Matt woke up. He was lying in a narrow hotel bed, covered in sweat. Shaking the sensations from his body, the dream was still fresh in his mind as he headed outside to the cool, fresh air.

CHAPTER
23

'I'm knackered. I'm gonna hit the sack early,' Stumpy said, standing to help clear away some of the dishes while licking the last of the red claw from his lips.

'Me too. I can't move after that feed. I'm as full as a fat man's undies,' Slim added.

'Yeah, I reckon I'll be asleep before my head even hits the pillow,' Jimmy said, yawning. 'I have a big few days ahead of me. Can't say I won't miss you all, but I'll see you next year. Judy and Steve have asked me to come back next season and I told them I'd love to.'

'That's great news, Jimmy. But what do you mean, a big few days?' Sarah mumbled, feeling the exhaustion of the day creeping up on her.

'I'm heading back to Mareeba the day after tomorrow,' Jimmy said. 'Georgia's offered to drop me at the bus station in Mt Isa.'

'Shit, that soon, Jimmy? I thought you weren't leaving till next week!' Sarah said, suddenly awake.

'I was gonna leave next week, but we finished up the last of the mustering today, so I'm not really needed any more. It's my dad's birthday next week and I'd like to be home for it if I can.'

Sarah's mind raced with sudden possibilities. A yawn came from nowhere and a second wave of tiredness washed over her.

'Liam and I'll clean up tonight, Sarah. After that effort I think you deserve a break from the washing up.'

'Thanks, Patrick. I'll help you carry everything in,' Sarah said gratefully, standing up to gather everybody's plates.

The guys helped her, grabbing a handful of dirty plates and bowls each to carry into the kitchen.

'Are you sure you two don't mind?' Sarah asked.

'Of course we don't, mate! Now you tootle off to bed. You look knackered,' Liam replied.

*

By four in the morning Sarah had had enough of trying to sleep. She kicked off her sheet in a huff and wandered out to the kitchen to make herself a cuppa. She went out to the patio and sat in her usual spot, waiting for the sun to rise and pondering what she should do.

She was meant to stay on for another couple of weeks at the station, but the work had basically wound up for the season. She was pretty sure Judy and Steve wouldn't mind if she left now. That way she could give Jimmy a lift back to Mareeba. It was a long trek for her to do on her own, and she would appreciate the company. And she could make life easier for Matt – he wouldn't have to avoid her until she left. It had been pretty obvious from his reaction that he didn't want to see her again. She figured she'd be doing him a favour. She took a deep breath and shut her eyes. She knew what she had to do, but it was going to break her heart to do it.

As soon as the men had left for work Sarah headed out the door. When she'd mentioned the possibility of a lift to Jimmy over breakfast, he'd been excited at the chance to go home with her instead of catching the bus. The men had reacted slightly differently. They'd sat in front of her without a word, shocked by the news that she might be leaving so suddenly. She did her best to act cheerfully and hid her feelings, explaining that she was feeling a bit homesick. Since the season was almost over and she could take Jimmy, now seemed as good a time as any. They'd accepted her reasoning, visibly saddened by the thought of her leaving them. Her heart ached at the sight of their faces, and she barely knew what to say when they told her she'd better be back to cook for them next year. She knew full well that she would probably never set foot on Rosalee Station again. She'd stuffed it up well and good. It was time to go home and restart her life back on the fruit farm.

Sarah pulled up outside the homestead. She was absolutely petrified of running into Matt and prayed that he was off working on the station somewhere. She took a deep breath and hopped out of the LandCruiser. Judy answered her knock at the homestead with her customary warm smile. 'Come in, darling. Do you want a cuppa?'

'That would be lovely, Judy. Thanks.' Sarah followed her into the kitchen, keeping an eye out for any sign of Matt.

'So how're things, love?' Judy asked, pouring hot water into a cup and jiggling a teabag.

Sarah felt a lump in her throat as she began to talk. 'Well, Judy … I, um, well …'

Judy looked up from the kitchen bench as tears filled Sarah's eyes. 'Oh, love. What's the matter?'

Sarah burst out crying. 'I think I'm gonna head home tomorrow, Judy. Sorry for the short notice, but I just feel like it's the right time to go.' She pulled back from Judy's embrace and grabbed a tissue from the box on the bench, blowing her nose loudly.

Judy's dismay was obvious. 'If you're leaving because you're worried about not having any work once the men go, then don't go, Sarah. There's plenty you can do until we need a cook again. We'd all love you to stay. I hope you know that.'

Sarah smiled beneath her tears. 'Thanks, Judy. That means a lot to me. Thanks for being so lovely and for treating me like one of the family. But I just feel it's time to go home.'

Judy nodded. 'I can understand that, love. I hope you're going to come back and work next year.'

'I'll definitely consider it.' Sarah sniffed a little, the tears drying on her cheeks.

'Why so sudden, love? You know, wanting to leave and all? I thought you'd be here for at least a week more.'

'Jimmy mentioned he was heading home on the bus tomorrow afternoon and it seemed a shame for him to have to catch the bus when I could give him a lift. Plus I thought it would be nice to have company to drive home with. It's silly to wait a few weeks more here, only to drive home on my own. Dad could probably use a hand on the farm too.' Sarah hoped her white lie was convincing.

Judy shrugged her shoulders. 'Yeah, it does seem like a good opportunity to take. After all, it is a long drive you've got ahead of you. Please keep in touch, though, won't you, love? We're gonna miss you around here. Georgia and Steve should be back this arvo – drop in to say bye. If you want to say goodbye to Matt, though, you might have to give him a call on his mobile when you're passing through Mt Isa. He and Brooke had a massive argument last night and he took off for a few days, saying he needed time to clear his head. God knows what took place, but he was really upset. I thought it best to let him go without bombarding him with questions.' Judy's face creased with worry as she spoke.

Sarah felt a rush of guilt. She hoped and prayed that the argument between Matt and Brooke wasn't brought on by her. She was suddenly filled with a desperate need to run from the house, pack her bags and leave. God, imagine if she ran into Brooke. Matt had obviously told Brooke what happened. She felt sick with anxiety at the thought of seeing Brooke. She wouldn't know what to say to her.

Sarah sipped the hot cup of tea that Judy had just made her as fast as she could, while listening with half an ear to Judy jabber on about how poorly Brooke treated Matt. She sat there inwardly cringing – little did Judy know, she thought sadly. Trying to gulp down mouthfuls of the scalding tea, Sarah burnt her tongue, but finally her cup was empty.

'Well, I have to run, Judy. The men are home for lunch today and I've loads to pack before I hit the road.' She reached out to give Judy a hug and Judy responded warmly, hugging Sarah until she could barely breathe. Judy walked her to the door of the homestead, wiping a few tears away.

'Drop by before you leave and say goodbye to Steve and Georgia, won't you? And please let me know when you're home safe and sound. You have my email address, so don't be afraid to use it, okay?' Judy said, holding Sarah's hands.

Sarah squeezed Judy's hands in hers. 'I promise I'll keep in touch, Judy.'

Sarah waved from the LandCruiser as she started the engine and then drove back to the cottage. She was going to miss Judy and her welcoming home. Sarah knew a piece of her would remain here no matter what, and the thought of it brought tears to her eyes. That piece of her heart belonged to Matt, the man she had fallen deeply in love with.

Sarah packed most of her clothes while waiting for the men to come home for lunch. The room looked so bare already, and it made her sad to think she only had one more night in her bed here. She had enjoyed so many nights under the roof of the cottage with the blokes. It had changed her life being out here, and she wondered if her family would be able to see the difference. The trauma of her break-up with Brad, his shocking accident and her growing feelings for Matt, along with the rough and tumble of daily life with the men, had all contributed to the change she felt within herself.

She gathered up the mound of tissues on her bedroom floor. The tears had rolled freely and endlessly while she had been packing, but now she had to pull it together. She was not about to let the men see how upset she was. It would worry them all too much, and that was the last thing she wanted to do. She was so deep in thought that she nearly hit the roof when there was a gentle knock at her door. 'Come in!' she called, quickly wiping her face to remove any residue of the tears. She hadn't expected the men home for another hour.

'Hi, mate,' Patrick said as he came through the door. 'Shit, it looks empty in here!'

'My word it does, Patrick. I'm gonna miss this place.' Sarah sat on the bed and gazed out the window, trying to avoid eye contact with Patrick, knowing full well that the redness of her eyes would give her away.

Patrick sat down beside her on the bed. 'Sarah, you can tell me to mind my own business if you like, but I know there's something wrong. It's just not like you to up and leave so suddenly, and last night you looked like you'd been crying.'

Sarah couldn't contain her emotions; fresh tears ran down her cheeks as she saw the concern in Patrick's face. 'You're right, Patrick,' she said through her tears. 'There *is* a reason, but I'm afraid you might judge me horribly if you hear it.'

Patrick smiled warmly at Sarah. 'You're one of my best mates here, Sarah. Nothing is gonna change my opinion of you. Trust me. Unless you've had sex with a horse or something – then I might have to rethink our friendship!' His feeble attempt at a joke made Sarah smile.

Patrick listened intently as Sarah filled him in on all the details of what had transpired with Matt the day before.

Sarah felt her face go red as she explained that she'd realised she was in love with Matt, and it was just going to be too painful to be around him after the reaction he'd had yesterday.

Patrick wrapped his arm around Sarah's shoulder. 'Oh, mate. You poor bugger. You should've talked to me about it last night. It might have made you feel a bit better rather than keeping it all to yourself. I can understand you wanting to leave now. I just wish it was different, though. You and Matt would be a match made in heaven. Brooke doesn't deserve him, and we all know it.' He paused for a moment, lost in thought. 'Matt's got pretty strong morals when it comes to cheating, though, and it must be killing him to think about what happened. Whatever you think, it's not your fault, Sarah. He can't blame you for the kiss. And after all, that's all it was – a kiss.'

Sarah shook her head. 'I'm not so sure, Patrick. He jumped back from me like I was a venomous snake, leaving me there on the ground, and said it had been a mistake kissing me. And then he didn't say a word to me all the way home. I felt like I was the one who'd done something wrong.'

Patrick put his arm around Sarah's shoulder and gently kissed her on the forehead. 'Well, we all love you, mate. If you can, don't worry about Matt. He'll sort himself out and hopefully come to his senses. Whatever you're feeling, don't blame yourself. Go home and have a great time with your family back in the tropics. But don't forget us all now, will you?'

Sarah sniffed and gave Patrick a smile through her tears. 'How in the hell could I forget you blokes? You're all one of a kind!' Not for the first time, she realised how lucky she was to have good mates to look out for her.

*

Sarah threw the last of her things in the back of the LandCruiser and whistled for Duke to jump up in the back. Victory was happily munching away on his hay in the float. She hoped he'd travel as well back to Mareeba as he had on his way to the station. Jimmy was packed too, and they were set and ready to go. Stumpy, Slim, Patrick and Liam gave Jimmy a firm handshake each before turning to Sarah and giving her a quick hug. She couldn't help letting a few tears fall once again. 'Now you boys be good, or be good at it!' she said, hoping to put a smile back on their faces as she hopped up in the driver's seat.

'I think I'd rather be good at it!' Liam joked back.

'See you all round like a rissole!' she called out her window with Jimmy waving from the seat beside her. The men waved back until she couldn't see them any more. As the LandCruiser approached the gates, Sarah found herself involuntarily slowing down, not wanting to say her final goodbye to the station that had given her so much. She whispered a private farewell as she looked in her rear-vision mirror, watching her life of four months disappearing in a cloud of dust, her heart splitting down the middle. So much for holding it together – the tears started again, and she wept openly as she drove. Jimmy tried his best to console her. It was going to be a long, sad journey home.

Chris walked out of his bedroom and straight past Patrick, Liam, Stumpy and Slim in the lounge room without bothering to say a word. Patrick watched him with dislike. Now that the season was almost over, it wouldn't be too much longer he'd have to put up with him. The front door closed behind Chris as he headed outside. Patrick took a swig from his beer bottle, his curiosity screaming loudly in his head. It hadn't been a great day – Sarah and Jimmy had left in the morning, and the mood at the cottage was low. Patrick couldn't shake Sarah's story out of his head, and he missed her already. What he needed was something to take his mind off things.

'Who's up for a bit of fun then?'

Stumpy squinted to see the time on his watch. 'Bit late for fun, isn't it? Whatever it is, count me out, I'm afraid. This old bugger needs to get to bed. I need my beauty sleep.'

'I'm always up for some fun!' Liam said eagerly. 'What exactly would you be proposing?'

Slim put his hands up in the air and stretched. 'Anything would be better than this crap on telly. What did you have in mind?'

'I wanna know what that bugger is up to at night.' Patrick pointed towards the front door.

'Ah, you're going to play Sherlock Holmes?' Slim smirked.

'Seriously, he's been disappearing out there most nights, and I reckon it's about time we knew what he was up to, don't you?' Patrick asked.

Liam bounced on the couch. 'God, yeah! I'm up for it!'

An amused look crossed Slim's face at the thought of snooping around in the dark. 'Me too.'

Stumpy laughed and shook his head. 'What are you gonna do? Run around in the dark and hope you bump into him? You lot are gonna look like right criminals.'

Slim, Liam and Patrick rugged up in preparation. The days were still fiercely hot but the nights were often icy cold. It paid to be warm, and the men had no idea how long they'd be outside.

To help conceal themselves in the dark, they painted each other's faces black with a tin of old boot polish they had found in the back of the laundry cupboard. It was a bit over the top, but it was worth the laugh it gave them all. It was Patrick's idea but Slim and Liam were willing participants, although most of the boot polish ended up on their jeans. Stumpy took a photo, teasingly saying that he was going to get it enlarged and then hang it on the wall in the lounge room as a reminder of what loonies the three of them could be.

'So are we right to go then?' Slim said, still chuckling at the sight of them, his big belly bopping away with his laughter.

'We sure are. Let's get a move on. We don't even know where to start looking and there's a lot of ground to cover out there,' Liam whispered mysteriously, trying to keep a straight face. As they were heading out the door, he grabbed his camera from his room and hung it around his neck.

'I think I know where to start, you two. Just follow me!' Patrick said once they were on the porch, putting on his best commando voice. That set them off again.

Stumpy grinned from the door. 'Will you lot piss off? I can't look at you any more without laughing.'

The three headed in the direction of the stables to begin with, and the darkness and cold was surprising after the warmth of the cottage. Suddenly the whole excursion didn't seem as much fun. Patrick pulled the hood of his jumper over his head. 'It's that windy out here it would blow a dog off its chain.'

Slim shivered at the cold breeze that whistled through the trees eerily. 'It's bloody cold too.'

Liam scoped out the area as they snuck about, wearing his head torch as their light.

'You look like a right idiot, Liam,' Slim said.

'Yeah, but it was a bright idea to wear it. Get it – ha ha!' Liam laughed.

Patrick smirked at his brother. 'You should've been a comedian. I'm sure you could even make a cat laugh.'

'I second that,' Slim added.

There was no sign of Chris in the stables, and it wasn't getting any warmer.

'Let's go and check out the hangar next. What do you two reckon?' Liam was trying to look serious but not succeeding with the light mounted on his head. He resembled a glow worm.

He switched the head torch off and they walked up to the hangar in the dark. It was no good trying to sneak up on Chris with the torch announcing their presence. They searched around in the dark, bumping into fuel drums and each other, but it was soon obvious that Chris wasn't there, or if he was, he was hiding somewhere pretty good. The absurdity of their excursion struck the men and Liam started to chuckle a bit. Once he'd started Slim joined in, and soon Patrick joined them in roaring with laughter in the darkened hangar. No matter whether they found Chris or not, at least they were having fun again.

Liam let out a ripper of a fart that broke the silence of the night like thunder. He broke out laughing again, crawling fast along the ground to get away from the stench. It was so bad he had to hold his breath.

'Shit, Liam! Any more choke and you would've started. It stinks that bloody bad!' Slim chuckled, trying his best to get away from the odour.

'Sorry about that, guys … but Fluffy wanted to be let off the chain!'

Patrick rolled his eyes at his larrikin of a brother while holding his nose.

'So where are we gonna look next, Patrick?' Slim enquired once the laughter had settled.

'I've got a bit of a hunch, lads. Just trust me … but we're gonna have to be extra quiet, because we've gotta sneak around the back of the homestead,' Patrick said.

'Shit, Patrick. I don't know about going up near the homestead. I don't wanna get the sack if we're caught,' Liam said nervously.

'If we're extra quiet we'll be all right. Where are those big tough man balls of yours you always talk about? Let's add some spice to the adventure.' Patrick was smiling, but on the inside he was as edgy as a long-tailed cat in a room full of rocking chairs.

'I'm keen, mate,' said Slim. 'I love a good adventure. But remember to take into account I'm not the easiest body to hide, given these curves of mine.'

'Just stand still if anyone spots you – they'll think you're one of the bottle trees,' Liam said.

'Oh, hardy ha, Liam. Always the kidder!' Slim retorted.

The plan was decided, and the three snuck up to the homestead, hiding in the shadows of the trees whenever they thought they'd heard something. Once they reached the fringes of the main property they went right into commando mode. Using simple hand gestures to point the way, Patrick led. He knew exactly where he was heading, manoeuvring his way around the house like a panther, avoiding any spots where light was seeping out from a window. Finally he motioned for the guys to join him at a sheltered spot behind an old molasses tank, lowering his voice to a whisper. Liam and Slim had to lean right in to hear what he was saying.

'I've had my eye on Chris for a while, and I reckon my hunch is just about to be proved right,' he said. 'I bet you that Chris is in there with Brooke.' He pointed to the granny flat out the back of the homestead.

'Are you serious? How in hell did you come up with that one?' Liam whispered, clearly shocked.

'Well, where do I start? Matt's gone to Mt Isa for a few nights because he and Brooke had a fight last night. And obviously he's in Mt Isa a bit anyway, delivering cattle. Isn't it funny how Chris stays out late on the nights when Matt's away? And I don't know if you guys noticed at the rodeo, but Brooke and Chris couldn't take their eyes off each other. I reckon Chris's been paying Brooke a few late-night visits, and we can only hope it's more innocent than it sounds,' Patrick explained.

Slim sat deep in thought for a few moments before nodding his head in agreement. 'Now that you mention it, yeah, I did notice them at the rodeo. And there have been a few other things too. You might just be right.'

It was clear from Liam's voice that he wasn't convinced. 'Okay, big brother. I hope you're right, 'cause if Matt hears about us spying on his missus for no apparent reason he'll have our balls on a dinner plate.'

They went from tree to tree near the fence line, sticking like glue to the shadows until they reached the granny flat. Short of walking up to the front door and heading on in, Patrick wasn't sure how to check whether Chris was there. But then he spotted a sliver of light falling on the ground from an open curtain. He pointed it out to Liam and Slim and they nodded in agreement. They eased their way around to the window, trying not to step on any twigs. All around they heard the scurry and whisper of night animals and the occasional call of an owl. Eventually they found themselves sitting on the ground below the window. Patrick decided to do a quick recon, and knelt up slowly. He was right, the curtain wasn't fully drawn, and he put his eye level with the windowsill to peer in.

Brooke was on all fours on the bed completely naked, with Chris behind her, holding her hips with his hands as he pumped into her rhythmically, his white arse bobbing backwards and forwards. Brooke was thrashing about like a croc with prey in its mouth.

Slipping back down from the window, Patrick's face told the story. Liam and Slim carefully peered through the window while Patrick sat below them, shock twisting his features. As quietly as he could, Liam brought the camera around his neck up to the windowsill and pressed the shutter a few times until he couldn't take it any more.

The men snuck back the way they'd come to the safety of the dirt track that went back to their cottage, none of them saying a word. Once they made it to the track, Patrick broke into a run, and Liam and Slim followed suit, the three of them running like mad until they reached the front door.

Patrick grabbed three beers from the fridge and handed one each to Liam and Slim as they went to the back patio, trying to process what they'd just seen. Slim was still trying to catch his breath. 'Shit. I don't know whether I'm just unfit or still in shock!'

'What are we gonna do now?' Liam asked, before taking a long scull of his beer.

'Well, we've gotta tell Matt as soon as he gets back, I reckon. That's the only decent thing to do,' Patrick said, his face clouded with worry. 'I can't believe Matt is in Mt Isa worrying about a little kiss when Brooke is doing the wild thing with Chris under his own roof!'

'What kiss?' Slim asked, curiosity written across his face. Liam looked equally puzzled. 'Yeah, what kiss?'

'Oh shit, me and my big mouth. Well, I s'pose I have to tell you both now I've just stuck my foot in it,' Patrick huffed. He filled the guys in on what Sarah had told him yesterday.

'I always thought there was something between those two. You could see it when they were around each other,' Slim recalled, shaking his head.

'All that aside, I'm gonna have to break the news to Matt about Brooke. You know what they say about being the bearer of bad news.' Patrick sighed.

*

The men were on the patio having breakfast, filling Stumpy in, when they heard the crunch of tyres at the front gates. Patrick knew it'd be Matt, and felt his stomach do a 360 at the thought of having to tell him the horrible news. Chris was still asleep.

Patrick ran for the front door, hoping to catch Matt on his way down the drive. The camera was burning a hole in his pocket and he had to say something to Matt before Chris woke up. Spotting Matt heading towards the homestead, he knew it was now or never. He waved the truck down and Matt came to a halt, winding down the window as Patrick approached.

'Morning, Patrick. What's up, mate? Looks like you've seen a ghost,' Matt said, a smile on his face.

Patrick felt the colour drain from his face as he cleared his throat. 'Mate, um, I have some shitty news to tell you. I don't know how to break it to you gently, so I'll just put all the cards out on the table.'

Matt's face immediately changed from a friendly smile to a look of grave concern. 'Right. This sounds serious. Is anyone hurt?'

'Not yet, buddy,' Patrick answered warily.

Matt looked confused. 'Okay, mate. Lay it out for me without any sugar coating. What's up?'

Patrick cleared his throat again. 'Matt, I found out something about Brooke.'

Matt's jaw clenched and his hands rolled into fists on the steering wheel. He didn't utter a word and sat deadly still, his breathing becoming audible. He looked as though he was about to do his block.

Putting his hand through the window and touching Matt gently on the shoulder, Patrick said, 'Mate. Brooke's been cheating on you with Chris.'

Matt reacted instantly, punching the steering wheel hard enough to draw blood on his knuckles. 'How do you know?' He turned to Patrick with eyes ablaze.

Patrick hesitated before answering, his voice quivering. 'We've got proof, but are you sure you want to see it?'

'Of course I do!' Matt growled.

Patrick pulled out Liam's camera and turned it on. He grimaced as he saw the first photo briefly. The shots of the naked bodies were even more graphic in the light of day. Matt swallowed hard as he flicked through the photos, shot after shot of Brooke and Chris doing things in *his* bed, under *his* roof. His hands started to shake so much that it was hard to stay focused on the camera screen.

Finally Matt looked up at Patrick. 'Thanks, mate, for coming and telling me about this. It means a lot to me. I know it would've been hard. But of course I want to know how in the hell you got these photos.'

Patrick screwed his face up like a naughty child. 'Do you really want to know?'

Matt stared back at him, steely-eyed.

'Well, I had a funny feeling that Chris has been up to something for a while. He was going out after dinner some nights and not coming back until all hours of the morning. After a bit, I realised it was on the nights that you were away driving the cattle to Mt Isa, or out shooting with your dad. I didn't put Brooke into the picture until that day at the rodeo, when she and Chris were stuck together like glue. Last night the lads and I were a bit bored, and I finally decided to see whether my hunch was correct. Of course I hoped I was wrong. When Slim, Liam and I got to the granny flat, one of the curtains was slightly open, and we were able to look in without them even knowing. What are you gonna do now, Matt?'

Matt lifted his hat and wiped the sweat off his brow. 'I'm going home to kick the cheating bitch out of my house. Then I'm coming back to fire Chris. He can drive Brooke back to Mt Isa – they're welcome to each other.

This is probably a blessing in disguise. By the way, is Sarah about?'

Patrick shook his head. 'There's more bad news, mate. She and Jimmy drove back to Mareeba yesterday.'

Matt felt his throat close over with emotion. He couldn't believe Sarah was gone. He'd spent most of the past forty-eight hours thinking of nothing but her. He'd made up his mind to break up with Brooke, and use the kiss as a way to end things with her. It'd been a long time coming, and he'd finally realised how strong his feelings were for Sarah. He'd thought it was going to be clear-cut, but now, Sarah was gone. He wondered briefly if he'd had anything to do with her sudden departure.

He hid his disappointment, not wanting Patrick to see he was taken aback. 'Shame I didn't get to say goodbye to Sarah. She was a good worker. Anyway, Patrick, I've got some shit to deal with at home. See you back here soon.'

*

Brooke was sitting on the couch when Matt walked in the front door, slamming the flyscreen behind him and nearly ripping it off its hinges.

'Hi!' Brooke called in a cheery voice, as though their recent argument was completely forgotten. 'I haven't had breakfast yet but maybe you feel like being kitchen bitch and making me something?'

There was no reply from Matt, who'd headed straight to the kitchen to grab a garbage bag, and then headed to the bedroom. He started shoving Brooke's clothes and possessions roughly into the bag, and as he worked he felt himself calm down. No matter what happened, Brooke wouldn't get the better of him now.

He could hear her calling him from the lounge room, and after a couple of minutes she appeared in the doorway of the bedroom.

'That wasn't much of a hello, was —' She stopped short. He watched panic rise on her face.

'What the hell are you doing with my things, Matt?'

Matt looked up at her, his nostrils flaring like a micky bull. 'You cheap little *floozy*. Who do you think you are, inviting men into our bed when I'm not here?' He felt his temper rise and the words flew out of his mouth like flying bullets. 'I thought you were in love with me, Brooke, but you only love yourself. I cannot believe I've wasted years of my life with you! I want you the hell out of this house and the hell off this station today. You can catch a lift with Chris, who'll also be leaving.'

'Have you lost your mind, Matt? What are you on about? I love you, and wouldn't do anything to jeopardise our relationship,' Brooke said, her eyes pleading with him. 'I don't know who's been telling you what, but I'll give them a good piece of my mind!'

Matt turned to her briefly and smiled cynically. 'Don't try and look sweet and innocent, Brooke. You're far from it. I don't want to hear any of your cock and bull stories. I don't owe you any explanations, but there's some pretty hardcore evidence that proves you've been up to a lot more than you might admit to. I've seen photos of you and Chris going for it in *our* bed. Now get the hell out of my sight, and take your shit with you!'

Matt threw the filled garbage bag at Brooke. It landed with a crash at her feet. 'Fine, Matt. It's your loss anyway!' Brooke said, her eyes flashing. 'You don't know a good thing when you've got it. *That's* why I ended up with Chris – you didn't give me what I needed. You *drove* me into another man's arms!'

Matt bared his teeth like a dog about to attack. 'How dare you accuse me of not appreciating you, Brooke? I've always done my best to treat you with love and respect, and this is how you repay me! I cannot believe you. Now get the hell out of my house! You're enough to give diarrhoea the shits!'

At his words Brooke fell to the floor and started sobbing, but Matt was past caring. He tried to step over her and she grabbed his leg, trying to hold on to him weakly.

'I mean it, Brooke. I'm gonna stand at the front door until you walk out of it. You better go now before you miss your lift with Chris! I'm not bloody driving you to Mt Isa.'

After a few moments, Brooke stood up and tried to compose herself. Taking deep, gaspy breaths, she grabbed her bag of clothes off the floor and raised her head high in the air. 'I'm glad to be leaving. I hate this dust pit,' she spat.

'Fuck you!' was all that Matt could muster as he watched Brooke walk out the door. He hoped he never laid eyes on her again.

*

Stumpy, Slim, Patrick and Liam were sitting in the lounge watching telly when Matt walked in the door. On the drive from the homestead, Matt had told himself over and over not to do anything stupid to Chris, even though every bit of him wanted to lay him out.

'Where's the bastard?' Matt asked as the men looked up from the telly.

'He's in his room, mate. Do you want us to join you?' Stumpy asked.

'Nah, I can handle it,' Matt replied as he punched his fist into his hand. He headed down the hallway and bashed on Chris's door.

A muffled voice shouted back from inside. 'What the hell do you want? I'm sleeping in here!'

Matt didn't bother to answer. He shoved the door open and in two strides had crossed the floor to the bed and grabbed Chris by his singlet. They were close enough for Matt to feel Chris's nervous breath on his chin. Sweat beaded Chris's forehead as he saw the anger in Matt's eyes.

'You get the hell off my property, and if you try any funny business I'll have your guts for garters,' Matt growled. He could smell the fear pouring out of Chris, who remained speechless. He looked like one of those painted metal clowns at the fairground, his mouth hanging open ready for punters to drop a ball into.

Matt filled in the deafening silence. 'I think you know what I'm on about, Chris. How dare you cheat with Brooke, especially under my roof? Where's your respect? You only operate by your dick. Now pack your shit and bugger off – and make sure you take Brooke with you.'

He let go of Chris, and the sweating man crumpled back onto the bed, shaking like a leaf. With one last look at him, Matt went out to the lounge to sit with the men. Minutes later Chris slunk past them all, holding his bag and quickly pushing his way out the front door. 'You can all go to hell!' he screamed from the safety of the porch.

'See you there!' Slim yelled back, smirking.

*

Matt, Slim, Liam, Patrick and Stumpy watched from a distance as Brooke and Chris stood together under the cluster of paperbark trees. They were waiting for them to leave. Matt wanted nothing more than to see the dust trailing from the back of Chris's ute as the pair of them drove away. While he waited, his thoughts kept returning to the moment he had shared with Sarah by the dam. He felt his heart ache, wondering if he was ever going to see her again. He'd royally stuffed that one up.

Finally Chris and Brooke loaded up the ute and, with a slamming of doors, headed towards the gates.

'Good riddance to bad rubbish,' Matt mumbled as the pair drove off the station and towards Mt Isa.

CHAPTER
25

Sarah pulled the doona up and over her head as Lily sat down on the edge of her bed. She didn't want to face yet another tear-filled day. Lily placed her hand gently on Sarah's doona.

'Mate, I'm begging you. You gotta try to let him go. It's been almost a month since you've been home, and we've barely seen you smile. I know it's tough when you have a broken heart, but please don't shut all of us out. We love you, Sarah.'

Sarah sighed and pulled the doona down so her eyes were visible. 'I know you love me, Lily, and I'm sorry I'm an absolute sad case ... but I just can't stop thinking about him and what could have been. Life just isn't fair sometimes. I can't pretend I'm happy when I'm not.'

Lily smiled lovingly at Sarah. 'I'm not asking you to pretend, mate, I'm just asking you to at least try to have a bit of fun. And yes, you're right, babe. Life isn't always fair, but it's at these moments that you have to decide whether you're gonna be a victim or a survivor. And you, Sarah Clarke, are a survivor.'

Sarah couldn't help but smile. Lily always knew just what to say to make her feel better. 'Oh bloody hell, I know you're right, Lil. I *want* to get my sorry arse up and enjoy the day, but then once I'm up all I wanna do is go back to bed and cry. Matt is probably off enjoying himself with Brooke anyway. I just need to get over him.'

Lily slapped Sarah's shoulder gently. 'That's the spirit, my friend! Now get up and help me pick up all these tissues on the floor. What are you trying to do, sponsor Kleenex?'

Sarah peered over the edge of the bed and grimaced. There would have been easily two boxes worth of tissues thrown haphazardly about the floor. 'Oh my goodness! I've been crying a river, haven't I?'

Lily nodded. 'You have, mate, but that river has dried up now, right? There's life out there to be living!' And with those words, Sarah couldn't help but believe her.

Lily helped Sarah tidy up her room, ripping her sheets off for a well-needed wash. Sarah caught a glimpse of herself in the mirror as she was tidying up and frowned. 'Shit, Lily. I look like death warmed up.'

'That's what happens when you cry all day long and don't get any sunshine,' Lily replied. She walked over and pulled open Sarah's curtains, coughing at the dust that had built up over the last month. 'There's a party tonight at Jimmy's farm. Daniel and I are going. Are you gonna come with us?'

Sarah knew it wasn't really a question. She threw her hands up in the air. 'Yes, I'll come. I'll never hear the end of it if I don't.' She screwed her face up as she got a whiff of her underarms. 'Man, I'm in desperate need of a shower. I smell like a mountain person!'

'Tell us about it! Now go and hose yourself down, and I'll make us a feed for breakfast. Bacon and eggs sound good?'

'Just what the doctor ordered.' Sarah smiled, feeling a little spark of life bubbling in her belly. It felt good to smile. The last month she hadn't known herself. She had never been so torn up before. Every thought she had revolved around Matt, and she'd replayed the scene at the dam so many times in her head that it was starting to feel like a dream. But the awful, bone-crunching knowledge that Matt hadn't wanted anything to do with her was not a dream, and thinking about it even now hurt her heart too much.

But Lily was right, life was meant to be lived, not spent pining away. Sarah decided she would throw herself back into it and enjoy the time with her family and friends. Christmas was next week, and she hadn't even begun to buy gifts for everyone. There would be plenty to keep her busy.

*

Maggie jumped up from her seat the minute Sarah walked into the kitchen, freshly showered and smiling. 'Good morning, my love! Glad to see you've finally decided to join the land of the living! We've missed you.' She gave Sarah a big cuddle.

Sarah squeezed her mum back tightly. 'I've missed my mum! Sorry I've been so down and out. I just needed a bit of time to get over a few things, but Lily has helped me out of it. Enough moping around, I reckon.'

Maggie stood back and put her hands on Sarah's shoulders, looking deeply into her daughter's eyes. 'That's so good to hear, darling. We knew you'd snap out of it eventually. You just needed time to heal. Don't be too hard on yourself for it now, you hear?'

Sarah smiled at Maggie, her heart filling with emotion. 'You're the best mum ever. Thanks for being so understanding. Love you!'

'Love you too, Sarah.'

'One egg or two?' Lily asked from the stove, dishing up breakfast.

'Three, I reckon! If there's enough, that is.' Sarah was feeling her appetite return with a vengeance.

Lily laughed. 'She's definitely back!'

At that moment Daniel and Jack stepped into the kitchen, covered in mud. 'Gee whiz, you two look lovely this morning,' Sarah said.

'Blocked pipe,' said Jack shortly, before realising it was Sarah speaking. A smile cracked his face, and Daniel beamed from ear to ear. 'Ah sis! You're back from the upstairs bedroom!' He ran over to give her a huge hug, covering her in mud.

'Oh bloody hell, Dan. I've just showered and all!' she squealed, cuddling him back in spite of herself.

Jack walked over and gave Sarah a ruffle on the head, messing up her wild curls. 'Feeling better now, sweetheart, I see.'

'Sure am, Dad.'

'Good on you, my girl.'

*

The party was in full swing by the time they arrived, and Sarah felt the adrenaline start to flood through her as she heard the low thump of the bass. Jack had dropped Daniel, Lily and Sarah off at Jimmy's place with strict instructions to call him if they needed a lift home, mumbling that he would rather them wake him up in the middle of the night than for him to get a call from the hospital because they had caught a lift with some drunken idiot. In case they wanted to stay the night, Daniel had brought the swags.

Sarah's excitement rose as they approached Jimmy's farmhouse. It was going to be a great night, catching up with mates she hadn't seen for four months. She could just make out the orange glow coming from a huge bonfire. Jimmy usually had one at his parties. This wasn't Jimmy's actual home – it was a little shack on his family's property that had been the scene of many a wild night. Everyone called it the Sugar Shack – all the seats inside were made from bales of sugar cane mulch – and you knew if there was a party at the Sugar Shack, it wasn't one to miss.

'Shit, watch out girls!' Daniel yelled, pushing Sarah and Lily out of the way as a bush basher came around the back of the shack with Jimmy and a bunch of his mates hanging out the window, hooting and hollering. The horn was stuck on, and the noise was close to deafening. Every single panel of the car was bashed in, and the back tailgate hung by a thin sliver of metal as it dragged along the dusty ground, banging and clattering over every rock. The large crowd gathered in front of the shack quickly jumped out of the way, cheering and clapping as the driver began to spin the tyres. The smell of burning rubber filled the air and smoke surrounded the beast of a car. Seconds later, one of the back tyres exploded, the rim of the disintegrating wheel throwing out sparks. The horn was finally silenced and Jimmy emerged from the passenger seat, holding a beer bottle up in the air in triumph. Sarah rolled her eyes and laughed. From the state Jimmy was in, it looked as though the party had started earlier than expected.

Sarah found herself with her fourth or fifth Bundy and Coke in hand, standing near the bonfire with Lily and Daniel. Suddenly Johnny Marsh went tearing past the crowd on his imaginary horse, butt naked, with just his hat covering his manhood, singing out *giddy up* at the top of his lungs. Everyone burst out in fits of laughter, and Sarah laughed so hard she had Bundy and Coke coming out of her nostrils. Before she knew it her legs had given way, and she laughed even harder as she fell on her butt. Lily tried her best to help her stand up, but Sarah's legs refused to carry her. Lily finally gave up and flopped down beside Sarah, laughing so hard she was snorting, which in turn made Sarah laugh even more. Daniel swayed above them, holding out a hand to each of them.

'Nah, you're right, Dan. I reckon I might lie here for a few minutes until the sky stops spinning so much,' Sarah said. 'I feel like I'm on a bloody merry-go-round.'

'Me too!' Lily exclaimed, burping loudly. 'Oops, pardon pigs in front of hogs!'

'Hey! Who you calling a hog?' Sarah asked, hiccuping loudly.

'Come on, you two. Let me help you back up!' Daniel laughed.

Sarah and Lily held out their hands and Daniel wobbled and swayed, finally getting the girls to their feet. The people gathered around the bonfire cheered when the girls were up, and Sarah held her thumb up in the air triumphantly.

Someone turned the stereo up, and the Dixie Chicks 'Sin Wagon' blared out of the speakers. Sarah threw her hands up in the air and stomped her boots on the ground, singing along to the song at the top of her lungs. She felt alive for the first time in weeks, and revelled in the feeling of dancing, letting herself go with the raw earth beneath her feet. Goose bumps ran up her spine from the sheer joy of it all. She twirled around in circles, taking pleasure in the motion of her own body and the feeling of the alcohol coursing through her. She was so happy to be back. Lily and Daniel threw their arms over her shoulders and the three of them bumped and jived together in a line, trying to imitate line dancing but failing miserably.

The music played on for the rest of the night, the crowd dwindling as the hours passed, and before long all that was left were hot embers of the bonfire and snoring bodies in swags.

*

Sarah squinted as the sun beamed down on her, rudely waking her from her drunken slumber. She sat up and surveyed the sugar shack in the harsh reality of the morning light, groaning as her head started to ache. Her mouth felt like it was a dried-up riverbed and she needed a glass of water like it was going out of fashion.

Lily and Daniel were beside her, slowly stirring from their sleep, looking a bit worse for wear. Sarah wondered how she looked after seeing the state of them. She tried to run her fingers through her curls, but they were matted and refused to untangle. She could feel something sticky in there too, and grimaced as she wondered what it might be. She vaguely remembered throwing up at some stage, and hoped Lily had been there to hold her hair back. Otherwise that was probably what was acting as an unwanted styling product this morning.

Johnny Marsh waved at her from his place beside the smouldering embers; he was still butt-naked, except for his akubra over his manhood, and obviously slightly embarrassed.

Sarah wriggled free of her swag – she might as well go look for Johnny's clothes for him before the rest of the partygoers woke. 'Hey mate, where's the horse you were riding last night?'

Johnny blushed slightly. 'Oh, man, I must have looked like a right tool. The guys bet me a hundred bucks to do it, and you know me – I love a challenge.'

'Where do you reckon your clothes are?'

Johnny shook his head, making sure to keep his hat in place. 'Your guess is as good as mine, mate.'

'Well, I'll have a look for them. Can't leave you naked all day, Johnny. Your arse would get sunburnt!'

Johnny smiled. 'Thanks, Sarah.'

Sarah eventually found Johnny's clothes inside the sugar shack under a sleeping body. Johnny breathed a sigh of relief when she came back and handed them to him.

'Oh thank Christ for that. I was afraid I'd have to go home without any bloody clothes on.' He stuck his hand in the pocket of his jeans and proudly pulled out a hundred-dollar note, grinning. 'And they even put the money in there for me. What great mates I have!'

Sarah laughed, looking away so Johnny could get dressed. 'Yeah, great mates, Johnny. Ones that send you riding an imaginary horse through a crowd of people at a party, singing out *giddy up* at the tops of your lungs!'

'Did I make you laugh?' Johnny did his best to get dressed while still holding onto his hat.

'You sure did.'

'Good. That's what life's all about. Having a laugh.' Johnny smiled, a lot more relaxed now he had his jocks on.

'You're right about that, Johnny! I really enjoyed last night. I was in desperate need of a laugh, and you larrikins certainly made sure of that. I didn't realise until now how much I missed Mareeba and everyone here. I'm so happy to be home.'

Johnny put his arm around Sarah's shoulder. 'Well, we're chuffed to have you back, Sarah. You know how to let your hair down and have a good time, and from what I remember last night you certainly did that!'

Sarah nodded and grinned. She felt in high spirits, despite her massive hangover, and knew in her heart that it was time to get on with her life. Matt was part of her past now and she had to let him go – it was time to look forward to her future. She had so much to be grateful for, like great mates and a loving family. She was home, and like the saying goes, home is where the heart is.

CHAPTER

26

The Clarke family sat in their cosy lounge room, wrapping paper covering the floor, while 'Jingle Bells' sang out from the radio station. Sarah leant over and gave Jack a kiss on the cheek, handing him his gift. 'Last one, Dad. Merry Christmas!'

Jack gave her a smile as he took the present, eagerly unwrapping it. His eyes lit up when he saw what it was. 'Thanks, love! This is just what I needed.' Jack happily held up the handmade sign that read *Clarkes' Farm* for everyone to see. ''Bout time I changed the one out the front, Sarah. You can barely read it now.'

Sarah grinned, glad Jack was impressed by the sign.

'Now all the gifts are unwrapped, who's up for brunch?' Maggie asked.

Sarah tidied up the lounge room as Maggie went into the kitchen to prepare brunch. Daniel, Peter and Jack went outside to hang up the sign. Since Jimmy's party she'd been feeling better, but even though she was smiling on the outside, her heart was still aching for Matt. She'd tried her best to distract herself, helping out on the farm and going shopping for Christmas presents, but he was still on her mind. She found herself wondering what he was doing for the day, and got a sudden urge to call the Walsh family. She could easily avoid talking to Matt – she'd just ask for Judy. Sarah hadn't spoken to her since she'd made it safely back to Mareeba.

She stuck her head into the kitchen. 'Hey, Mum. Do I have time to make a phone call before we all sit down to eat?'

'Of course, love. I'll call you when it's ready,' Maggie called from the sink.

Sarah picked up the hallway phone and noticed that her hands were shaking. She placed the receiver back down and took a huge breath. She was so afraid that Matt was going to answer the phone, but part of her desperately wanted him to. What would she say to him? She reasoned that Judy would be the one to answer the phone, since she was the one who was always pottering about the house. She picked the phone up again and dialled the Walshes' number, her heart racing. It rang three times and then Matt's husky voice spoke into the receiver. 'Rosalee Station, merry Christmas!'

Sarah felt her whole body go into shock. She wanted to hang up but she was frozen solid. She stood, holding her breath, praying that the Walsh family didn't have caller ID, wondering if she should hang up or take the plunge and speak.

'Hello, anyone there?' Matt called into the phone. 'Hello?'

Sarah knew she couldn't hang up. She had to find the strength to speak. She cleared her throat nervously. 'M–merry Christmas, Matt.' Her voice was quivering, and she felt as though her heart was going to bash its way out of her chest.

There was a short silence before Matt answered. 'Sarah, is that you?'

'Yeah. It's me. Long time no hear, hey?'

It was Matt's turn to clear his throat. 'Um, merry Christmas, Sarah. How — how are you?'

'Oh, I'm okay. How's everyone?'

'Mum's in the kitchen cooking up a storm as usual, and Georgia and Dad are fighting over the remote for the telly as we speak.'

Sarah couldn't help but smile, picturing the family in her mind. She missed them so much it hurt. She realised that Matt hadn't mentioned Brooke and her heart fluttered a little. 'How's Brooke?'

'Oh,' Matt said, and paused for a long moment. 'We broke up, Sarah. I thought you would have heard about it through the grapevine. I found out she was sleeping with Chris. She left the day after you did.'

Sarah was lost for words. A new lease of life had entered her body, and she felt like singing and dancing with exhilaration. She had to swallow hard to contain herself. 'Oh, I'm so sorry to hear that, Matt.' She *was* sorry for him, but she could barely believe it. She rummaged around in her mind to find another subject. A brief silence ensued, and Sarah blurted out the first thing that came to her. 'I miss you, Matt. I haven't stopped thinking about you since I left. I wish we could see each other for Christmas.'

The line went quiet again and Sarah kicked herself. Why had she said that? He wouldn't want to see her anyway, regardless of whether he was with Brooke or not.

Matt exhaled deeply. 'I miss you too, Sarah. There's so much I need to say that I never got a chance to. I thought you would never want to speak to me again after the way I left you lying there after we kissed. I just, um, I just didn't know what to do. I didn't want you to think I was a man who would cheat. I would never normally do that, Sarah, you *have* to believe me, but you – you're different, I have feelings for you that I've never had before.'

Sarah gasped. She couldn't believe what she was hearing. 'Oh, Matt. I thought *you* weren't talking to *me*. I thought *you* regretted it and wouldn't want me around Rosalee any more. The kiss was incredible – I felt so much passion in it. That's why I was so confused when you reacted the way you did.'

'Can I come and see you when I get some time off, Sarah?' Matt asked.

'I'd love that. The sooner the better. Oh, you have made me so happy!'

'And you've made my Christmas the best one ever. I wish you weren't so far away – I would grab you and kiss you under the mistletoe right now if I could,' Matt said with a sexy undertone.

'Don't tease me – not while you're not here next to me,' Sarah pleaded.

'I promise I won't be far away for long,' Matt said. 'Would you like to wish Mum a merry Christmas?'

Sarah was reluctant to let him off the phone, but she *had* rung to talk to Judy. She could have sat and listened to Matt all day, basking in the sexiness of his voice. 'Yes please. Can she pull herself away from the kitchen for a minute?'

'I'm sure she'd love to if she knows you're on the blower. I'll talk to you again soon, hey?'

Sarah wanted to reach through the phone and grab him, tell him that she loved him, but she wanted to say it when she was looking into his beautiful brown eyes.

Sarah heard Judy squeal in the background. She could just picture Judy wiping her hands on her apron before grabbing the phone.

'Sarah, love! It's so nice to hear from you!'

Sarah smiled into the phone. 'Hi, Judy! It's great to be talking to you too.'

*

Matt hadn't needed much more of an invitation to visit Sarah. Since she'd left things hadn't been the same at Rosalee. He knew in his heart that he had fallen deeply in love with her. He'd never felt this way about a woman before, but after Sarah had taken off back home without even saying goodbye, he'd been convinced she'd never want to see him again. Now he knew what was really the case – she'd been open and honest with him on the phone, telling him everything he'd been dying to hear. He wanted to leave right now, throw his bag in the truck and hit the road. He might be able to see Sarah by daybreak tomorrow morning if he was lucky. He was filled with a craving that wouldn't be satisfied until he could see her, smell her, touch her, kiss her. He knew what he had to do.

Once Christmas brunch was done, he found Judy in the kitchen and put his arm around her shoulders. 'Mum, what do you reckon about the idea of me getting in the truck right now and driving to see Sarah for Christmas?'

Judy put the tea towel down and looked deep into her son's eyes. She smiled tenderly. 'I think it would be the best darn Christmas present you could give her, Matt. And the best one you could give yourself, too. You've been moping around the place ever since she left. Love does crazy things to people. Go son, go and get your girl!'

Matt smiled at Judy incredulously. 'How do you know these things?'

Judy tapped her nose. 'I'm a mum, Matt. Mothers know everything. Now go, and drive safely. Call me when you get there, okay?'

Minutes later, Matt was throwing his bag on the passenger seat of the truck and checking his watch. He had a sixteen-hour drive ahead of him, but it would feel like nothing. He pushed play on the CD player and smiled as Garth Brooks sang out of the speakers. He was going to win Sarah back, and this time he wasn't going to let her go.

*

Sarah took the last sip from her glass of mulled wine and yawned, deciding it was time to hit the sack. She was bored to death of all the Christmas shows on the telly.

'Night, Mum, night, Dad.' She kissed them both on the cheek.

'Night, love,' they replied in unison.

Sarah lay in the darkness of her room and thought back to the conversation with Matt. She had to pinch herself when she got off the phone; it was hard to believe he had said all those wonderful things to her. Lily was right, she and Matt *were* meant to be together. Fate had made sure of that.

*

Duke was barking like a maniac. Sarah rolled over and looked at the time on her clock beside the bed. It was four in the morning, and she was annoyed at being woken up at such an ungodly hour. She could tell Duke knew whoever it was that had pulled up from the way he was barking. She pulled on her robe and shuffled her way down the steps, narrowly missing Harry, who was sleeping in the middle of the stairs as usual.

Sarah opened the door and Matt's chocolate-brown eyes met hers. Before she could speak he reached out and pulled her close to him. She felt her legs go weak as his lips met hers and she felt sudden heat rush through her body like a freight train. She fell into him and wrapped her arms around his broad, muscular shoulders. Their tongues explored each other, teasing and caressing. Matt ran his hands down her back and lifted her tenderly up off the ground.

'Hello, my beautiful lady,' he whispered in a husky tone.

Sarah gasped, trying to figure out if she was dreaming.

'How – when – oh my goodness, I'm so glad you're here, Matt!'

He looked so handsome. The dimple on his chin showed from the devilish smile he was wearing. 'I needed to come as soon as I could. I wanted to hold you and tell you how much I love you.'

Sarah met his penetrating gaze. 'I love you too, Matt.' She gently touched his face. 'You must be exhausted after such a long drive. Come inside.'

'Your wish is my command.'

Sarah led the way quietly up the stairs and into her room, hoping her parents didn't wake up. Matt gently placed her on the bed and lay down beside her, holding her close to him as stroked her hair. God, he had missed her. They fell asleep in each other's arms, content to finally be able to hold each other.

CHAPTER

27

Sarah smiled as she opened her eyes and felt Matt lying beside her. The fan was above her twirling madly, doing its typical wobbly routine, and the electrician still hadn't been to fix the air conditioner, but Sarah didn't care. She was so happy that nothing could faze her.

She rolled over and watched Matt sleeping for a while, his tanned chest rising and falling with each breath. Then she leaned over and kissed him softly on his delicious lips. He blinked his eyes open and gave her a wide grin, before rolling over quick as a flash and pinning her down. Once he started tickling her she begged for mercy. As they were wrestling together, they accidentally rolled off the bed and landed on the timber floor with a loud thud, giggling like a pair of schoolkids. 'Shit, Mum and Dad are going to wonder what in the hell I'm up to. They don't even know you're here!' Sarah giggled.

'Well, in that case, I better spruce up a bit then go down and introduce myself,' Matt replied, kissing Sarah fair on the lips.

*

When Sarah, Daniel and Peter were kids, the smell of Maggie's cooking had always magically drawn them out of their rooms and down to the kitchen in the mornings. A hot breakfast had been Maggie's secret way of getting the kids fed and off to school on time, and it still worked wonders. Sarah and Matt found themselves drawn to the kitchen by tempting aromas, and saw Daniel and Lily emerging from their bedroom at the same time. The shock on Lily and Daniel's faces when they spotted Matt was priceless.

'Holy shit! When did you rub the magic lamp and make him appear, Sarah?' Lily squealed.

Sarah put her finger up to her lips. 'Shhh, Lil, Mum and Dad don't know Matt's here yet and I want to surprise them.'

Daniel gave Matt a friendly handshake. 'Good to see you, mate. Sarah hasn't shut up about you since she got back.'

Sarah slapped him lightly on the arm. 'You don't have to tell all my little secrets, Dan!'

Matt beamed as he looked at Sarah. 'Is that so?'

Sarah tiptoed into the kitchen, holding Matt's hand. Jack and Maggie had their backs to them at the kitchen sink. Sarah cleared her throat loudly and they turned around.

'Dad, Mum, this is Matt.'

Maggie's face lit up and she smiled knowingly. 'Hi Matt, nice to meet you, love.'

Jack grinned, wiped his wet hands on his stubbies and held one out for Matt. 'Welcome to our home, Matt. Great to finally meet you – I feel like I know you already since I've heard so much about you.'

'It's fantastic to finally meet you guys too,' Matt said, smiling.

Maggie cooked a feast fit for a king. By the end of it, there wasn't a single bite left.

'That was fantastic, Mum, thanks,' Sarah said, licking the last of the sauce from her lips.

'You're welcome, love. Glad you enjoyed it.'

'Matt, would you like to come out with me for the morning and I'll show you around the farm? I have some odd jobs I have to get done, so I thought you might like to tag along with me,' Jack asked.

Maggie turned to Jack before Matt had time to answer. 'What a great idea! It might be nice if me, Sarah and Lily went out for the day.' She looked at Matt. 'That's if you don't mind hanging out with the old bugger, of course.'

'That sounds fantastic. I'd love to check out the farm.' Matt beamed.

'Excellent. We better make a move, then,' Jack said, draining the last of his third cup of coffee. He gave Maggie a quick kiss on the cheek. 'Now you girls behave yourselves and don't go too mad with the credit card.'

Maggie rolled her eyes at Jack. 'We don't even have a credit card, love.'

'I know, but isn't that what you say when a group of women hit the shops? Just trying to be hip.'

'Oh Dad, you're so corny sometimes!' Sarah said, laughing.

Matt gave Sarah a quick kiss before heading out the door with Daniel and Jack.

Maggie fondly watched Matt leave before turning back to Sarah. 'You seem so happy, Sarah. And Matt is absolutely genuine, and you can tell he loves you to bits. Blind Freddy could see it.'

Lily nodded her head in agreement. 'Yeah, I like him too. He's a true gentleman, and easy on the eyes.' She winked at Sarah.

Sarah blushed a little. 'It makes me really happy to hear that. I think it's safe to say I'm pretty madly in love.'

'I thought maybe things were moving too fast – after all, it wasn't too long ago that you were with Brad, and in a serious relationship – but I can see that I was wrong now I've met him,' Maggie said. 'I think it's a match made in heaven, really!'

'So what are we going to do today, girls?' Sarah asked, desperate to change the topic to save herself from blushing even more.

'Um … Well, firstly I think I need to go to the toilet!' Lily said suddenly, abruptly standing up from the table, her chair toppling over behind her, and heading in the direction of the bathroom as quickly as she could, her hand clutched over her mouth.

Maggie screwed her face up. 'Poor bugger. I wonder what's up? Hope it wasn't my cooking.'

Sarah could hear Lily throwing up in the toilet, and knew she should help, even though the sound of someone riding the porcelain bus always made her feel sick herself. 'I better take her a glass of water or something. She sounds like she's having a hard time in there. Maybe we should take her to the doctor's?'

'Wait a sec,' said Maggie, getting up to rummage in a cupboard. 'Give her some of these tablets. They'll help soothe her belly. And ask her if she'd like me to call the doctor.' Maggie passed Sarah a packet of tablets.

Sarah made her way to the toilet and knocked on the dunny door. 'You right, mate?'

'Yeah, I think so. I feel really ill, big time, and it just came out of nowhere.' Lily's face appeared in the crack of the toilet door, looking pale. 'I think you two better go without me today. I need to lie down. I'm just not feeling good at all. Sorry, mate.'

Sarah pushed the door open and put her arm around Lily. 'Don't apologise. It's not your fault. Do you want me to call the doc's for you?'

'Nah. It's probably just a virus or something. I've felt really woozy these past few days and my boss was off sick at the beginning of the week, so maybe he's given me whatever it is he had, the bugger. You go and have a good day with Maggie.'

'I'll have my mobile, so just ring if you need me and I'll come home straightaway, okay?' Sarah gave Lily's shoulders another quick squeeze and passed her the packet of tablets. 'Mum said these'll help.'

'Thanks, mate. I'm gonna go lie down now before I chuck everywhere again. Have fun today.'

Lily did indeed look ill, and Sarah helped her upstairs and back into bed, making sure she was tucked in with a bucket beside her before heading downstairs to Maggie.

*

Jack spent the morning showing Matt around the farm while Daniel and Peter got on with the tractor work. Matt was enjoying his time with Jack. Like Sarah had said, Jack was a lot like his own dad Steve. And with their mutual interest in farming, Matt and Jack had no shortage of things to talk about.

Around ten a.m., Jack pulled up at the dam to check on the pump. Matt went to step out of the ute to help.

'Just wait here, Matt. All I've gotta do is turn the pump on, so it's a one-man job. It'll only take a minute,' Jack explained as he stepped out.

Matt watched Jack walk over to the pump and go about his routine of turning switches and dials. Then to his horror, a snake raised itself from under a dead tree branch that was lying near the pump. As Matt watched in terror, the reptile lashed out at Jack. Jack jumped back in fright but the snake was so fast that he didn't even have time to get away. It struck at him over and over and Jack's face contorted in pain and fear.

In panic Matt fumbled for the door handle, desperately trying to get to Jack. The seconds seemed like hours before he pushed the door open and sprinted to Jack's side, anxiously scanning the area to make sure that the snake had disappeared.

'Shit, Jack, are you all right, mate?' Matt said, tearing his own shirt off. Not waiting for an answer, he started ripping the shirt into strips. He knew he had to get the shirt wrapped around the bites to try and stop the venom from spreading through Jack's body. He worked fast, wrapping the make-do tourniquet tightly up Jack's leg from the ankle, knowing full well that time was of the essence. Jack didn't say a word the whole time, his face still frozen in shock, but Matt could see that he was in pain. Once Matt was satisfied that he had secured the shirt as well as he could, he gently helped Jack up and over to the ute.

'You have to try and stay calm, Jack. The more you panic, the worse it will be. Take deep steady breaths and you'll be right,' Matt said, trying hard not to let his own panic show.

Jack nodded his head, looking dazed. Matt called 000 on his mobile and as he was connected, Jack mumbled woozily, 'Tell them a taipan. It was a taipan.'

Matt explained the situation to the emergency line operator and watched Jack lean out the car door and vomit. As the venom worked its way through Jack's body, Matt knew the nausea would only get worse.

Matt hung up and quickly started the ute. 'They're sending an ambulance, Jack, but I'm gonna start driving you into town and they'll meet us on the road.'

He threw the ute into gear and spun the tyres wildly. Jack slumped in the passenger seat, holding his chest. He looked like a lead weight was pressing down on him, and his breathing was strained. Matt pushed his foot down harder on the accelerator and drove like a bat out of hell down the gravel road, feeling the back end of the ute flick out as he swung out onto the bitumen road that led to town. This was one of the times where he couldn't have given a shit about how fast he was driving. He wasn't stopping for anything other than the ambulance. As the ute sped down the road, Matt stared straight ahead, willing the red, flashing lights of the ambulance to appear. Time seemed to freeze as the kilometres flashed past, and each glance in Jack's direction told Matt that he had no time to spare.

Halfway into town he finally saw the lights of the ambulance coming towards him and he frantically flashed his headlights. The ambulance abruptly pulled over to the side of the road as Matt pulled in beside it and ran to the passenger-side door to open it for the paramedics. As he did so, Jack began to convulse, and Matt was horrifed to see the shirt he'd used on Jack's leg soaked through with blood. He stood back and watched helplessly as the two paramedics lifted Jack out of the car and into the waiting ambulance.

'Are you going to follow us, mate?' one of the men asked. Matt nodded his head swiftly and ran back to the ute.

It was a nerve-racking drive. Matt followed the ambulance at breakneck speed, hoping and praying he'd done enough to get Jack safely to hospital. Luckily, it took only minutes to get to the emergency doors of the hospital. Matt pulled the ute to a sudden halt in a loading zone, and ran to Jack's side as the medics wheeled him into the hospital. As they approached a set of large doors, one of the medics stopped him.

'You'll have to wait here, mate. I'm sorry, but you can't come in. I'll let you know what's happening as soon as we get him looked over, okay?'

'He said it was a taipan,' was all Matt could say, watching helplessly as Jack was wheeled out of sight. Matt could feel tears beginning to sting his eyes. He put his head in his hands and let the tears fall, and prayed with every bit of his being that Jack would be okay.

*

Sarah was in a clothes shop with Maggie, looking at summer dresses, when she heard her mobile ring. Rummaging through her bag, she pulled it out and saw the caller ID was Matt.

'Hi babe! Missing me already?'

There was a silence on the other end of the line, and then she heard Matt clear his throat. 'Sarah, listen to me. Your dad's been bitten by a taipan.'

Sarah felt her hands tremble and she clutched the phone like it was a lifeline. 'Oh my God. Is he okay? Where are you now?'

'I'm at the Mareeba hospital with him. They've taken him into the emergency room. I can't give you any more information than that, babe. Can you come down here as quickly as you can?' Matt's voice broke.

'I'll be with you in a minute. I'm only just down the road.' Sarah was finding it hard to get her words out. Maggie had dropped the dress she'd been looking at to stand by Sarah's side, and as Sarah hung up the phone she almost fell into Maggie's arms.

'Dad's been bitten by a taipan, Mum, and Matt has taken him to the hospital. It's not sounding good.' On her last word, her voice cracked and she started sobbing.

Maggie wrapped her arms around her daughter's shaking shoulders. 'Oh, Jesus. Oh no, Oh Lord, no. Please, not my Jack.'

Sarah pulled her head up and looked at her mother through tear-blurred eyes. 'Come on, Mum, we have to get to the hospital.' She groped in her bag for the car keys as they ran out of the shop and dashed to the Jag. Sarah drove through town in a daze, while Maggie sobbed uncontrollably beside her. Sarah knew that nothing she said would help, but she stroked Maggie's leg all the way to the hospital, trying to calm her down a bit. Once they arrived they saw Jack's ute near the entrance and parked beside it. Matt was nowhere to be seen at first, but they spotted him hunched over in a chair with his head in his hands. Sarah's heart dropped, fearing the worst. Without warning Maggie collapsed on the ground next to her. Matt looked up and rushed over as Sarah fell to the ground beside her, but she was out cold. Two nurses ran to Sarah's aid, checking Maggie's throat for a pulse. All colour had drained from Maggie's face and she lay deathly still on the cold hospital floor. As Sarah stared at her mother in panic, her head started to spin and she felt like she was going to scream.

'Has your mum got any medical problems?' one of the nurses asked Sarah in a soothing voice.

Sarah could hear the nurse speaking to her but it sounded like she was speaking in a tunnel. She tried to clear her head. 'My dad was bitten by a snake. I think ... I think Mum has gone into shock.'

On the floor Maggie started to mumble, and Sarah grabbed her hand anxiously. 'Mum? Are you okay? You just fainted.'

'Your father. How's your father?' Maggie asked in a trembling voice, her hands shaking uncontrollably.

Sarah turned to Matt for the answer. He looked down at the floor, not knowing what to say, the words threatening to get stuck in his throat.

'He's been induced into a coma and taken by emergency helicopter to Cairns. They'll administer the antivenin there. He's in such a critical condition that they couldn't wait for you to arrive. I'm sorry, babe.'

Sarah clutched Matt's arm and let herself go, the tears flowing freely. 'No, Matt! I can't lose my dad. Not my dad.'

Maggie was sitting up now with the aid of the nurses and had heard Matt. She seemed to gather all the strength she could muster, and stood on her shaky legs.

'Well, we must get to Cairns. I've been by Jack's side for twenty-nine years, so by hell or high water I'm going to be there when he wakes up. And I promise you, love, he *is* going to wake up. Your dad is a fighter.'

Maggie's eyes were suddenly fiery, and her determination brought Sarah to her feet. Her mother's resolute words had lifted her spirits, and she realised she couldn't wallow in self-pity and distress.

Leaving the ute parked at the hospital, Matt, Sarah and Maggie got in the Jag and pulled out of the carpark for the one-hour drive to Cairns. Matt was happy to drive and focus on the road, giving Sarah and Maggie some time to come to terms with it all.

Sarah rang Peter and Daniel from the car and brought them up to speed. As she spoke to Daniel, she could hear Lily wailing in the background. Once she'd hung up the phone Sarah closed her eyes and prayed for her dad whom she loved with all her heart, begging for him to live. She had so much more life to share with him. There were so many more happy moments to come. She clung to the belief that he was going to make it through.

CHAPTER
28

It had been an agonising twelve hours. Sarah, Maggie, Daniel, Lily and Peter had sat huddled in the waiting room of the Cairns hospital, drinking coffee and trying to sleep on the hard seats while they waited for news about Jack. Doctors came in and out, keeping them updated. Jack was critical but still alive. The staff had already administered two vials of antivenin, and were looking at giving Jack a third. His heart had stopped twice and both times staff had fought hard to revive him. Sarah was beginning to lose hope. Her eyes were red and swollen from the amount of tears she had cried. It felt like sheets of sandpaper were ripping at her eyelids with every blink, and she just couldn't cry any more. There were no tears left.

Matt sat by Sarah's side the whole time. Neither had spoken much. They didn't know what to say. The silence was beginning to sound deafening. All Sarah could hear was the ticking of the clock on the wall in the waiting room. She felt like ripping the darn thing off and smashing it against the floor. Her nerves were on the brink of explosion.

Just when she was ready to give up, she spotted a white coat floating towards them. The doctor's face was tired but when she caught his eye he smiled, and she knew from that simple expression that Jack was going to make it.

The doctor spoke to them in a calm, professional voice, measuring his words carefully. 'Well, I've got some great news for you. Jack's going to be okay. He's in a lot of pain at the moment, but he *will* pull through. He's one tough man. You should all be very proud of him.'

Maggie wept openly now, her determination no longer needed. 'Can we see him?'

'Yes, you can, but please remember he's still very weak. Don't ask him any questions. Just let him know you're here for him,' the doctor answered. He led them down the hall and to the door of the room Jack had been placed in. He nodded and gently opened the door, leaving them be.

As she slowly filed into the room, Sarah put her hand on her heart when she saw Jack. He lay in the hospital bed, shrunken and pale, barely recognisable. He had a drip coming out of his arm and his face was hardly visible beneath the oxygen mask. His skin was an unnatural shade of grey, and one of his arms hung limply over the edge of the bed. Sarah carefully lifted it up and placed it back onto the bed.

They huddled around Jack, the floor soon spotted with the tears that rolled off their cheeks. Some cried for pure relief and others at the thought of how close they had come to losing him. But one thing was the same for all: Jack was the heart and soul of the Clarke family, and if they had lost him, nothing would've been quite the same ever again.

Jack opened his eyes and slowly scanned the faces in front of him. A weak smile cracked across what little they could see of his face. He turned to Maggie, who was clutching his hand. She ran her other hand over his clammy face.

'Don't talk yet, love. You just rest. You had us all scared out of our wits. We love you very, very much. You know that, don't you?'

Sarah watched a lone tear fall from her father's eye. She had never seen him cry. She realised he must have believed he would never see any of them again. Her breath caught in her throat at the thought of the narrow escape he'd had.

Jack tried to speak through the mask. His voice was muffled but Sarah could hear what he was saying.

'I love you too, with all my heart.'

Once he finished speaking, Jack closed his eyes, and it was soon clear that he was asleep.

*

The family slept on the uncomfortable lounges in the waiting room, not wanting to leave the hospital. Sarah woke at the crack of dawn, her back aching badly from tossing and turning all night long. She made her way to the toilets and gave her face a quick wash, rubbing at her teeth with her finger seeing she didn't have a toothbrush handy. She looked at herself in the mirror and shook her head. Could her life get any more dramatic?

For the rest of the day, the family took turns sitting with Jack, spending the rest of the time getting food, bringing coffee up from the cafeteria or just getting a bit of fresh air. Jack came to every now and then for a few minutes, and then would slip back into sleep, giving in to exhaustion. By early evening, Sarah felt like her emotions had been pushed through the wringer. They had all been in the hospital for over twenty-four hours now and she couldn't help feeling slightly relieved when Maggie insisted that everyone go home. 'There's no point all of us hanging around here. We don't know how long Jack might be in hospital. Drive home, sleep and don't worry. I'll call you the second I have any more news. You all need some rest.'

Sarah tried to talk Maggie into letting her and Matt stay, but Maggie put her foot down. She begrudgingly followed the stern orders and left, getting into the Jag with Matt. They headed back up the range to Mareeba, occasionally glancing out at the endless blue ocean beyond them. Sarah recalled all the times she had spent out on the aqua-blue water with Jack and her brothers, fishing and catching mud crabs. They were happy times, and she longed for more of them.

The drive seemed to take forever, and Sarah had plenty of time to think over the last two days. The idea of living away from her parents had suddenly become unthinkable – it was amazing how quickly things could change. She and Matt hadn't had a chance to talk about the future, but Sarah now knew that she could never live away from her family. What would Matt think? she wondered anxiously. She knew he was close to his family too. She couldn't walk away from Matt, but she couldn't leave her family either. She wished there was some way she could have it all, but she knew that to be with Matt she would have to live away from all the people that meant the world to her.

Matt noticed the furrow in Sarah's brow. 'Are you all right, sweetheart?'

Sarah nodded softly. 'Yeah. It's just really scared me nearly losing Dad. Makes me so glad I was back home and not at Rosalee when this happened.'

Matt sighed. He knew it had been hard for Sarah being away from all her family and friends when she had worked on the station.

'Sarah, I have something I want to share with you. It may come as a shock.'

Sarah turned away from the car window and her introspective thoughts to look at him. She plucked her sense of humour up from within the depths of her misery. 'Shit, Matt. You're not gay, are you?'

Matt smiled for the first time in hours. 'You cheeky bugger! I wanted to let you in on a little secret of mine. I've never told anyone else, especially not my family, but I reckon I'll have to tell them some day soon. I've never really wanted to take over the station.'

Sarah raised an eyebrow quizzically. 'I thought it was your dream to run your own station, Matt. What are you on about?'

'You're right, I've always wanted to run my own station, but not Rosalee. Georgia's there for Dad, and I know how much she wants to run the station. I don't want to disappoint Mum and Dad, and they've always just assumed I'd be the one to take over when they finally decided to throw in the towel, but I've never had my heart set on it like

Georgia has. She's definitely got the guts and the strength to do it, and I want her to have the station, not me.'

'But if you're not running Rosalee, what will you do?' Sarah asked.

'From the very first time I saw the ocean, I knew that I couldn't live out the whole of my life in the outback,' Matt said, gazing at the road. 'I have this dream – I'd love to live closer to the coast and breed cattle on my very own piece of dirt.'

'Are you serious?' Sarah asked, pleasure shining on her face. 'I think the shock of the last twenty-four hours has gotten to you.'

'No, babe. The last few days have just confirmed how short life can be. Like I said to you that day by the dam when we were fishing, you've gotta follow your heart and your dreams, and live life to the fullest every second of every day. I love this area, and I know it would mean the world to you to live closer to your family. Maybe we can make both our dreams come true.'

Sarah felt like she was on an emotional rollercoaster. Her heart was still filled with sorrow, but suddenly the sorrow lifted, if only for a moment, and her face lit up like an outback star-filled sky.

'Matt! That would be amazing, but I don't want you to do this for me. Is this what you *truly* want? I'd be over the moon if you lived here.'

'So you wouldn't object if I said I might have a look at a few properties in the Tablelands?' Matt asked, knowing full well from the look on Sarah's face that she wouldn't object at all.

Sarah leant across the car and gave Matt a tender kiss on the cheek, continuing down his face and his throat as she caressed his shoulder.

'Steady on!' Matt said, trying not to get distracted from driving. 'Hold that thought till I don't have a steering wheel in my hands.'

'You'll keep,' Sarah said, backing off with a light kiss, a sexy smile on her lips.

Matt rubbed the stubble on his chin, still thinking. 'Guess I should tell Dad and Mum soon then, hey? Better to get it over and done with. I'm really nervous about telling them I don't want to work on the station. I'm just hoping they understand.'

'Judy and Steve are the nicest people, Matt. I just know that they'll appreciate you being honest with them, and after the initial shock, they'll support you one hundred and ten percent …'

'I hope you're right, Sarah.'

*

That night the Clarke household felt empty without Jack and Maggie around to make the place warm and homely. Sarah, Matt, Daniel and Lily were all too knackered to even think about cooking, so they ordered in pizzas and went for quick showers before their dinner arrived. They chowed down on the feast, devouring the lot. Once their bellies were nicely full, Sarah shot Matt a quick glance, and cleared her throat.

'Guys, Matt's decided that he'd like to live somewhere near here. He's gonna start looking at properties in the Tablelands. Could you give him a hand, Lily?'

Daniel and Lily's faces showed their surprise and happiness. 'Wow!' Lily said, finding her voice first. 'We'll all be neighbours! And I'll make sure I get you a bloody good deal on a place, too.'

'That's great news. I wasn't looking forward to doing that sixteen-hour trek to Rosalee on a regular basis to visit you, sis,' said Daniel, his look of relief evident. 'While we're on the subject of news, we have something to tell you guys too.'

'You go ahead and tell them, honey,' Lily said to Daniel, who was wriggling like a worm in his seat.

'Lily and I are pregnant!' Daniel said, a huge grin on his face.

Sarah jumped up from the couch with a whoop of excitement, scaring the crap out of Harry the cat, who was curled up at her feet. She wrapped her arms around Lily and Daniel. 'Oh, I'm so happy for you both. What a brilliant end to a very stressful day! I'm gonna be an aunty to my best friend's baby – wow!'

Matt stood to shake Daniel's hand. 'Congratulations, mate.'

'Mum and Dad are gonna be over the moon when they find out!' Sarah squealed.

'We'll tell them soon, once we know Dad's on the mend. Don't want to shock him too much just now!' Daniel said jokingly.

'We only realised yesterday, anyway. Turns out it wasn't a virus after all,' said Lily, a wry look on her face. 'It was a big surprise but I'm really happy about it. I'm just not enjoying this bloody morning sickness thing.'

The phone rang, interrupting their celebration. Sarah had a feeling it'd be Maggie, and ran for the phone.

'Hello, darling,' said Maggie when Sarah answered, her voice sounding exhausted.

'Hey, Mum. How's Dad doing?'

'He's improving, love. I think they're going to let him come home tomorrow afternoon. They just want to monitor him overnight, and if all his vitals look good they'll discharge him tomorrow, but under strict instruction to get plenty of bed rest. He's already started bossing the doctors and nurses around, which is a sure sign he's feeling a little like himself again. It'll be a while before he's given a clean bill of health, but at least he's still with us, Sarah.' Maggie's voice cracked and Sarah wished she could reach out and hold her mother in her arms.

'Oh, Mum, that's great to hear. And I know what you mean. It makes you rethink your life, and it's a reminder to not take anything or anyone for granted. I wish I was there with you right now.'

'Darling, I'd love your company, but I'm glad you went home. I'll be fine after a bit of rest. They've set up a camp bed up in your father's room so I can stay with him all through the night. Anyway, I better go back and sit with him again. I'll call you in the morning, okay, love?'

Sarah wished she could tell Maggie the fantastic news about Matt staying around Mareeba, but she wanted Jack to be there to hear it. She bit her lip in an attempt to not blurt it out.

'Okay Mum, good to speak to you. Thanks for ringing. Love you.'

Sarah hung up the phone and stood for a moment in the dark hallway of the house. She found that she needed a few minutes alone to get her head together. It felt like the last twenty-four hours had happened to someone else, or was something she'd dreamt. It was a strange sensation. She closed her eyes and thanked God that he had left her father on earth instead of taking him to heaven.

Lily and Daniel said their goodnights and trotted off to bed. Sarah stretched her arms in the air and yawned.

'You want to hit the sack too, Matt? It's been a long day, hey?'

Matt leant over and kissed her, letting his tongue slide seductively over her lips as he pulled away. 'I want to make love to you, Sarah. I can't wait a minute more.'

Sarah reached out and pulled him into her, kissing him passionately. They continued as they stumbled up the stairs and into her bedroom. Sarah lit a candle and lay down on the bed, enjoying the rugged handsomeness of Matt's face in the candlelight.

He joined Sarah on the bed and slowly took off her silk robe, the flickering flame revealing her soft sweet skin beneath it. He kissed every inch of her as he went. He stopped every now and then and held her gaze, running his fingers through her long blonde curls. She could feel him devouring her with his eyes. It was so intense she could barely breathe. He knelt and kissed down her legs, making his way to the heaven that lay between them. Sarah groaned in pleasure as his mouth explored her, his warm tongue slowly tasting her, exploring inside her. She couldn't take the burning need for him any longer and tore at his shirt. Running her fingernails over the hair on his chest, she kissed his lips hard and ran her tongue down his neck.

Matt pushed her down onto the bed and held her arms so she couldn't move. He whispered into her ear, 'Let me take control. I want to savour all of you. Let's take this slow and enjoy ourselves.'

Sarah gave into his wish and arched her back as he licked around her erect nipples, flicking his tongue over the top of them, teasing her, making her moan for more. He bit her neck and she pushed his head down harder until she could feel his teeth devouring her skin. Her whole body was pulsing with pleasure. Grabbing at his jeans, she carefully unzipped him and pushed them off with her feet. She let her hand slide over his erection and smiled as she watched him groan. She slid down so she could feel him in her mouth, and he cried out her name. When he could take no more he ran his hands over Sarah's face and pulled her up so she was kneeling, facing him on the bed. He ran his fingers through her hair and pulled gently to tip her head back, kissing her down the front of the throat. He met again with her breasts and bit down on her nipples, making her arch in pleasure. She held onto him and ran her fingernails up his back.

Matt gave into the moment and slowly slid himself inside her. He could feel her hands on his back, urging him deeper and deeper. Once he was deep inside her he kissed her with intense passion, enjoying the feeling of being at one with her. He pulled out and teased her with the tip of his cock before sliding back inside again. Never in Sarah's wildest dreams did she think a man could make her feel like this. Matt started to thrust hard and Sarah moved her hips in unison with his. They came together, calling out into the darkness of the night, gripping each other in pleasure. They collapsed on the bed beside each other and let the silence wash over them while they tried to catch their breath.

Matt propped himself up on his elbow and took in the beautiful woman that lay before him.

'I'm in love with you, Sarah. Every part of you amazes me.' He ran the tips of his fingers up and down her flat belly, circling her belly ring.

She felt like his fingertips were electrified. 'I'm in love with you too, Matt. I thought I was never gonna get the chance to say those words to you in person.' She reached up and kissed him gently on the lips. 'Thank you for coming all this way to see me, and thank you for saving my dad's life. I'm so glad you're here.'

'Oh, Sarah, please don't thank me for your dad. He made it through because of his pure determination to be here with his family. I just happened to be the one who got him to the hospital. And I'm glad I'm here too.' Matt smiled. 'That was pretty amazing, by the way. I'd like more of that in the future, please.'

'I promise there'll be plenty more of where that came from. I've got the munchies now. You want something to nibble on?' Sarah asked.

Matt playfully grabbed her and nibbled on her neck. 'This'll do me fine.'

*

The sun had risen and the birds were happily chirping outside the bedroom window. Sarah watched as Matt stood to pull his jeans on. She admired the tattoo on his back – she'd waited so long to see it in its entirety. The beautifully tattooed stockwhip snaked up the middle of his spine and finished at the base of his head. Sarah felt compelled to jump out of bed and run her finger along it.

'How long have you had this for, Matt?' she asked as she gently traced it with her finger.

'Oh, about four years now. Do you like it?'

'I love it. It's sexy as hell!'

'Good. I'll just turn you on with my tattoos in the future then.' He laughed.

'You turn me on with every inch of you, Matthew Walsh.'

'Likewise, Sarah Clarke,' Matt said as he kissed her lips again, savouring the taste of her.

Sarah whipped them both up a bacon and egg burger along with a cup of tea to wash it down with, while Matt enjoyed a cigarette on the back verandah. Sarah smiled as she watched Matt give Duke a scratch behind the ears. Duke had warmed to Matt from the very first moment they met, and Sarah believed dogs were a great judge of character.

She carried the tray of food out to the verandah and they sat at the table devouring the burgers, both ravenous from their romp between the sheets.

'So what made you decide you loved me, Matt?' Sarah asked boldly.

'I knew it when I kissed you by the dam. I knew it even more when I found out you'd left. My heart felt like it had been ripped out of my chest. Like I mentioned, I thought you must've regretted kissing me, and that was why you took off so suddenly,' Matt replied softly.

Sarah reached out and touched his hand. 'Oh, Matt. I thought *you* regretted kissing me! What a pair of idiots we are!'

'That makes us a perfect match,' Matt said, grinning.

*

The hospital discharged Jack the following afternoon. Within two hours of getting the call from Maggie, Sarah and Matt were in Cairns and waiting to pick them up. It was a slow drive home – the road back to Mareeba was full of curves, and Jack kept feeling nauseous. He never got car sick normally, but all the painkillers were playing havoc with his body.

Eventually they made it back to the farm, where Daniel and Lily were waiting to greet them. Sarah got Jack settled on the couch while Maggie made cups of tea and brought out the tin of biscuits. Once everyone was seated, Matt and Sarah shared the news. A cheerful smile spread across Jack's weary face, and Maggie was overjoyed.

'So this means you'll be staying here, Sarah? Oh, I'm so thrilled! It was a tough few months without you. Of course I was happy you were following your dream, but Rosalee's a long way away.'

'I thought the news would bring a smile to your dials. I'm thrilled to bits too. This smile has been plastered on my face since Matt and I spoke about it,' Sarah said, pointing to her face.

Lily leant in and whispered, 'I know what else is making you smile, my friend.'

Sarah blushed and playfully slapped Lily on the arm.

'Dad, Mum – we have some good news for you too,' Daniel said, smiling proudly.

Maggie sat forward on her chair eagerly. 'As long as it's good news, I want to hear it.'

'Tell them if you like, Lily,' Daniel said, suddenly shy, as he lovingly rubbed Lily's back.

'I'm pregnant!' Lily squeaked happily.

It was a happy morning for them all. They sat and talked about the wonderful things they could look forward to, and Sarah felt bathed in a tranquil river of happiness, an abrupt contrast to the raging rapids of the day before. It had taken a near-death situation to make Sarah realise how important her family was to her, and the discovery had thrown her into turmoil – could she live away from her family for the man she loved? But Matt's unexpected announcement had put her mind at rest. *Home really is where the heart is,* she said to herself, *and the beauty of it is I don't even have to choose.*

CHAPTER

29

Sarah and Matt were beginning to lose hope. It had been three weeks since Matt's decision to move to the Tablelands, and Sarah and Matt had looked at dozens of properties. Not one had grabbed their attention, despite Lily's help.

They'd decided to give it one last shot today, and then take a break for a few weeks. They met Lily at the pub in Tolga for lunch before going to look at some properties, and while they were eating Lily got a call from a potential seller about a property that she had viewed two weeks earlier. The seller had decided to go with Lily's company.

Once the brief conversation was over, she hung up the phone and smiled broadly. 'What a freaky coincidence is that! There's this property I looked over a few weeks back, and the guy selling has just rung to ask me to list it on my books. It's *amazing*, guys, and I think it'll be just what you're looking for. It's 150 hectares of prime grazing land over in Malanda. The couple who own it want to retire and they never had any kids to take over the farm. The bloke wants to sell the cattle along with the farm, so if you're interested I'm sure we can come to a good price for the lot. Oh, I just know you're going to fall in love with the place!'

Matt looked at Sarah and they both grinned. It sounded perfect.

'How much does the guy want for it, Lily?' Matt asked.

Lily flicked through her paperwork until she came across the scribble she had written down when she looked at the property. She scanned down the page of chicken scratch, tapping the amount once she found it.

'Well, it's a bit on the expensive side, but I swear to you it's worth it. I can work wonders when it comes to finalising the cost, and seeing it's for my best friends, I'll pass on my commission so you can save some money.'

'You're brilliant, Lily,' said Matt, flashing her a warm smile before grabbing Sarah's hand and looking deep into her green eyes. 'It sounds just right, doesn't it?'

Sarah smiled. 'It sure does, babe.'

Matt slapped his hands down on the table, making Sarah and Lily both jump. 'Let's get a move on, then! Can we go and take a look at the place today, if the owner doesn't mind?'

Lily fumbled for her phone in her bag. 'I'll call him back now.'

*

Sarah gazed out the window of Lily's car. The fields flowed out in front of her like a sea of green, spotted in every direction with cattle grazing lazily, swishing their tails in an attempt to ward off flies. The further into the Tablelands they drove, the cooler the temperature – a welcome change after Mareeba. Most people over in Malanda had fireplaces as the temperatures in winter dropped to single digits and very occasionally below zero. Sarah allowed herself a moment to visualise what it would be like lying with Matt by the fireside in their very own home.

She felt the car slowing and eagerly peered out the windscreen to see the place they might call home in a few months' time. There were big wooden gates at the front of the property, already open, welcoming them in. A large timber sign dangled from the corner fence post with *Tranquil Valley* written across it in bold blue writing. Sarah let her eyes focus on the horizon. Sprawling out beyond the property were endless fields of lush green grass, dipping and diving into valleys and continuing up into shadowed hills that lay beyond. A light mist hung in the distance, giving the impression that they were entering a land somehow closer to heaven than anywhere else.

'Lily, this is amazing!'

Lily nodded her head as she drove. 'I told you, didn't I? Don't get too excited, though, otherwise the owners will know you're keen and they won't budge on the price. Play it cool, okay?'

Matt gave the thumbs-up sign to Lily. 'I like the look of this. I promise I'll put on my poker face so they don't catch on, boss.' He squeezed Sarah's hand and she squeezed back.

The house came into view moments later. It was perched high up on the top of a hill, commanding a view of the entire property. The beauty of it all took Sarah's breath away.

'Pinch me, Matt. I think I'm dreaming right now. Am I dreaming?'

'No, sweetheart. This is damn real. Believe it, baby.'

Lily pulled up out the front of the house, and as they spilled from the Prado the owners came out to greet them. They were warm, welcoming, country people, but Sarah could see the pain in their eyes at the thought of having to let their beloved property go. Their grey hair and weatherworn hands told the story of their lives on the land. They told Sarah and Matt that it was getting all too much for them in their old age. It was time to move somewhere smaller and easier to look after.

Introductions over, the couple made themselves scarce while Lily showed Sarah and Matt around the house. Sarah pointed out the big fireplace to Matt.

He smiled at her, raising his eyebrows cheekily. 'Wonder what we could get up to in front of that?'

Sarah winked mischievously. 'Just what I was thinking! Great minds think alike.'

Lily rolled her eyes. 'Come on, you two. Let me show you the *bedrooms* then.'

The house was very impressive. The views from every room were out of this world, and the place was full of charm and atmosphere. After they'd had the tour, Sarah and Matt stood on the verandah and whispered excitedly about how they would spend their evenings outside enjoying the sunsets. It was all they had hoped for, and more.

Next stop was the land itself. The sheds, yards and equipment were all well looked after and in good working order. Sarah realised they would be able to basically walk in and take over from where the owners had left off. Most impressive of all was the cattle. They had big round bellies, no doubt full from the endless green fields surrounding them.

Lily went back to the house to talk to the owners about the details, leaving Matt and Sarah gazing out across the paddock of healthy cattle.

Matt looked enthusiastically at Sarah. 'What do you reckon?'

Sarah grinned. 'I love it, Matt. We'll have a really happy life here.' She took a deep breath and looked back at the miles of green, imagining the secluded and peaceful existence they would lead here, tucked away from the wider world.

Her reverie was interrupted by the sound of someone clearing their throat behind. Sarah turned to see Lily smiling at them both.

'How about we buy you guys a house?' she said, raising her eyebrows.

Sarah grinned back at her, holding Matt's hand firmly. 'Let's talk figures, Lily.'

CHAPTER

30

Sarah felt her heart leap with joy as Matt drove the truck through the front gates of Rosalee Station. She gave the puppy on her lap a scratch behind the ears and the little cutie tried to lick her hand. Judy had told Sarah a dozen times how much she missed having Duke around, and when a mate of Matt's in Mt Isa mentioned he had a few puppies for sale, Sarah knew a puppy would be the perfect gift.

Sarah glanced at the workers' cottage as they passed and felt a little pang of sadness. None of the blokes were there. They had all moved on to different jobs, filling in the time until they met back here again for the beginning of the new season. Sarah had a sudden flashback to just a few months before, when she had driven away with Jimmy in floods of tears at the thought that she would never set foot here again. Now here she was, with Matt and Duke by her side, returning to help Matt pack up and get ready for his move into their

new home. It had been tough for Matt to break the news
to his family, but once they'd got over the surprise, they'd
accepted Matt's decision. Judy and Steve were delighted for
Matt and Sarah, and Georgia couldn't have been happier –
she'd been dying to run the station for years.

Judy appeared at the front door of the homestead the
minute Matt and Sarah pulled up. Duke spotted her and
started jumping around the Cruiser like a fart in a bottle,
his tail slapping Sarah in the face. She pushed him away,
laughing. 'Oh, get out of it, you bloody bugger! That tail of
yours is lethal.'

Matt opened the driver's side door and Duke went
tearing towards Judy, trampling Matt in his haste to get
out. When the dog reached Judy he almost licked her to
death. Judy gave him a cuddle and then stood to greet
Sarah and Matt, spotting the bundle in Sarah's arms. 'Oh
my goodness! What have you there, love?'

Sarah passed Judy the tiny staffy puppy, smiling. 'She's
for you, Judy. She hasn't got a name yet but I'm sure you'll
think of a good one for her.'

Judy's eyes filled with happy tears as she took the little
black bundle from Sarah's arms. 'Oh, she's beautiful!
Thanks, both of you. Now let me give you a cuddle, Sarah.
It's been too long!'

Matt took the puppy from Judy before the little thing
got squashed, and Judy gave Sarah a good old-fashioned
country squeeze. Matt smiled as he watched the two women
hug. Anyone could see how much they adored each other.

Judy finally pulled away from Sarah and gave Matt a
cuddle and a kiss on the cheek. 'All right, you two. Steve

and Georgia won't be back for an hour or so, but I've got a kitchen full of food and a bowl of meat ready for Duke. I'll make another bowl up for this little sweetie!' She scratched the puppy's soft belly as she carried her inside.

As they stepped through the front door, Judy suddenly stopped dead and put her finger up in the air as if an idea had come to her. 'I'm going to call her Stella. Yep. I like that. *Stella.*' She nodded her head.

'I love it!' Sarah exclaimed. 'That's one of my favourite beers!'

'Oh, you!' Judy gave her a friendly slap on the butt. 'I'm not naming her after a beer, my love; I'm naming her after my great grandmother.'

Steve and Georgia came out to the back verandah an hour later, and when Sarah saw them she jumped up to give Georgia a hug, stopping in her tracks as she spotted Patrick standing behind her. 'Oh wow! What a surprise! Patrick!'

'Thanks, Sarah! Just bypass me then!' Georgia said, laughing.

'Sorry, mate. I just wasn't expecting Patrick to be here, that's all.'

Georgia smiled widely in response. 'Patrick finally asked me out.'

This time Sarah gave her an uninterrupted hug, and then stood back, her arms still around Georgia. 'That's fantastic! About bloody time, you two.'

Patrick leant in to give Sarah a friendly hug and a kiss on the cheek. 'It's good to see you, mate. And don't pick on me for being a bit slow in the love department. I got there eventually, didn't I? I was always afraid that Georgia would tell me to rack off if I asked her out, but hey, she didn't. Stranger things have been known to happen, I s'pose!' He looked over at Matt. 'And now you're moving to the land of green rolling hills, Matt, I can be here to help out. Assuming Georgia wants me to.'

Georgia smiled affectionately at Patrick. 'Of course I want you to be here, you dork!'

'Come on then, you lot. Two, four, six, eight, bog in, don't wait!' Judy sang out as she brought the first of many plates of food to set on the table.

They all followed her orders enthusiastically and dug into the feast.

'You want to go on a star-gazing date tonight, babe?' Matt asked as he licked icing off his fingers.

'I'd love to,' Sarah replied. It was such a simple idea, yet so romantic.

*

Sarah had never been on a star-gazing date before. It was the most romantic setting in the world, and she couldn't help smiling with delight at the dazzling beauty of it all. Matt had spread a blanket on the bonnet of the LandCruiser and she cuddled into him, enjoying his warmth in the chilly night air. The sky above them sparkled like a swathe of fabric encrusted with diamonds, the blackness of the night surrounding them and making her feel as though she was on the planet all alone with Matt. He pointed out all the different stars and constellations, and she was amazed by how many he knew. Snuggling closer still, she breathed in his fresh scent. He smelt so good, and she loved the way her body seemed to mould to his when they snuggled. It was as though they were made for each other.

With only moonlight to guide him, Matt pushed a ringlet of blonde hair off Sarah's forehead and kissed her gently on the lips, savouring the taste of her strawberry lip gloss. Running his hand softly down her face, he looked deeply into her eyes. 'I love you, Sarah Clarke, with all my heart and soul. I can't wait to begin the rest of our lives together.'

Sarah smiled back at him, her eyes luminescent in the faint light. 'I love you too, Matt. This is the life I've always dreamt of, and I'm sharing it with the most amazing man in the world. We were on different journeys in life a while ago, and now we're lying here together in each other's arms. It's absolute bliss!'

A peaceful silence descended, and they gazed at the stars for a few moments, lost in their thoughts.

'Hey, how about a song?' Matt said. 'Any requests?' He slipped gently out of Sarah's arms and slid off the bonnet, his boots stirring the dust as he landed. 'Hmm … I'm in the mood for some Garth Brooks.'

Matt flicked through his CD case and found the album he wanted. He put the disc in the car CD player and skipped forward to the song he knew would be right: 'To Make You Feel My Love'. It made him think of Sarah every time he listened to it.

'Oh, I love this song!' Sarah called out into the night as the first bars rang out softly. She sang along to herself as she waited for Matt to join her back on the bonnet.

Matt walked up to Sarah and held out his hand. 'Can I have this dance, princess?'

Sarah didn't think the night could get any more romantic, but it just had.

'Yes, you may,' she replied with a gentle smile.

She slid down off the bonnet and into Matt's arms, resting her head on his chest, lost in happiness as she listened to his heartbeat. Matt took the lead and waltzed her gently around, one hand cupping the slender curve of her back while the other tenderly held her hand. They danced, their boots sliding across the red earth beneath them, the moon spilling its silvery light across their faces.

I have found the love of my life, Sarah thought to herself. And above millions of stars shone down from the beautiful country sky.

ACKNOWLEDGEMENTS

To my beautiful little girl, Chloe Rose, thanks for allowing me to see the world through your eyes – it makes the world such a magical place. Your smiles bring so much warmth to my heart and you light up each and every day.

My mum, Gaye, you're my rock and my best friend. You never stopped telling me I was going to make it. Thank you for reading my very first draft and giving me loads of advice. I'm so fortunate to have such a marvellous mum and I love you dearly.

My wise and loving dad, John, you were my inspiration in so many diverse ways. Your country blood has made me the rural woman that I am today.

To my wonderful stepdad, Trevor, thank you for being the man you are. I'm blessed to have grown up with your positive outlook on life.

Edie, my cherished Nanna, you kept telling me to write a book. I finally listened to you and you were so proud of me becoming an author. I wish you had lived to see the book in print, but I know you are with me in spirit. I miss you every day and I love you with all my heart.

To my fabulous sisters, Karla, Talia, Mia and Rochelle, you all gave me support in so many different ways. I'm so blessed to have four beautiful sisters! And to my brother, Kane, your crazy antics gave me so many ideas for this book.

Aunty Kulsoom – thanks for being there throughout my endeavours. I look forward to the day you decide to retire and move closer, so you can put your teacher's eye to work on my drafts.

Fiona Palmer, you're the best! You've made me laugh so many times with your emails and I reckon if we lived closer we would be around at each other's place all the time. Thank you for reading *Rosalee Station* and allowing me to put your thoughts on the front cover.

Thanks to all those unique, memorable and remarkable country souls I have met in my life. You all know who you are; the unforgettable experiences I've shared with you have contributed to making *Rosalee Station* what it is.

And last but not least, thanks to you, the reader, for picking up *Rosalee Station*. I hope I've given you a taste of the outback, from the dust on your face to the country sun on your skin. Anyone for Vegemite on toast and a cup of billy tea?

Until my next book, keep smiling and dreaming…life is beautiful!

Mandy xo

MEET MANDY MAGRO

MEET MANDY MAGRO

What or who inspired *Rosalee Station*?

When I was 30 I was offered a job as camp cook out at Tobermorey Station in Central Australia – the middle of whoop whoop really! It was really exciting and an experience I will always hold dear, but it was also a very big lesson in life. Hard doesn't even begin to describe having to survive in such an unforgiving landscape. While out mustering for weeks on end my culinary kitchen consisted of a fire and a barbecue plate, and my bath time was hiding behind a clump of spinifex with a valued packet of wet wipes while trying to avoid being spotted by the chopper pilot – fun times! You don't really know how hard it is to come up with things to cook on an open fire for an army of hungry men until you try it. The days were scorching hot and the nights were freezing cold, and I spent most days on my own craving for a can of creaming soda. Weird, but when left for hours without anything to occupy yourself, the mind does strange things. We slept in our swags, the earth our bed and the dazzling star-speckled sky our ceiling. I remember waking up one morning and my rubber contour pillow was frozen solid! And there were dingoes in the camp most nights. The men would sit up half asleep, shotgun in hand, ready to defend our turf if need be – though thankfully it never came to that. The storyline, and the wonderful characters, are based on my experiences in the outback and all the unforgettable people I met while out there. The heroine, Sarah Clarke, is like me right down to the curly blonde hair.

What was the biggest challenge writing it?
It was my very first attempt at writing a novel, and I also had a one-week-old newborn baby, so what wasn't a challenge? Time, weariness, self-doubt, sanity…on replay over and over. LOL! Trust me to try and do everything on a grand scale, and all at once! My first round of edits hit me hard – I wasn't used to being critiqued so unforgivingly. But as hard as it was, it shaped the author I am today, and I wouldn't change a second of my writer's journey for anything or anyone.

Are there any parts of it that have special personal significance to you?
The title, *Rosalee Station*, came about from adding my middle name, Lee, and my daughter's, Rose, together – so that in itself is special. Matt and Sarah, the hero and heroine, are very dear to my heart. They were the first characters I brought to life and fell in love with along the journey, as too were all the stockmen and the animals. *Rosalee Station* was

my very first book baby, so it will always have a very special place in my heart, and on my bookshelf.

Do you have a favourite character or one you really enjoyed writing?
I loved breathing life into Sarah, as she was all the parts of me I wanted to share with the world. And Matt, well, what isn't there to love about the hunky spunky man. I also adored Slim – his larrikin humour and big heart were a joy to write about.

If you've had other jobs outside of writing, what were they?
I've had quite a few other jobs. While at school I worked at an ice-creamery on the weekend. Yum! I then worked at a chemist and when I left school I went on to do a hairdressing apprenticeship. Once I graduated I opened my own salon and worked in that for about 10 years, going on to do mobile wedding hair once I sold it. I've also worked as a therapeutic masseuse, marketing manager, nightclub promotions manager, in advertising and just recently as a creative writer for PBR – Pro Bull Riding Australia.

How would your family describe you, in three words?
Loving, spontaneous, stubborn.

Do you have a special 'spot' for writing at home? (If so, describe it)
I sure do. I have a desk in the open living area. From it I can see outside and I can man the kitchen while dinner cooks

in between writing – very handy! I have photos of loved ones around me and my desk is extremely tidy – I am a neat freak and can't work in chaos.

Do you like silence or music playing while you're writing?
While I'm writing I need complete silence. Editing, I like to have some background music on – preferably some old school country, like Waylon Jennings or Johnny Cash. Or if I'm in a hyper mood a bit of psychedelic trance (I did mention I was spontaneous)…I'm a raver from way back. ☺

Any other quirky writing habits?
Not really…maybe I should find some and then I might stop sidetracking on social media when I should be working. ☺

When did you start writing?
When I became a mum, so 33.

Did you always want to become an author?
I always loved English, and it was the subject I excelled in at school, but no, it wasn't a lifelong dream to become a writer. Although now I'm doing it, I feel like I've found my niche.

What star sign are you and are you typical of it?
I'm an Aries through and through – headstrong, creative, passionate, loyal, fiery at times, and very very stubborn.

What are your three favourite things?
Other than my family and friends, if I have to pick, food, music, and travelling – all three at once is perfection!

What three things do you dislike the most?

Confining to the expectations of society – I like to have freedom of expression and live life the way it makes me happy – apricot chicken makes me gag, oh, and bad smells.

There's a new instalment to Sarah and Matt's story coming soon. Can you give us a tiny hint about what's to come?

Return to Rosalee Station is a beautiful yet tragic and harrowing story, and will tug at the very core of every parent who reads it. Make sure you have plenty of tissues nearby! Most of the characters make a comeback, even some of the animals. There is love, loss and also times of off-the-cuff fun…all the things you'd expect from a sequel to my very first novel about life and love in the magnificent Australian outback.

Turn over for a sneak peek.

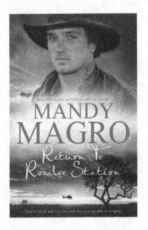

Return To Rosalee Station

by

MANDY MAGRO

Available November 2018

PROLOGUE

Malanda, Far North Queensland
Present day

Something needs to change ... the ultimatum circled torturously in Matthew Walsh's mind.

As much as he hated to admit it to himself, he had to agree. Self-medicating with booze was doing neither him, nor Sarah, any good. Her words played over and over again in his head, every one of them so very true.

Shifting uneasily, he hung his dusty, wide-brimmed hat on his knee and tried to stop from shaking. Sitting still was no easy feat these days. Not when it felt as if the weight of the world was pressing down upon his chest, and every one of his nerve ends hummed. Like a moth to a flame, he couldn't help himself when the drink gave him some reprieve – but it was high time he found a way to control it. The heartbreaking letter Sarah had left him on the dining table felt as if it were burning a hole in his pocket. He choked back tears – he didn't deserve to cry. His darling wife had reached her limit, and after the godawful year they'd had, he couldn't blame her one little bit.

Staring in a daze at the pile of magazines on the coffee table, and noticing that one of them was almost two years old – so much for fresh tabloid gossip – he tried to steady his breathing. The last patient of the day, he was thankful for the empty waiting room. Late afternoon sunshine poured through the glass front door and bathed the Malanda Medical Centre in golden light. What Matt would give to be lying in the sun in one of his paddocks instead of sitting in a doctor's surgery facing his fears. His leg bouncing anxiously, he watched the sixty-something secretary gather her things at the desk and then hurriedly shove them in her handbag before reapplying her already bright pink lipstick.

Rubbing her lips together she bustled over to him. 'The doctor knows you're here, love. He's on a phone call and won't be much longer. I'd usually wait around with you but I need to run, have to pick the grandkids up from daycare for Marne.' She dashed past him, frazzled but smiling. 'Say hi to Sarah for me, won't you?' she called over her shoulder.

'Will do, Shirl. And say g'day to Bob for me too.' Matt tried to smile as he watched her wrestle the door open and then disappear outside.

The surgery door opened and Doctor Lawson stepped out. 'Sorry to keep you waiting … come on in, Matt.'

His Akubra in hand, Matt stood up, wandered in and sat down awkwardly. He hung his hat back on his knee and drew in a slow, steadying breath. 'Thanks for seeing me at such short notice, Doc. I know you're staying back later than usual and I really appreciate it.'

The doctor followed Matt in and settled himself in his high-back leather chair, and folded his legs. 'Not a problem at all. I realise you've been having a hard time of late, which is to be expected after what you and Sarah have been through.'

A hard time? More like the worst time of his thirty-four years on this earth. Matt nodded, knowing full well the entire town would know of his situation at home, including the doctor, so it was no surprise to hear him say so. 'Yeah, it's been a damn tough year, that's for sure.'

'I have no doubt.' His lips set in a grim line, the doctor clicked and unlicked a pen – the sound grating on Matt's already frazzled nerves. 'So tell me, what can I do for you today?' His kind eyes moved over Matt as if already assessing him.

His heart in his throat and his stomach churning with nerves, Matt dug deep and found the nerve to open his heart just enough to get what advice he needed from the doctor. Each and every word was a struggle, an admission he needed help – and that made him feel even less of a man, and even more like the drunken fool he was. He was ashamed it had come to this, abashed he'd denied it for so long – but there was no more hiding from it, or from himself for that matter. Sarah was right. Enough was enough. If he wanted their marriage to have any kind of hope for a happily ever after, he needed to stand up and be the man he once was. The stench of stale alcohol was his shadow, as too was the past that haunted him every waking hour, even reaching into his nightmarish dreams that held him hostage every single night. He needed to find a way to climb out of the dark hole he'd fallen into.

The words tumbling from him, he finished his last sentence with a self-conscious smile, and then waited for a response he was almost too scared to hear.

'Well, you've come to the right place, Matt. I can most certainly help you through this.' The doctor's compassionate smile almost brought Matt undone.

'Great. Excellent.' Matt could hear the strain in his voice, and he coughed to try to cover it up. He wished he could rid the horrific images and the bloodcurdling screams from his head without the aid of alcohol, but he'd learnt all too well over this past year it was impossible. His only option had been to drink himself into a stupor to silence it all, if only for a little while. 'Sarah's right, I'm slowly killing myself, and ruining the hope of there ever being any chance of our marriage working.' He choked back a sob. If he allowed himself to cry, he was afraid he'd never be able to stop. And men weren't supposed to break down – it was his job to try to keep it together, to hold the fort, to make sure all the special women in his life were looked after. And he'd failed with that, miserably.

'Matt, you've taken the first step in asking for help.' His brows furrowed, Doctor Lawson adjusted his thick glasses and then folded his hands on his desk. 'So how many drinks, per day, would you say you're having?'

Ashamed, Matt's initial reaction was to lie, but he knew that wasn't going to get him anywhere. 'Probably eight or nine, maybe more on the really bad days.' He decided to leave out the fact he could devour an entire bottle if the moment called for it.

'I see, and what's your drink of choice.'

'Whiskey, sometimes rum.'

The doctor drew in a slow breath. 'Although the initial stages of alcohol withdrawal are over in a few weeks, your dependence may take anywhere from six months to a year to totally overcome, and even then you'll have to be mindful of falling back into the trap of thinking alcohol will solve all your problems for a few years after that.'

'I know it's going to be a tough journey, Doc, but I'm willing to give it my best shot.' Turning his gaze to the family photo of the doctor, his wife, and their two children in their twenties, Matt had to fight from feeling resentful. So, looking anywhere but, he tried to remain calm, steady, focussed – a hard thing to do when he was craving his next drink like a parched person craved water.

'Righto, well, let's get this show on the road. Are you open to taking some medication, to help with the side effects of withdrawal that you're most certainly going to experience?'

Drugs to get him off the drink? It didn't make an ounce of bloody sense. 'Nope, I'm not open to that. I just want you to let me know what I'm in for, and how to handle it, without making me addicted to another kind of drug in the process.' It was said a little too harshly, and Matt regretted his tone instantly. This is what he always did to people who tried to help – took his frustration out on them. Poor Sarah. He bit his lip shut to stop from saying any more.

'I see.' The doctor's gaze narrowed.

Silence hung heavy. Matt hankered to escape the confines of the little room, but he planted himself firmly in the seat and gritted his teeth. It had taken him a long time to gather the courage to come here, too long in the grand scheme of things, and he wasn't about to chicken out now.

The doctor readjusted a few already straightened papers on his desk. 'I *really* do think you need to reconsider my suggestion for medication, Matt.' His tone was serious and authoritative. 'It's no easy feat, getting off the drink. And I would suggest you also think about going to counselling.'

'Go to a counsellor? No, thanks.' Matt shifted uncomfortably beneath the doctor's unyielding stare. 'And I *really* don't want to do this with pills, either.' Acknowledging the doctor's disapproving expression, Matt shrugged. 'Sorry, but taking something to get off something is just jumping from the frying pan and into the fire, in my opinion.'

'As you said, that's your opinion, Matt, and with all due respect, I totally disagree with you. The medication is offered for a very good reason … especially if you're thinking about doing this in the middle of the outback where help isn't at your beck and call, as you mentioned when we spoke on the phone.'

'I'll have plenty of help there, if I need it – my mum and dad, my sister, my best mate.'

'That's all well and good, but they can't do what medication will do.' Doctor Lawson breathed a weary sigh. 'Look, I totally understand your concerns, but the Valium will help in the short term, and then the Naltrexone will guide you through until you feel strong enough to do it on your own.'

'Thanks, but no thanks … it'll be another thing I need to ween myself off.' Determined to stand fast with his decision to go cold turkey, Matt cleared his throat and feigned a confidence he was far from feeling. 'If it makes you happier, though, I'll take a script for both, just in case of an emergency.'

Doctor Lawson held up his hands in defeat. 'Okay, but for the record, I really don't like the idea of you going it alone out there, Matt.' He reached for his prescription pad. 'Can you do me a favour and fill the scripts, so you have the tablets on hand if you get to the stage where you feel you need them? There's not many chemists out near your parents' station, I'm gathering.'

'Correct.' Happy to meet on middle ground, Matt nodded. 'Yup, it's a done deal, Doc. I'll make sure I have the tablets with me before I head out to Rosalee … but that doesn't mean I'm going to take them.' Matt's word was genuine – he would get the script filled at the very least.

'That's a good start …' Doctor Lawson stopped writing and looked up. 'So thank you.' He tipped his head a little to the side. 'May I ask, on more of a personal level seeing you and Sarah are like family to Marg and me, how is she feeling about you heading out there and doing this without her around?'

Matt swallowed. Hard. 'I haven't told her yet.'

'Oh, right, okay. That's probably something she should know sooner rather than later, don't you think?'

'I know, I'll tell her.' Unable to look him in the eye any longer, Matt stared down at his weather-beaten boots. 'I just want to stop. Now. Before it's too late.'

The pen still poised, Doctor Lawson raised his eyebrows. 'Too late for you and Sarah? Or too late for you?'

Matt suddenly realised what the doctor was asking him. His throat so tight with emotion he couldn't speak, he quickly shook his head, and then stole a few moments to recover. 'I'm not suicidal, if that's what you're asking.'

'Are you one hundred and ten percent sure of that?' The look in the doctor's eyes suggested he was unconvinced.

Even though he'd contemplated it many times, and come very close to following through with it, Matt rolled his eyes and forcefully made himself appear completely shocked by the accusation. 'Of course I'm sure.'

The doctor regarded him over the rim of his glasses, to the point that Matt squirmed in his seat, and then looked back down at his prescription pad. 'Be sure to talk to someone if you do feel suicidal at any time, okay?'

'Yup, of course.'

Ripping the sheet of paper off, he passed it to Matt. 'Like I explained, after drinking so heavily for the past year, you're going to experience the height of the withdrawal symptoms in the first few days. Irritability, poor concentration, feeling shaky, irregular heartbeat, difficulty sleeping and nightmares, just to name a few.' He smiled sadly. 'And then there's the physical symptoms ... trembling hands, sweating, headaches, nausea, vomiting, lack of appetite, and possibly even hallucinations. So please, don't try to be a hero – use the tablets if it gets too bad.'

'You have my word, Doc, thanks.' Matt took the script, folded it, and then shoved it in his pocket along with Sarah's letter. He was terrified of what lay ahead, both for him and his marriage. How in the hell were they ever going to get through this, and out the other side, if he didn't rediscover the man he once was, the man that Sarah had fallen head over heels in love with?

BESTSELLING AUSTRALIAN AUTHOR

MANDY
MAGRO

Novels to take you to the country...

Available in ebook   Available in ebook

mira

LET'S TALK ABOUT BOOKS!

JOIN THE CONVERSATION

HARLEQUIN
AUSTRALIA

@HARLEQUINAUS

@HARLEQUINAUS